THE TITIAN PORTRAIT

DEREK ANSELL

Copyright (C) 2021 Derek Ansell

Layout design and Copyright (C) 2021 by Next Chapter

Published 2021 by Next Chapter

Edited by Terry Hughes

Cover art by CoverMint

This book is a work of fiction. Names, characters, places, and incidents are the product of the author's imagination or are used fictitiously. Any resemblance to actual events, locales, or persons, living or dead, is purely coincidental.

All rights reserved. No part of this book may be reproduced or transmitted in any form or by any means, electronic or mechanical, including photocopying, recording, or by any information storage and retrieval system, without the author's permission.

THE PRIVATE JOURNAL OF QUEEN MARY I

GUILDHALL, LONDON FEBRUARY 1554

It is February 1554 and I prepare to make one of the most important speeches of my life.

It is an icy-cold day with frost-encrusted roads, buildings, carriages, and stone edifices everywhere. The carriage rattles and crunches along slowly, dipping unceremoniously into the potholes and rising again with a shudder and squeal to continue its rocky journey. People are abroad and on the move along the highways, huddled into their smocks and coats, hats and caps pulled down tightly over their heads in attempts, mostly futile, to keep out the cold. Most of them stop their movement and take off their hats and caps, bow towards the carriage and wave to me. I raise one hand repeatedly until it positively aches with lifting continuously, as we progress. I should smile more, and I am aware that I could make the effort and indeed I determine in my mind to do so. The people expect it, and I should accommodate them; I need their support and intend to acquire and keep it.

The Strand is packed with people, all excited, some cheering, others making a strange guttural murmur. They spill out across the road, impeding the progress of our carriage and those following. I am irritated at the number of stops and starts we are obliged to make. The officials herd people and push them back towards the edges of the buildings and we move forward again, the horses spurred on to run a little faster. I lean back against the cushions and take a few deep breaths. As we draw up outside the Guildhall finally, I am losing patience with a journey that appears to have taken far too long but I must keep my irritation in check, or I shall lose focus on why I am here and what I am resolved to do.

Lord Howard and the courtiers escort me through the building and into the Great Hall. The people are crowded into the hall, jostling each other and the murmur of voices, magnified by the sheer numbers of those present, appears to my ears like a subdued roar. Looking out at the mainly ragged, bustling assembly in front of me, I suddenly feel a spasm of panic. Stephen Gardiner, Bishop of Salisbury and my Lord Chancellor, is smiling.

"Your chance, Majesty, to rally the troops," he says, grinning.

"Easier said than done, Stephen," I tell him with a frown.

"Just seek out one head in the middle of the hall," he suggests reflectively. "Focus on that one head throughout and it will be just like speaking to a single person, I assure you."

I raise an eyebrow and give him a sceptical glare.

"No, really, Your Grace, it works, believe me," he continues, eyes glinting. "Just try it."

They are all there in front of me, a large and motley assemblage indeed. Farm workers and labourers, carters and coachmen, cobblers and candle-makers, bakers and beggars. Friars and ferrymen. Blacksmiths and butchers. All waiting patiently for me to speak.

Howard asks if I am ready.

"As ready as I ever will be, My Lord," I tell him. "Let us begin."

I approach the rostrum and take another deep breath. I

nod towards Howard and he bows briefly. I take a deep breath in readiness.

"I am come to you," I begin, "in mine own person, to tell you that which already you do see and know, that is how traitorously and seditiously a number of Kentish rebels have assembled themselves against both us and you." The murmur of sound in the hall rises perceptibly for a few seconds and subsides to uneasy silence as they wait upon my next words.

I sense already the collective mood of these good people, that they are with me, their queen, and the silence all around me is only an indication of their shock and dismay. I see on their faces, those closest to me at any wise, the sense of outrage already building.

"Now, loving subjects," I go on, "what I am you right well know. I am your queen and at my coronation, when I was wedded to the realm and the laws of the same, ye promised your allegiance and obedience unto me."

Murmurs of assent are now heard in the hall and I remind them that I am the right and true inheritor to the crown of this realm of England and again assert that acts of parliament confirm this.

I tell them, raising my voice slightly, that I do not believe they will not suffer so terrible a traitor as this Wyatt has shown himself to be, to subdue the laws to his evil and give scope to rascally and forlorn persons to make general havoc and spoilation of their goods. I pause briefly to breath in and take measure of the atmosphere in the hall. They are with me to a man; I can sense it – I can almost feel it.

It is time to consolidate my advantage. I must take immediate advantage of the sympathy I feel coming from the people in front of me.

"I cannot tell how naturally a mother loveth her children for I was never the mother of any but certainly a prince may as naturally and earnestly love subjects, as the mother loves her child. Then assure yourselves that I, being sovereign lady and queen, do as earnestly and tenderly love and favour you. And as you heartily and faithfully love me again; I doubt not, but we together shall be able to give these rebels short and speedy overthrow."

The cheer that erupts from the hall is deafening. Some raise their fists in salute, but all are vocal, whether moving or still. I pause, breathe deeply once again and look over to my right and receive a glance acknowledging the success of the speech from the expression on my Lord Howard's face and the lingering smile on the face of William Paulet, my Lord Treasurer. Gardiner too is grinning contentedly. I permit myself the very ghost of a smile on this sombre, momentous occasion and raise my hand to request silence. What more to say? I realise I cannot conclude my speech without reference to the stated cause of the uprising and I assure them that I entered into the intended marriage only with the advice of my privy council, the same to whom the king, my father, committed his trust. "And they not only thought it honourable, but expedient, both for the wealth of our realm and of all our loving subjects."

I assure them heartily that I would not put a wedding and my own lust first but would be prepared, with God's blessing, to continue as a virgin. "But it might please God that I leave some fruit of my body behind me, to be your governor. I trust you would not only rejoice but also find it great comfort."

I go on to say that I would enter no marriage that would not be to the benefit of the whole realm and receive the approval of the nobility and commons in the high court of parliament. "If this marriage be not for the singular commodity of the whole realm," I say with measured, grave tone, "then I will abstain, not only from this marriage but also any other whereof peril may ensue to this most noble realm."

Cheering breaks out once again, louder this time than before and longer sustained. It was always my intention to finish this speech with a suitable rallying call that had to be exactly right. If my memory or even speech should falter for an instant, I might lose any advantage and support from my subjects that I had gained. I incline my head to give the signal to Howard and he hands me the parchment where the words are written out. I begin slowly.

"Wherefore now, as good and faithful subjects, pluck up your hearts and like true men stand fast with your lawful prince against these rebels, both our enemies and yours, and fear them not; for I assure you I fear them nothing. I will leave you with my Lord Howard and my Lord Treasurer to be your assistants, with my Lord Mayor, for the defence and safeguard of this city from spoil and sacking, which is only the scope of this rebellious company."

When the uproar of applause, stamping and shouting abates at last and the good people start to move towards the doors, I turn away myself and walk over to my councillors.

"It's up to you now, William," I tell my Lord Treasurer.

"That was a magnificent speech, Your Majesty."

"Yes, very well done indeed," Bishop Gardiner agrees.

"You think so?" I walk slowly with him, Gardiner and my Lord Treasurer William Paulet into the adjoining chamber where they are preparing to serve refreshments. "Not a little overdone, you might think?"

"Most certainly not," Howard says soberly, waiting until I am seated before joining me on my right-hand side. So now, I suggest carefully, measuring my words slowly, he would be able, would he not, to raise sufficient numbers of militia to crush these vile rebels?

"I am confident," he responds swiftly.

"Sufficient numbers, William, sufficient numbers. And we would need several thousand."

The servants are bringing in roast boar, chicken with cherries, artichokes and large tumblers of sweet French wine. Good, crisp bread, freshly baked, is also provided and I do not stand on ceremony but begin to eat, thereby allowing my councillors to follow suit. The food is good, well roasted and refreshing after my long speech. I eat quite heartily, which is unusual for me but then these are unusual times and there is a rebellion to be suppressed. They add roasted swan a little later and I indulge as it is a delicate meat of which I am particularly fond. Everybody seems to be in jubilant mood so my speech must have made an impact.

"What say you, William?" I ask, addressing Paulet.

"I agree," he replies, hastily emptying his spoonful of meat back to the plate to answer. "You would need at least 10,000 men, though."

"Possibly more," Howard chips in. "Quite a lot more, I'm thinking."

"It's up to you, Howard," Gardiner tells him, "to secure the numbers. Look to it heartily."

"Yes," Paulet concurs, "I do agree."

"Well, don't delay, My Lord," I urge anxiously.

The people are with me, Howard tells me, and always have been. "Remember last year?" he asks.

"How could I forget?" I wonder. As the meal continues, my mind is in turmoil.

Sometimes I wonder why I have been so troubled and punished in my life. It should have been so straightforward and uncomplicated. The only daughter of the popular and just King Henry VIII and Queen Catherine of Aragon, we were happily united in all wise happenings for many years until my father, in his wisdom, concluded that his marriage was illegal and set out to have it annulled. Whatever possessed him to desert my mother and deny the authority of the Holy Roman Church, I shall never know. When I made it clear that I could never accept another religion and my allegiance, like my mother's, would always be to Rome, I knew the full force of his dissatisfaction with me. What happened after that, appointing himself as head of the

English church and taking another wife, I cannot bear even to think about.

"The attempt by your half-brother, Edward VI, to alter the line of succession and put your cousin Lady Jane Grey on the throne was always doomed to failure," Howard is musing. "Look how the people rallied around you then and aided the overthrow of the usurper."

"Yes, well, that young woman has been a thorn in my side these last six months or more," I say bitterly. "I still don't know what to do with her but I've resisted all the advice by my ministers to have her executed."

"She is dangerous," Howard suggests tentatively, "and fully committed to the new English church."

"More dangerous than she looks, I grant you," Gardiner adds, looking at Howard.

"She will be dealt with," I advise acidly. "And we are not inclined to continue with this conversation."

"No, I spoke out of turn. My apologies," Howard hastily replies. Gardiner nods to indicate agreement.

Sweetmeats are brought in for our consideration; marzipan, fruits and jelly in an imaginative mould. I allow a servant to serve me an exceedingly small portion as I really wish only to take a little sweetmeat to cleanse my palate. Howard takes a plateful of sweetmeats, attacks them greedily and asks me if I will be leaving London during the next week as he recruits his volunteers for the fight with Wyatt's villains.

"As I have made quite clear to you and others," I insist, "I intend to stay right here. Most likely at Westminster Palace."

"We thought, for your safety," he begins nervously, "you would be much safer in the country, Majesty."

"If I am not in London," I respond irritably, "the rebels could attack government and attempt to overthrow me. No, I stay right here."

"Windsor would be a safe haven," Gardiner opines. "I commend it to you."

"Not even Windsor, Your Majesty?" Paulet enquires.

"Not Windsor, not even 10 paces from Westminster. I know what I am doing and there will be no further comment on our decision."

Howard nods his understanding to me; Gardiner and Paulet follow suit and resume their attack on the sweetmeats. I take a drink of wine from my goblet and reflect that sooner or later, before I am done, these officials and others will realise that the words and decisions of a queen have equal import with those of a king.

QUEEN MARY'S DIARY

WESTMINSTER PALACE, EARLY FEBRUARY
1554

LATE AFTERNOON ON A GREY DAY. SOME SMALL BRIGHTNESS LICKS at the lattices of the window and filters light into the chamber. It soon fades. I dislike winter days and especially as the light dims early and plunges us into night and darkness. The candles can be lit early on and usually are at my discretion, but a gloom still pervades the chamber at this time of year. The deep-brown panelling around the room seems to lose its sheen as night starts to fall. Even the colourful tapestry on the far wall appears pale and lifeless at this time of day.

I dismissed all my ladies-in-waiting a short while ago as I felt the need to be solitary and my Lady Margaret Douglas was beginning to irritate me with her tiresome anecdotes about past queens that she had heard from her many admirers. After sitting here for a while in the ever-encroaching gloom, however, I am feeling the need of at least one companion. I send for more candles and have them lit, deciding that artificial light is preferable to no light at all. I send next for Jane Dormer for, if I am to have one companion who will not irritate and darken my mood, it is she. Jane is of a bright and cheerful disposition almost always and rarely fails to brighten my mood. She is in no wise a handsome creature, but her soft features and ready smile are good enough for me; I tire very quickly of pretty women who are always preening themselves. Jane too, is small in stature, has copper-coloured hair, clear eyes and we are not unlike physically and in deportment generally. Like me, she is very short, has red hair and plain, wan skin but bright blue eyes. Physically, too, it seems, we have much in common.

She enters the chamber with a warm, bright expression on her face that cheers me immediately. I send for sweet French wine and raise my goblet with Jane. Sweet, with a hint of bitterness and as refreshing as could be desired, it perks me up immediately. Jane thinks that I look quite pleased about something and tells me so.

"You know, I was just reflecting on my speech at the Guildhall," I confess. "My Lord Howard was gracious enough to call it magnificent."

Jane raises an eyebrow slowly.

"What, you think I exaggerate or did not deserve the compliment?"

Jane utters a short, tinkling laugh. "I'm sure you deserved every word, although we should perhaps bear in mind that if you said black was white Howard would agree with you."

"He wouldn't," I protest, unable to suppress a smile. "Anyway, you may scoff but it had the desired effect. Who could have dreamed the man would recruit 20,000 men to the militia in less than 24 hours?"

Jane agrees immediately on that point and expresses wonder that Wyatt and his rebels were crushed so swiftly and convincingly so soon after he had been successful early on in his disastrous campaign. She finds it impressive that Wyatt was lured in towards the City of London and then had the gates at Ludgate closed against him. On the other hand, she whispers satirically, it would be difficult for the finest warriors in the world to resist 20,000 armed and bloodthirsty soldiers coming towards them.

"Not all 20,000 at once," I say, keeping a straight face and a bland expression.

"No, not that," agrees a laughing Jane.

At any rate, it is done now and over and I can continue with my policy of restoring the authority of the Holy Roman Church in our land, safe again from those who would overthrow me, doubtless take my life and put my half-sister Elizabeth on the throne of England. It will be a long and painful process and may not even be achieved in my lifetime, but I will never rest from my attempts to complete it. There is much to do also in building up our navy to resist all attempts by those who would invade our shores and colonise us.

"When is his trial?" Jane asks.

"In a few days' time, I am informed."

"So soon?"

"The sooner the better. He can have no defence of his infamous behaviour. We will have his head on a spike before March is out."

"Indeed."

As soon as Wyatt is locked securely in the Tower, my trusted officials will interrogate him vigorously to ascertain what part Elizabeth played in this uprising. If the plan were to overthrow us and put her on the throne, I cannot believe that she was not a willing conspirator with them or, at the very least, knew of the plan and heartily approved it. He may not wish to implicate her or admit her involvement, but my interrogators are advised by me to be very, very persuasive. The truth will come out, of that I am sure. As it is a concern and worry to me, I mention my fears to Jane.

"She wouldn't dare openly ally herself with Wyatt, surely?"

"How can I tell, Jane?" I enquire sombrely. "Members of my own family have hurt and attempted to break me as much as my worst enemies. My father, my half-brother, Lady Jane Grey and my half-sister, Elizabeth."

Jane's expression conveys to me that she is shocked and sympathizes with my predicament. She is a goodly friend and, I think, of all my ladies, the one I trust the most as loyal and true. She is one of few intimates to whom I have opened my heart in discussion; she knows the pain I endured when my father annulled his marriage and sent my faithful, God-fearing mother away into isolation. I never saw her again after that and I suffered grievously as a result. Worse was to come when my father, with his new wife, that Boleyn woman, had a daughter and I was assigned to wait upon her as a servant. After that, how could I ever have a normal bond with Elizabeth? Only Jane knows the full details of these transgressions against me as I had to confide in one good friend or I fear I should have gone mad.

"I can't believe Elizabeth would be so foolhardy," Jane muses quietly but I see from her expression that she is as doubtful as I.

"It is not just her," I continue irritably. "Jane Grey has languished in the tower these past six months and now that her father and brother took part in Wyatt's rebellion and traitorous upsurge, I have little choice but to have her executed. As she is my cousin, I resisted all attempts by my councillors to have her sent to the block, but I fear I can no longer do so. She is a symbol for the English church that Wyatt and his motley crew wanted to perpetuate, and she must, I regret, go to her death."

"If that is what you must do, Mary, you will do it," Jane says. "You are much stronger than your enemies have ever realised."

I smile. She is right, of course. Have I not resisted an attempt by my half-brother to have me eliminated from the line of succession to claim the throne that is rightfully mine? Have I not resisted and crushed an attempt to overthrow my government, have me killed and put my half-sister on the throne? And have I not resisted the strong advice and attempted persuasion of my councillors to abandon my plan to marry Price Philip of Spain and wed an English noble?

I remind Jane of these achievements and she nods in agreement. "So what of young Philip?" she asks.

"He is tall, handsome," I tell her cheerily, "and he will make a wonderful husband."

"Where and when did you first meet?" she asks, grinning at me. "Tell me all."

"We have never met," I admit, quietly. "Yet."

"Never met?" she says incredulously. "And never spoken?"

"Well, no, he speaks extraordinarily little English, I am informed."

Jane laughs and shakes her head vigorously. She says I never fail to surprise and sometimes amaze her, but she knows, well enough, that I must have a plan and, knowing me, it is one that will work. She is sincere, too; I can see that in her face and the way she speaks. So many of my ladies of the court just want to please me and flatter me and I see through them all. They are tiresome. Jane is an exception.

"But how on earth will you communicate?" she wants to know.

"Come with me," I say, rising and signalling to a servant to open the door, "and you shall see."

We walk into the corridor and move along until we reach the chamber where I keep my most prized possessions. On the wall that receives the most lighting from the window lattices hangs a magnificent portrait. I turn to Jane and invite her to take a good look.

"So this is Prince Philip?"

"It was sent to me from another Mary, in Europe," I murmur softly. "They say it should be returned later."

"And will you return it?"

"Never."

Jane lets out a high pitched, tinkling laugh. She adds that it is, indeed, a striking portrait.

"Isn't it? Painted by Titian and who better in Christendom to produce a more faithful likeness?"

"Impressive," Jane breathes quietly, nodding as she looks at the portrait.

"Is he not the boldest, the most handsome man you ever set eyes upon?" I ask her. "I often come in here on a bright morning when the light is best and gaze at the portrait for ages."

I take a step back, the better to admire the large picture and its imposing subject. The light is fading now so this is not the best time to study it although I am held, entranced by the painter's work. And the man represented therein. I am impressed by his choice of apparel and the bright colours but most of all it is the figure and the upright bearing of the man himself. Those eyes, the straight nose and his firm chin from which sprouts the neatest, small, pointed beard. I am informed that Phillip arranged for this portrait to be sent to me as an indication that he would be a suitable husband. Well, I am convinced, to be sure.

"It isn't just that a marriage like this, linked with Spain will be fortuitous to our realm," I tell Jane as we return to my smaller, privy chamber. "There is the question of leaving an heir who will continue the Tudor line."

"But a Spanish prince?" Jane begins, confused.

"One who will have no authority whatsoever in this land," I inform her brightly, "should he outlive me. I have made sure of that and my government has ratified it. Philip was not happy about signing away such influence, but he agreed to it, reluctantly, as a way of ensuring that the marriage should go ahead."

"Oh, I see."

We settle back down in the chamber as the light begins to fade further and, at a movement of my hand, further candles are lit. More wine is brought, and our goblets recharged. Outside, beyond the window lattices, I hear the early chiming of bells, calling the people to evening prayers. A servant builds up the fire, which burns brightly and sends waves of heat and shadows across the chamber. The sounds of heavy cartwheels can be heard passing below the window in the street outside. The scent of cinnamon rises and pervades the dusky room.

"And he will have little or no authority in the country during our lifetimes," I continue. "My government was firm on that point, and I agreed readily as the basis for their support of my marriage to a foreign prince."

"Even though they were set on your marriage to an Englishman?"

I raise an eyebrow slowly. "It is whom I wish to marry that carries the full weight," I say. "Not what the government suggests."

Jane nods and I note the wonder in her eyes that such arrangements have been concluded to my satisfaction.

"Nor will he have the authority to take us to war with any other nation unless it is with my approval."

"What will he have authority to do, for heaven's sake?" Jane asks mischievously, her eyes glinting.

"Provide me and our realm with a son and heir," I tell her joyously. "Although a daughter will be acceptable now that I am established as England's first queen regnant."

Jane laughs, a fluttery sound that echoes round the chamber.

"Such times we are living in."

"Indeed we are."

A courtier enters following a rap on the door just as Jane and I are settling in again and taking draughts of wine freely. I cannot hide my annoyance at this unwanted interruption to our repose but bid the man state the purpose of his visit immediately.

"Bishop Stephen Gardiner, Sir Francis Englefield and ambassador Renard are here," he states flatly. "They wish to speak with you, Your Majesty, and state that it is of an urgent nature."

"Do they, indeed?" I reply harshly. "Very well, I will see them. Jane, join the ladies and bid them prepare for supper. I will join you all very soon."

QUEEN MARY'S DIARY

WESTMINSTER PALACE, FEBRUARY 1554

I LET THEM STAND FOR A WHILE. I AM IN NO HURRY, NOR INDEED have I any desire to make them feel particularly comfortable. It is late in the day and I have no stomach for affairs of state at this hour. Gardiner is tall and stately with dark brown hair and beard but not particularly pleasing to the eye in appearance. Francis Englefield, I have always liked and found a wise and considerate adviser. He has soft blue eyes and light brown hair. He too is tall, smart in general demeanour and appearance and I would never allow either of them to be upstanding when I myself am standing; my diminutive stature gives me an unpleasant disadvantage. Renard, the Spanish ambassador, is not tall but rotund with very dark hair and beard and, I think, a somewhat sour expression.

"Please be seated, gentlemen," I say when I have composed myself.

"Your Majesty, I regret this intrusion at such an hour, but I must request that you make an immediate decision regarding the Lady Jane Dudley, as she is now styled, presently languishing in the Tower of London," Gardiner states flatly.

"I know well enough where she is, Stephen," I state acidly.

"As to a decision concerning her fate, I will make that at my convenience, nobody else's."

"Of course, of course," he agrees, looking uncomfortable. "But things move on apace. You know I have repeated many times that she is seen as a figurehead to those who would usurp the crown and return us to the misery of the English church and ruin the good work you are engaged upon in fully restoring us all to the legitimate Roman church."

"Have I not dealt with the recent uprising and ordered the execution of Wyatt and his fellow conspirators, including the girl Dudley's father?"

"Yes, Majesty," Gardiner states, looking pained. "Yet the maid, his daughter, still lives."

I wave him away impatiently and remind him yet again that I have always been inclined towards showing mercy to young Jane. She is but a slip of a girl, just 16 years of age and no possible danger to anybody on this earth. I also remind him, once again, that she is of royal blood and my cousin.

"It didn't stop her accepting the crown of England for herself," he replies heatedly, "and leaving you to the mercy of the notorious Duke of Northumberland."

"Your description of Northumberland is accurate indeed," I tell him. "He is the real villain here. He sought to take control of the throne himself by marrying his son Dudley to young Jane and he almost got away with it, I may remind you. Jane was just a pawn in his vile treachery."

I am aware of three pairs of eyes scrutinising me and all holding the same somewhat hostile glare. I begin to feel I am in a minority and it is not a situation I am prepared to tolerate. I tell them acidly that I will give the matter of Dudley close consideration and let them know my decision.

"With the greatest respect, Your Majesty," Gardiner goes on anxiously, "we are of opinion that the matter should be addressed now. Immediately."

Veins stand out on his forehead; it is something I have noticed happening any time he feels he is under strain or in a difficult situation.

"Are you, indeed? Perhaps you'd like to sit upon the throne, Stephen, and rule the country?"

He shakes his head vigorously and I am amused to see the veins turning purple on his brow. I look to Sir Francis who has always been a loyal and considerate servant to his queen and, indeed to kings and queens before me. "How say you, Francis?"

His expression gives me my answer before he says a word. "I regret that I do feel action should be taken now, Majesty," he says in that soft, soothing voice that I normally find so comforting.

"Well, I will not be rushed," I affirm with a brief toss of my head as I turn to Renard.

"Now sir, what news of the Prince of Spain?"

The ambassador regrets that Prince Philip does not see the little Lady Jane as an innocent but rather as a rallying point and symbol for traitors and those that would overthrow a Catholic queen. In time, the followers of the English church would rise and use her to start a new rebellion. The prince regrets that he will be unable to come to England while the girl is living.

That is a blow that I have not seen coming. I lean back in my chair and sigh. I will do whatever is required of me for my people and my country, but I will never, ever, give up the man I intend to marry; a man I feel that I know intimately already, even though we have never set eyes upon each other. I remain silent for some time before turning in my chair and facing Gardiner directly. "Very well. I will sign the death warrant tomorrow noon. She will be dead in two days."

Gardiner's veins are subsiding back to normal. There is relief in his expression. He is about to speak.

"There is one other matter, Majesty. Might I suggest that Lady Jane be given the opportunity to renounce her religion and return to the Holy Catholic church?"

I smile. "She should have that opportunity, I suppose. Who to send, though?"

"Your chaplain, Majesty. John Feckenham, Dean of St Paul's."

"Yes," I whisper thoughtfully. "Ideal."

Sleep will not come. I have endured a night of tossing and turning in bed and fitful, brief minutes of sleep that evaporate and bring me back to full wakefulness. It is still dark, and I can barely make out even dim shapes in the bedchamber, even though the curtains are partially drawn, and I can just see the fading red glow of the fire that has been kept burning through the night to keep me warm. There is just the first faint greyish-white light glowing through the lattices of the window now so the dawn must be fast approaching.

I close my eyes again and keep them tightly shut. I count to 100, try to empty my mind, but the ghosts still appear before me in front of my closed eyelids. My mother sent into long, lonely exile in the country, comfortably accommodated but with no freedom of movement whatsoever. Lady Jane Dudley, her young head severed and lying in a pool of her blood on the cobbles. Red-stained straw. It is this last and most fearful image that tortures me the most and prevents sleep. The fresh face of that young girl will probably haunt me in my dreams for years. Sleep will not come. There is to be no peace or comfort in remaining in bed. I ring my night bell for assistance.

"Fetch my robe and footwear," I instruct. "And request the Lady Margaret to come to me."

Margaret Douglas looks sleepy-eyed and pale of expression, which is little wonder as I have roused her from peaceful slumber. When we are installed in my morning chamber with the fire banked up and fruit and soft drink in front of us on the table, I tell her I am sad to have had to disturb her, but my ghosts will give me no peace and sleep is impossible. She assures me that she is content to be here, ready to serve and is not a heavy sleeper herself at the best of times. Margaret is always a good and sympathetic listener, and I can forgive her many of her sins and caprices for, when my spirits are low, she is my best companion of the night. Or any time, for that matter.

"Was it a very bad dream, Your Majesty?" she asks sympathetically.

"Several dreams, Margaret," I respond. "All with blood flowing freely and a young girl's face that is haunting both my days and sleepless nights."

"Oh, how awful."

"The ghosts will not leave me alone, Margaret. It is to be expected, though. In the first dream my mother Catherine came to me looking as she did when I last set eyes on her, many years ago. Somehow, I had travelled to Kimbolton and I was in her presence. She told me to beware of Wyatt's remaining men."

"What can it mean?" Margaret asks, wide eyed.

"Oh, the first dream is plain enough and to the good," I explain readily. "The ghost of my mother was warning me of the danger from Wyatt's soldiers who escaped capture recently. Those who would rise up and revolt against me once again."

Margaret shakes her head as though unable to comprehend any of it. I feel the warmth of the fire and pull up the collar of my robe as the first grey light of dawn seeps through the window. Extra candles are lit as the light is poor and slow to break through.

"The second dream was the bad one," I continue. "The ghost of Jane Grey came to me and she just stood there, looking at me and accusing me silently. Then her head was off in a pool of blood at her feet but still her eyes looked upwards, accusing me."

"Oh don't, Your Majesty, please," Margaret pleads. "I can't bear to think of how you suffered."

"It is what I must live with," I say gently. "You know, Margaret, I can send any villains like Wyatt to the block happily and dance on their graves afterwards but that young girl…" My voice tails off to a whisper.

"She was a traitor, though."

"Was she? I rather think she was a victim, manipulated by ambitious men for their own ends."

I begin to muse very quietly about dreams and the way the ghosts come to us to warn us or prepare us for events that are not obvious in our everyday lives. It is God's way of sending us messages from the living and the dead of which we would not necessarily be aware. Margaret has closed her eyes and is fast asleep. I smile. I have dragged her out of her warm bed, and I will not waken her now. As daylight slowly brightens the chamber, I feel calmer now and more at peace. There was, after all, no other way that I could have avoided passing sentence.

The amazing thing, to me, is that Jane never wavered for an instant in her faith in the English church. She clutched her prayer book to her chest all the way to the scaffold, mounted it, knelt at the block and died with her faith intact. Feckenham's robust attempts to dissuade her and bring her back to the Roman church came to nothing. She would not be moved, and her faith sustained her right to the end. Contrast that with the ready and willing action of renouncing their English faith practised by The Duke of Northumberland, Jane's father and all the rest of them and her faith becomes even more surprising and impressive. So many men, so many traitors and all so eager, at the end, to renounce the faith they claimed to hold so dear.

It is, though, this false religion that has proved the downfall of so many good men and good women. I would never accept my father's self-appointment as head of the Church in England. Even though he roared and cursed furiously, "Do you defy your father and God's representative on earth, unnatural girl?" I stood firm in what I knew to be just and correct. Which was, of course, my downfall, just like that of my mother and all the good people who lost their lives. So peaceful and pleasurable, though, was my early life as a child when my father was the most popular and loved king in Christendom. He could hold a sword like no other, ride a horse with impressive skill, win a joust as easily as breathing and he was, in truth, an exceptionally fine figure of a man. He loved my mother then and it could be plainly seen, and he loved me. "One day, Mary," he would say, "your little brother, yet to be born, will be king and you will be one of the most loved women in this realm." He was always so certain that he would have a son and gradually became so impatient for the child's arrival that he lost all affection for my mother and me.

When that son finally arrived, it was not my mother or the Boleyn woman but his third wife, Jane Seymour, who delivered it to him. I liked Jane very much and she was a good friend to me. She paved the way for my father to forgive me and bring me back to court, even if I had to accept, finally, that which is most abhorrent to me; to recognise him as head of state and church.

Poor Jane died shortly after childbirth and her boy, Edward was always a sickly and unhealthy child. When he became king, he fiercely championed the new Church of England that my father instigated. When I saw him, I tried hard to get him to reverse his changes, but he was adamant.

"I may lack the physical attributes that made our father a great king, but I can atone and increase my own prestige by taking his changes to our church and implementing them completely. I will advance our new religion far beyond what he envisioned." My protestations went unheeded. Worse still, he harassed and chivvied me to drop the Roman church and cease holding the Mass at home. I never complied.

We were always at odds but when he died, sick and withering at just 15 years, he applied the final insult by removing me from the line of succession in his will and naming Lady Jane Grey as his successor.

Margaret stirs fitfully in her chair but does not waken. She is making up for the sleep of which I deprived her. although I am surprised that she seems so comfortable where she sits. A bell tolls somewhere in the distance and she awakens precipitously. He eyes widen and she looks momentarily astonished as she turns to face me.

"Oh, Your Majesty, a thousand apologies. I have fallen asleep in your presence and that is unforgiveable."

I laugh out loud. "Do not fret, Margaret. All is well."

"Please forgive me."

"It was I who robbed you of your precious sleep to begin with," I tell her, smiling. "The debt is repaid."

My thoughts are still with Lady Jane and her terrible demise, but I must put it all behind me for the sake of my sanity. I console myself with the thought that there is nothing now to impede my forthcoming marriage to the Prince of Spain. With ever-fading reluctance, my councillors, government officials and the clergy have accepted the alliance with Spain and my wedlock. I fought tirelessly to persuade them all and have gained acceptance. My own Spanish blood will be mingled with Philip's and that stately prince will, I hope sincerely, provide me with son and heir. The Tudor line must be retained but allied to the church of Rome. And while it shall last, that alliance will help safeguard our realm from the French and any others that would seek to invade us.

"It must be breakfast time by now," I speculate cheerily.

"Yes." Margaret looks relieved.

"First though, come with me, Margaret," I say. "I want you to see the portrait of my prince. I know you will like what you see."

SIR FRANCIS ENGLEFIELD'S PRIVATE DIARY

⌘

WHITEHALL, LONDON, APRIL 1554

LIVESTOCK ON THE ROADS IMPEDES MY PROGRESS ON MORE THAN one occasion. I urge the coachman to "run on" but he is reluctant to kill or injure sheep or even geese. "Run through them," I instruct him and the coach lurches forward and there are animal screeches and cries from the herdsman but what of that? It will only afford some fortunate common people a dinner for which they will praise God and never forget as long as they may live. An early-morning ride through the streets of London is not a welcome occupation or one I would normally embrace but today is a mission I can hardly avoid. The cobbles shine with recent rain, but the sky is clearer now. It is not so cold as yesterday but fresh indeed. Aldgate is quiet, with very few people abroad but there are more down near the river.

The façade of the Tower of London is bleak, grey and cold this morning, as though the very stonework is aware of what will happen in a few hours' time. More people here are abroad, the early birds seeking a good place to stand. They shuffle resolutely upwards, some heeding the calls of the purveyors of pies or relics depicting the execution scene, who are selling their wares from their barrows.

We draw up outside the residence of the Lieutenant of the Tower and, as I alight from my carriage, Sir John Brydges is already out on his front steps in the fresh morning air.

He greets me cheerfully. "Step inside, Francis," he bids me. "The cold can seep into a man's bones at this time of the morning."

It is indeed cold and will not, I fancy, become much warmer in the next hour or two. April weather can be changeable and capricious, so I am glad to walk into the sanctuary of Sir John's quarters. He enquires if he can get me something to keep out the cold.

"A tot of whisky might do the trick," I respond with a smile.

"Indeed, Francis, I wager that it will."

When we are settled in big chairs with the whisky goblets in our hands, he observes that the crowds are gathering early on this morning. I look out of the window at the newly constructed scaffold and the block on the green.

"So you are here to see justice done, then?" He suggests quietly.

"Not by personal choice or desire, John," I assure him.

"Ah, I thought not."

"Her Majesty wishes me to observe and remain until the deed is done."

"Ah. You are here at her Majesty's pleasure."

I fill in the details for him. "The queen has expressed a loathing of Thomas Wyatt that knows no bounds. She will not be happy until he is dead, his head spiked, and his body quartered. I have advised her in many matters over the past months but never known her to be so agitated over one specific traitor. She has indicated that she will rest content when she knows he has been straitly dealt with. I have not known her previously to be so set on sealing the fate of one man, but he has represented a dangerous threat for some time now and she wishes, no doubt to see the matter finally finished and done with."

"Apart from the treacherous Wyatt," Brydges enquires, "how is her Majesty faring?"

"She is in good heart, John."

He taps his whisky goblet thoughtfully and tells me that Wyatt had requested an interview with Edward Courtenay this very morning. "What was that about, do you think?" I enquire.

"I gather that he sought to get Courtenay to admit his involvement in the rebellion."

"Good luck to him with that one."

"Yes, that's what I thought."

Sir John rises and indicates that a replenishment of our goblets will do no harm and continue to keep out the cold. I too rise and walk over to the window. There is much more activity now and the crowds have grown considerably. The stewards must work hard to keep the rabble back and hold them at a safe distance from the block and some of the most vocal must be encouraged to move by the point of a pike. I turn away from the crowds outside and accept my second measure of whisky.

"On the subject of involvement in the rebellion," I say, "the queen appears convinced that the Lady Elizabeth was involved, and, to that end, I understand, Wyatt's stay in the Tower has been less than comfortable."

"It has indeed," John tells me sombrely. "Although I can tell you that at no point was he prepared to admit to her being involved. Not even, I must say, when he was in the most acute pain from the close attentions of the interrogators."

"That is unfortunate," I murmur. "She will not be pleased. Mary wrote to Elizabeth and requested that she come to London but received reply that her half-sister was unwell with cold and pains and unfit to travel. The queen sent her

THE TITIAN PORTRAIT

physicians to Ashridge and found Elizabeth was indeed in her bed, unwell. The queen was most displeased with that news."

"No sisterly love there then, Francis."

"I doubt there ever has been."

I pause for a moment to reflect that the Lady Elizabeth is at this moment not far from where I am sitting, here in the Tower. I doubt not that she is in comfortable accommodation and being looked after carefully but she must, I feel, be sick at heart wondering what will become of her. And, in truth, if there is any suggestion even, never mind proof, that she was in any way involved in the plot to bring down the government, she will receive no mercy from Queen Mary, blood ties or no.

"I must admit to forebodings," John tells me, "concerning what Wyatt will say when he makes his final speech from the block."

"Yes, that had occurred to me too," I admit.

"If he condemns the Lady Elizabeth from the scaffold, nothing can save her."

"Will he do that, though?" I wonder, speaking the words simultaneously with my thoughts.

"We will find out soon enough, Francis," my companion says.

The sky outside is darkening. Rather than a brightening of the day as the morning progresses, we are seeing the opposite. So much rain this year that we are almost permanently waterlogged. Then the rapid splatter of rain against the windowpanes is heard. Sir John rises and approaches the window to look out.

"Just what we needed," I whisper.

"It will probably pass," John forecasts. "It is April."

Sir John lets out a sudden guffaw as he watches the crowds outside. He reports that none of the people are moving, merely pulling their capes, coats or smocks more tightly round their bodies and huddling closer together.

"They do not want to miss the show," he tells me and advances back into the chamber.

I ask him if he has spoken much to the Lady Elizabeth since her arrival, but he shakes his head. Only a few brief words have passed between them since he escorted her to the royal apartments on the 16th day of last month.

"To be honest, Francis," he begins, "when I do speak to her, her voice is hollow and, although she appears calm and polite, I do sense the fear and horror that is enclosing her."

"Poor girl, she must be terrified," I speculate.

As we walk out of the residence and on to the green, the rain subsides, as Sir John had forecast. Bright, crisp but somewhat damp air is now surrounding us as we move along and take our place facing the structure. The damp cold suddenly bites into the flesh of my face and I shudder, partly from the chill air and partly because of what I am about to witness. If a scene like this is what haunts Elizabeth, who could blame her? It can so easily become her fate and the man who can seal that fate is about to walk across the green to his death.

Thomas Wyatt strides out, gaolers on either side of him and walks down the green to the platform with a defiant expression on his face. His beard has been trimmed right down and finishes beyond his chin in a precise point, looking very neat. He is wearing just a bright white shirt and breeches and must be freezing cold. Perhaps it matters not as he will soon be dispatched to somewhere extremely hot indeed if the scriptures are accurate.

He mounts the steps in jaunty fashion and nods to the executioner, who tightens his grip on the axe. Sir John's deputy leads him towards the block, and he moves swiftly, kicking surplus piles of straw out of his path. Then he is invited to make his final speech and he begins with only the faintest whisper of fear in his voice.

"And whereas it is said and whistled abroad," he begins, his voice faltering almost imperceptibly, "that I should accuse my Lady Elizabeth's grace and my Lord Courtenay; it is not so, good people. For I assure you that neither they nor any other was privy to my rising or commotion before I began. As I have declared no less to the queen's council. And this is most true."

Loud cheers erupt and are soon mixed with a chorus of jeers and hooting. Wyatt turns and bows low to the crowd and then, defiantly, makes an obscene gesture to the section of the crowd where the jeering appeared to come from.

"He's cleared her name," Brydges says. "Good man."

Before I can reply I see Wyatt led to the block, watch him kneel and see the executioner's axe come down with incredible speed and accuracy. The head drops down with a sickening thud that carries across the green and then it rests in a pool of bright, red-stained straw. A collective intake of breath is heard and then, momentarily, silence.

I turn my head away and notice Sir John looking at me interrogatively.

"I only hope the queen accepts his vindication," I say as I feel I need to speak to cover up my horror at what I have just witnessed. "I fear she may not."

"She cannot proceed against her now, though," he replies.

"No. What next?" I ask, nodding towards but not looking directly at the platform.

"The body will now be quartered then taken, with the head to Newgate, parboiled, nailed up and the head placed on a gibbet at St James's," he says. "But we need not wait here longer," he adds, sensing my revulsion.

"No," I agree, turning.

"You could do with another whisky, old chap."

"I do believe I could," I agree. "And I thank you for your hospitality."

"Queen's business, Francis," he says. "Queen's business.

Nothing too good for a servant of the queen working on her behalf."

Sir John is surely immune to executions here, having seen so many. I have not avoided so many in the past but still experience that pang of discomfort if I am close enough to witness the act. I tell him that I have witnessed the execution and can inform Her Majesty of the fact.

"If she requires word about the quartering and spiking, I must exercise my imagination."

I feel immediately warm and comfortable once we have gained access to Sir John's residence. He brings the whisky, and I am immediately warmed and buoyed by the liquid as I take a sip. I take another drink almost immediately and Sir John watches me, bemused; he has probably seen others frequently behaving as I have done but continues to find it fascinating. He shakes his head and then grins.

"Well, it is over now, Francis. Such a foolish man. He should have stuck to writing sonnets like his father."

"The older Wyatt actually invented them, I believe."

"So, what of you, Francis?" he asks jovially. "It is some time since we met and dined or talked together."

"I am certainly kept busy," I tell him. "Mostly at court."

"Yes, but your work is mainly in Berkshire surely? Sheriff of the county and MP?"

"I was sheriff, now I am MP for Berkshire," I admit. "Not much time to spend at Tilehurst Manor these days, though, John, not since I was elected to the privy council."

"Ah yes, Her Majesty is keeping you busy looking after her."

I make a deprecating gesture and smile. "Along with many others, yes."

When I make my departure, I thank Sir John for his kind attention to my comfort and hope sincerely that we can meet again very soon under more pleasurable circumstances. As the coach rattles over the cobbles and another downpour of rain thrashes down, I sit back against the cushions and hope sincerely that the demise of Wyatt will help to focus the queen's mind on other matters of state and erase at least some of her fears of treachery and rebellion from those who follow the new Church of England. She has already started to reinstate the Holy Roman Church back into prominence, but I fear there is much more to be done.

SIR FRANCIS ENGLEFIELD'S DIARY

WHITEHALL PALACE, LATE APRIL 1554

THE COUNCILLORS ARE ASSEMBLED, AND NONE LOOKS HAPPY. My Lord Bishop Stephen Gardiner has an irritated expression as he glances briefly at me and then rolls his eyes upwards to the Tudor Rose in the ceiling. Lord Paget is inspecting his fingers as though he expects them to yield up some fascinating secret. Feet are shuffling constantly. We are often kept waiting for long stretches and the actions taken individually seldom vary. My own distraction has been the raindrops dripping down the windowpanes and I wonder, idly, when and if we will ever receive clement weather this year.

When we hear the first scuffle outside and the door creaks open, we all jump to our feet like Jacks-in-the-box. Queen Mary strides in imperiously and sits at the head of the table.

"Please be seated, gentlemen."

She says we all know why we are here and what she is going to say. I cannot speak for the others, but I can certainly make an educated guess for myself.

"Francis you watched the execution and quartering of the vile Wyatt and heard his last words from the scaffold?"

"Indeed, Your Majesty, I did."

"And what was the gist of his final words?"

"He exonerated the Lady Elizabeth from all involvement in his uprising."

The queen shakes her head vigorously. She indicates testily that she is no fool and ventures the suggestion that the previous interrogators gave her an easy time, bowing and scraping to her as though she were a creature of some importance. She would like to see far more vigorous questioning because she does not doubt Elizabeth's involvement and even, possibly, participation. I wonder how on earth she could have managed that but keep my own counsel.

"So, what say you, Francis?"

"It's difficult to know," I begin cautiously. "Wyatt exonerated her, but he may have wanted to present himself in a gentlemanly light."

"We should perhaps remember," Gardiner suggests, "that she vigorously denied all charges and never wavered for an instant under constant questioning."

"As well she might," the queen says acidly. "As did her mother, the Boleyn woman. But she was found guilty of all charges and, speaking for myself, I was pleased to see her head rolling and turning the straw red."

"Would you be prepared to see Elizabeth executed?" Gardiner asks suddenly.

"I would execute all traitors," the queen replies briskly. "Man, woman or child."

There is a silence in the chamber as everybody except the queen looks down at the table or around the room. My Lord Paget leans across and whispers softly into my ear that blood is thicker than water, he will wager.

"If you have an observation, My Lord," the queen says quietly, "I'm sure we should all like to hear it."

Paget shakes his head and says he was just thinking that it must be exceedingly difficult for her, the queen, to do the right thing. I glance at him and raise an eyebrow slowly, but he looks down at the table.

The queen looks annoyed and her face is turning red. She reminds us angrily that she had to fight for her right as the legitimate queen and next in line in the succession against considerable odds and defeat a huge army of followers of the Church of England under the Duke of Northumberland. She has just put down an uprising by Wyatt and several followers that would have killed her and put Elizabeth on the throne and here she indicates Lord Howard and praises his military skill and courage. Howard inclines his head. "What I am not prepared to do," she continues resonantly, "is allow this young woman, daughter of the abominable Boleyn, to rise up yet again and threaten our kingdom."

We are all completely silent. The Wyatt rebellion has hurt her more than even I thought possible.

"I want her questioned thoroughly once again, pressed hard for answers, forcefully if necessary. Threaten her with the loss of her life if you must. And do not, as one interrogator did inadvertently, refer to her as 'Princess Elizabeth'. Her illegitimacy remains intact."

There is a low murmur around the chamber and some councillors even whisper an obsequious: "Hear, hear."

"We should be pleased if you would take on the assignment, Francis."

I nod acceptance of the task, but Gardiner is looking agitated, and he clears his throat noisily.

"With respect, Your Majesty," he says crisply, "I feel that as Lord Chancellor and Bishop of Winchester, it is a task that I should undertake."

"You will not change her religious beliefs, Stephen," she tells him. "She is her father's daughter in that respect and much more than I could ever be or wish to be. Go though, with Francis, if you so desire."

Gardiner does not look happy. I rather think he felt the assignment should be his alone and without my contribution.

"There has been much discussion about a letter Wyatt is

said to have written to Elizabeth," the queen says, "informing her of his plan to attack me and put her on the throne. She, in fact, denied it in a letter she sent to me just prior to her arrest in March. I did not believe her then and I do not believe her now. Find out the truth, gentlemen, whatever you have to do to get at it."

As we leave the chamber, I am ill at ease at the thought of the task ahead. Gardiner may relish interrogating the Lady Elizabeth, but I am much less enthusiastic. The queen appears to be obsessed with concerns regarding treason from her own half-sister. How have we come to this?

We are shown into the Bell Tower where Elizabeth has now been domiciled. It is sparse indeed, with the stone walls grey and forbidding. There are three small windows and a large fireplace but little in the way of comfort or furniture of any kind. Gardiner wanders over to the terrace and stands looking down. I join him and gaze below at the flowing river with many merchant ships moving slowly and a goodly view, from here, of royal palaces. The water on the river sparkles where a brief burst of sunlight hits it. Gardiner shakes his head and wonders at the extent of views of London available from this vantage point. My thoughts begin to wander, and I recall that Sir Thomas More occupied this very tower once. And look what happened to him.

As we return to the room, the Lady Elizabeth walks in, escorted by two jailers. I know not where she has been taken but it is idle to speculate. I greet her cordially as Gardiner follows me in and greets her stiffly but relatively politely. She looks lost and forlorn somehow, dressed in a brown-and-black kirtle and a plain skirt of dark grey. Her mop of ginger hair is brushed out but not particularly groomed. She is obviously choosing to dress in plain and even dark and sombre clothing but all I can think is that she looks so young and her face so pale. Her eyes, I note, still retain a bright glint, perhaps of defiance and her nose, long and slightly hooked, is an outstanding feature. She is 21 years of age but looks younger in the bright daylight.

"Well, gentlemen, shall we begin?" she asks in a slightly faltering voice that she is obviously trying hard to control.

We sit on stools, brought in for the occasion and Gardiner asks her if she has anything to add to her previous statements.

"I have not indeed," she asserts. "I have been straitly questioned and accused over and, over again and have nothing to add for you, gentlemen."

"The queen is much troubled," I tell her, "concerning the traitor Wyatt's rebellion and his stated intention to overthrow her and put you on the throne, Lady Elizabeth."

"I am not responsible for the activities and intentions of that person," she replies haughtily.

"But you knew about his intentions," Gardiner almost snarls.

"Not at the time he was formulating his plans," she states boldly. "Nor for that matter while he was attempting to put them into action."

"But you found out about them later?" I suggest.

"Only much later when the good lieutenant here, Sir John Brydges, acquainted me of his treachery."

She is sitting very still and very upright, and her face is composed in a serious but relatively calm expression so that the only sign of agitation that I can detect is the continued clasping and unclasping of her hands, although she is mostly trying to keep them out of sight. I admire her strength and spirit. Gardiner is shaking his head and setting his face in such an expression that it is clear he does not believe a word she is saying. A bell starts to toll suddenly, a loud metallic clanging, and we all sit stock still waiting for it to subside.

"Let us turn to the letter sent to you just before the rebellion commenced," Gardiner says.

"What letter?" she demands to know, sullenly.

"Informing you of his intentions and his desire to see you installed as queen."

"I know of no such letter."

"We know of its existence," Gardiner continues hastily, "because it was intercepted by government officials and the contents noted."

"Well, it never reached me," she states with just a hint of agitation and fear entering her voice.

"You must be honest with us," I tell her gently. "It is your only hope."

She sits up straight in her seat and appears to grow two inches. Her expression is a compound of rage, fear and a sense of injustice that I can identify, watching her face and body as closely as I am. She repeats that she is telling the truth and would never lie. If she received such a missive, she would admit to it openly and she resents the suggestion of her dishonesty. Gardiner picks up a candlestick from the table and bangs it down furiously with a cracking sound that causes her eyes to widen.

"Do you take us for fools?" he roars. "By all that's holy, admit you received it, My Lady and we can move along. My patience is evaporating. Do you want to be put to the rack? Your thin frame would quickly wither and your bones break."

Now I do see fear in her eyes; she can hide it no longer. She is seething with pain and rage but somehow exercises remarkable control. I hear a sharp intake of breath as she composes her features and faces Gardiner.

"Sir, you go too far. You have heard the truth and nothing but from my lips. I am of royal blood and should not be treated in this vile fashion. I have nothing else to say."

"Perhaps we should take a short break," I suggest, uncomfortable with the way our interrogation is going.

"God's blood, no," Gardiner shouts angrily. "We will have answers and no breaks or rests until my lady Elizabeth admits what she knows and what reply she gave to that traitor."

Gardiner shouts out questions rapidly, not waiting for answers but moving from one to another rapidly and trying to unnerve and destroy the girl. He wants to know why she has been working endlessly to reinstate the Church of England when the queen has worked tirelessly since coming to the throne to outlaw it. He asks why she did not report the traitor Wyatt when he first approached her and why she was so great a friend of his. Lady Elizabeth remains very still, her face set hard and does not crack as most young women would, swiftly, in this situation.

After a pause in which the only sound is a horn from one of the merchant ships below, she speaks. Her voice is charged with emotion but remarkably clear.

"My Lord Bishop, I will not speak further with you. Sir Francis, will you tell Her Majesty that I have told the truth in every regard in this matter and assure her that I wish her only wealth, health and happiness and I am and will remain, throughout her reign, her most faithful and obedient servant?"

I incline my head but Gardiner, seeing my gesture, is enraged again and begins reciting in gruesome detail the fate that befell Thomas Wyatt and enquires if she would like the same treatment herself. Somehow, I manage to get him out of the Bell Tower and, at the bottom of the circular stone steps we are met by Sir John Brydges.

"Well, gentlemen, did you manage to loosen the lady's tongue?" he asks.

"We did not," I reply. "She is formidable in her resolve to prove she is innocent."

"Fitzalan, my Lord Arundel had several hours trying,"

Brydges responds with a twisted smile. "He was none too gentle in handling her but received nothing for his trouble."

The lieutenant indicates the passageway leading to his office and we follow dutifully along behind him. Gardiner is red-faced and still in a state of anger and frustration at our recent interrogation. Brydges offers us refreshment and we accept wine and sweetmeats from him once we are seated.

"I have a thought," he tells us. "As you know, Edward Courtenay, Earl of Devon, is incarcerated here and Her Majesty, I know, is convinced he was Wyatt's right-hand man in the uprising. He has more than once requested a meeting here with the Lady Elizabeth, which I have denied him. However..."

"If you have an idea, Sir John, let us hear it," Gardiner demands brusquely.

"Well, it is just this. If heavy interrogation won't loosen her tongue, perhaps talking to a friend might."

"I'm not sure they are still friends," I advise cautiously.

"There was talk of their marrying," our host reminds us.

"That idea was more in the frivolous mind of Devon than the lady's," Gardiner points out.

I am quick to suggest that it is surely worth a try. Gardiner shakes his head in a negative fashion as we wait but his expression changes as an idea occurs to him.

"Of course, if you had a spy who could be placed close enough to overhear, Sir John," he says.

"Which is, of course, precisely what I had in mind."

We clink vessels, three conspirators in agreement on a way to find out if Elizabeth is involved and give us something that will please the queen if we are successful. I thank Sir John for his well-made plan, and we head back to Whitehall. Carriages, carts and horses are in abundance on the roads as we return but traffic on the Thames appears sparse by comparison.

LADY ELIZABETH'S DIARY

THE TOWER OF LONDON, MAY 1554

I AM ALLOWED BOOKS TO READ AND PAPER TO WRITE ON, WHICH is more than my poor mother had when they brought her here to die. It is more than Sir Thomas More had when he suffered the same fate and, in truth, I do not know whether or not I will leave this beastly place alive. Courtenay, the Earl of Devon, is anxious to speak with me and has been granted permission. Well, so be it, I will speak with him but will not encourage him in any way. My time with that young man as a suitor has long since expired. I shall have my diary and will use it openly enough and, if he should protest, well, then the interview may end and he can go upon his way, I shall not be indisposed. He is only in the cell below so will not have far to travel.

The gates open with a loud metallic clang and Courtenay enters. He has a broad smile upon his face and no doubt thinks that he can charm me the way he did when I was a mere child of nine or ten years. His appearance is quite striking, it must be admitted; bright eyes, dark hair and a well-trimmed beard are the first features that I notice. He is a good-looking young man, no woman would deny the fact. His doublet is brightly coloured, and he wears pure silk hose.

Indeed, if he were looked upon purely to consider his appearance, he would surely melt any maid's heart immediately. Likewise, any noble lady that came under his spell. I know him however for what and who he is; a scheming, self-serving, never-to-be-trusted creature.

He gives a neat little bow to me and broadens that infectious smile as I acknowledge him and indicate that he may be seated.

"Elizabeth," he begins, "what has happened to the love we shared?"

"I don't know, Edward," I respond. "Gone, blown away in the wind, no doubt."

"We were so close, we had such plans," he says sadly.

"I think," I respond slowly, "you attached far more to what was merely a friendship than was merited."

"Oh, don't say that," he pleads sombrely. "You and I had such love for each other."

"Let me see now," I muse. "Was that before or after you professed such undying love for my half-sister, Mary, the queen?" I ask haughtily.

He bursts out laughing. He gets up and walks over to the terrace to gaze out at the blue sky and the birds flying past. His attentions to Mary were mere flirtations, he asserts, not to be taken seriously. She liked him, she always liked him and saw to his release the first time he was locked up in this place. He played along when she seemed to encourage his advances but there was never anything in it. I am the only true love of his life.

He returns to the table, sits and attempts to take my hand in his but I remove it speedily.

"Elizabeth," he says, frowning, "do you tell me you do not retain at least a scrap of love for me now?"

"Not a scrap, Edward, I'm sorry."

He shakes his head and his expression shows that he can scarcely believe what I am saying. He goes on to say that he is amazed, truly that I should ever have entertained any idea that he was enamoured of Mary. He always regarded her as a family friend, of course, but any other liaison, never. In fact, he muses, the last time he saw her he was somewhat shocked to notice how thin she was and pale of face. Her face always looked somewhat pinched, too, he continues recklessly, and her short stature would never suit him as a companion.

"Have a care sir," I say softly. "These stone walls have ears, you know."

"Yes, I suppose they do," he agrees softly, looking up at the walls expectantly. Then he takes on a serious expression and says that there is something of a more important nature he needs to discuss with me.

"I am in this place because I am suspected of being involved with the late Sir Thomas Wyatt and his infamous rebellion."

I smile because I know full well that he did not regard the rebellion as infamous and was, most likely, fully involved in it and hopeful of its successful conclusion. "I know," I say. "I too am falsely accused."

He lowers his voice to a barely audible whisper and inclines his head closer to me across the table.

"There is the question of this letter Wyatt wrote to you that is being discussed abroad everywhere."

"What letter?"

"You know," he continues whispering. "The letter stating his intention to overthrow the government and place you on the throne of England."

"I know of no such letter," I tell him in a normal voice.

"Oh, come on, Elizabeth. It was addressed to you, although, I have heard it whispered, intercepted by the government. Then sent on to you as the intended recipient. The Queen needs only proof that you received it and were sympathetic to its contents."

"Then all is well," I reply calmly, "because I never received it."

"I cannot believe you deny it," he says, shaking his head. "I need to know if that missive attempts to implicate me."

"Then you must seek out the true recipient," I tell him. "I cannot help you."

He looks angry. He gets up again and commences pacing the flagstones. I suggest that our discussion is at an end and he should be on his way. He walks back and faces me but does not resume his seat.

"You and I are in great danger," he whispers urgently.

"Do you think I am not aware of that?"

He shakes his head as though despairing of the caprices of a small child. I am glad when he is gone, out of my sight for, in truth, I do not like him or trust him. Were we once close and contemplating a union together? I think not. He was always too much in love with himself anyway and, as an incredibly young girl, I was confused and did not know what I wanted. He was a mere dalliance, a cocky young boy and in any event, I knew he had set his cap at Mary because she was next in line to the throne whatever horrors our father had placed in our paths. I was described as illegitimate to suit the whims of my father and his relentless, selfish pursuit of a male heir. Well, he got one eventually, my poor, sickly half-brother Edward VI, and his few brief years on the throne made little impact. We are now thrown back to the Church of Rome as Mary steadfastly undoes everything Henry and Edward did. And what more might she do, indeed?

I am visited by Sir John Brydges, Lieutenant of this Tower but he is a just and not unkind man so I bear him no ill will. He urges me to avoid Edward Courtenay in future, a policy with which I am more than willing to comply.

"I never want to set eyes on that man again, not ever," I assure him.

"That's good," he agrees. "It's not my business, Lady Elizabeth, but the rumours are rife, as I'm sure you are aware, even in this place. If Wyatt's plan were to remove Queen Mary and replace her with you and Courtenay as your husband, and that is indeed the story going around, the greater distance you are from him, the better."

"Well, I thank you for your concern, Sir John," I murmur softly, "although I need not remind you that you gave him permission to speak with me."

"And you agreed to the meeting."

I nod. "Yes, I did. I wanted to find out what he knew and if he was working in conjunction with the queen, perhaps placed in this place as a spy. At least I know now that he feels as threatened as I do."

"This letter from Wyatt," Sir John begins tentatively.

"Oh, not you, too, Sir John. I tell you as I've told all the others, I never received any such letter."

"No, no but may I put forward a suggestion, purely for the sake of argument?"

"Only for argument's sake?"

"For no other purpose whatsoever."

"Please continue."

His suggestion, tentatively suggested, is that if, just for argument's sake, I admit to receiving the letter but state that I destroyed it immediately, I would look far less guilty and bring to an end their persecution. After all, they know the letter existed as they have seen it.

"And I could say, just for argument," I venture carefully, "that I denied receiving it for fear that I would have been thought to be implicated in the plot."

"Exactly so."

"Although they still might not believe me," I speculate. "They seem determined that I should be guilty."

"I think it gives you a much better chance, Lady Elizabeth. And they cannot prove anything. They have no evidence."

"No, they haven't."

"It could hasten the end of the persecution."

"It could," I concede.

He tells me that he must now be about his business. The smooth running of the Tower will not continue without his close supervision. He rises from his stool to depart.

"Thank you, Sir John, for your suggestion. It was obviously made with good intention."

"Indeed."

"Not that it makes any difference. I never received any such letter, and I will tell them so if they persist in further interrogation."

SIR FRANCIS ENGLEFIELD'S DIARY

WESTMINSTER PALACE, MAY 1554

I AM SUMMONED TO THE QUEEN'S PRESENCE. THAT CAUSES A little prickle to the hair at the back of my neck because usually I am told that the queen has requested my attendance. If she is angry about something, I must always have my wits about me for her bad temper and occasional rages are in direct opposition to her usually quiet and relatively placid demeanour. Since the dreadful business of Wyatt's uprising, though, she has not been her usual self. I hurry to her. Her ladies in waiting are busily sewing or weaving and one or two look up and give me a look or a provocative smile.

"Really, Francis, we are most unhappy," she greets me and some of the ladies put hands in front of their mouths to hide their amusement. The queen shakes her head in annoyance.

"Come into the anteroom," she snarls, nodding to a servant who manages to open the door only just in time.

"I asked you and the chancellor to break Elizabeth and get a confession," she continues. "What is going on? Please tell."

"She maintains her innocence," I inform her. "And cannot be shaken."

"Cannot be shaken?" the queen shouts. "I'll shake her till

her eyes pop. I'll have her hung up by her toenails and have her scrawny body stretched."

The queen is shaking all over but as I maintain a controlled silence and she realises her undignified behaviour, she gradually calms down and lets out a loud sigh.

"What is going wrong with the interrogations, Francis?" she asks, quieter now. "Why are you failing?"

I tell her that we have been back again and interrogated the Lady Elizabeth but, short of using the most fearsome torture, have been unable to shake her insistence that she is completely innocent. I tell her that Sir John at the tower advised that we press her to admit that she received the Wyatt letter because he believed she would admit it. He was wrong. I remind her that since our last attempt she has been visited by Lord Arundel and Lord Paget and they, too, had failed to make any progress.

"Do not justify your failure by quoting theirs," she warns.

"That was not my intention," I reply haughtily.

The queen smiles. "All right Francis, don't get all arrogant."

I glare at her silently.

She becomes calmer now all round and sits back in her high-backed chair. "She is guilty, Francis, I know it. I feel it in my bones."

"Without evidence or a confession, though…" I say, and my words trail off so that I cannot continue.

"I want this matter resolved. Ambassador Renard warns of the consequences."

"Renard is here?"

She smiles. "I have him tucked away safely. Come along."

She whisks me out of the chamber and along the corridor at a rapid walking pace. None too regal or dignified but, when Mary is in a hurry, she is capable of a brisk walking pace. Her slight build, stomach cramps and general listlessness all seem to disappear temporarily when the queen is in a hurry. Ambassador Renard greets her, bowing low and bestowing a brief nod in my direction. The queen asks him to repeat what he said to her earlier today.

"I advised her Majesty," he begins unctuously, "that the King of Spain and his son, The Prince Philip, are fearful of an imminent uprising centred upon the Lady Elizabeth and the Duke of Devon, Courtenay. A Church of England uprising. Which, of course, would be catastrophic, considering all the good work Her Majesty has done to restore the Church of Rome to rightful prominence."

"Yes, I see," I respond.

"But do you, Francis?" the queen demands to know, looking agitated once again. "I will not risk my prince feeling unsafe and unable to travel to England. The future of our country and our Roman church depends upon it.

"My marriage to Philip is crucial to the safety of our realm," she continues. "It will confound the French and other enemies of our country. It will be a Catholic alliance that will strengthen us and Spain and the whole world will be safer."

She really believes that, I think, and she may well be right, all things considered.

"I will not have my prince feeling unsafe here. It is monstrous," the queen says, looking wounded. "And I will most certainly not have my marriage put in jeopardy."

Renard says that the queen is right, the danger is very real for everybody. I must bring pressure to bear to secure a confession because if not, he fears, the English church people will rise up in their hundreds and thousands and place Elizabeth on the throne. The queen tells me I must go back and freshen my approach. She requires results quickly and, if they are not forthcoming, there will be a heavy price to pay.

"And take Gardiner with you," she instructs. "He has the teeth of a tiger and a cruel streak, which is what we need in this situation."

"Might I suggest, Your Majesty..?" I begin but I am cut short.

"Why am I thinking you are about to say something that will not please me?" the queen asks stridently.

"I just wonder, Majesty, if we have not exhausted all possibilities. She has been remarkably consistent in her denials throughout."

"Time for some implements of persuasion, maybe? Go and speak to Gardiner, Francis. You have been a good friend and a wise adviser in the past. Let us not change that."

I walk briskly but without enthusiasm through the streets of Westminster. At Gardiner's house a servant escorts me to the garden, where I find him sitting in the arbour, a tankard of beer in his hand and a jug full of the liquid on a small table in front of him. The sun is shining and the fountain splashes out cool water constantly. A large blackbird alights on the flagstones in front of the arbour, but the bishop kicks out his foot towards it and it flies off hastily with a thrashing of wings. I walk across the flagstones.

"Let me guess why you are here, Francis."

"Three, if you wish."

"Don't need them. More pressure on Elizabeth?"

I nod and a servant hands me a tankard of beer on Gardiner's swiftly interpreted gesture. I take a seat and a welcome draught of the ale. It is pleasant in the sunshine and I yearn to return to Englefield House for a few days' rest. My London home is dark and forbidding, too big for my needs and I have never felt comfortable in it.

"Arundel and Paget got nowhere yesterday," Gardiner says, looking thoughtful.

"So I understand."

"Too soft and prissy. Both of them."

"We start again, then?"

"With a difference, Englefield, with a difference. The ironware implements of persuasion will be on display and they will be used this time."

There must be another way, I suggest but he grins, and I suddenly realise that there is no other way now. The very thought of inflicting severe pain on that young woman is utterly repulsive to me. As a privy councillor with several responsibilities in government, it is my duty to carry out any tasks set by the queen. Or resign from government. It is with this bleak thought in mind that I bid Gardiner good afternoon and retreat from his home. I cannot face the prospect of tomorrow's activities with any optimism.

Gardiner has a sickening expression on his face, as though he has enjoyed the last five hours. After such a long time in the dark spaces of the tower, where even the walls feel cold and wet, it is a pleasure to step out into the sunlight. The barge awaits us, gleaming brightly in the sun with a colourful canopy and the oarsmen waiting expectantly. We step on board and the craft moves out slowly, under St Thomas's Tower and on to the open waterway of the Thames. We settle down under the canopy as the barge heads out towards Westminster. The river is calm with silver fish jumping up intermittently. My Lord Bishop looks upwards to the sky and emits a long sigh.

"I will never go through a day like that again," I tell him sombrely.

"You are squeamish, Francis," he says quite jocularly. "Like a maid."

People are gathering on the green banks on either side of the river and some wave at us, thinking perhaps that our colourful barge is transporting the queen, hidden from view at the back of the canopy, behind us. Stephen Gardiner waves back, amused at the attention we are receiving.

"You must grow a thicker skin," he tells me. "Much worse lies ahead of you."

"I think not," I growl.

"Interesting, then," he muses, "to see how you avoid it."

I look straight ahead towards Westminster but all I see is Elizabeth's defiant face and all I hear are her repeated, horrified denials. The feelings of discontent and revulsion are growing inside me with every passing minute until I begin to feel quite physically sick. I breathe deeply, in and out, repeatedly, trying to calm my spirit and my soul.

"And all that pain inflicted," I say when I calm down a little, "all the abuse, accusations and threats, what did it yield?"

"Her disgust and fear," he replies. "Her futile attempts at dignity. Her supreme discomfort."

"You enjoyed that?" I ask in disbelief.

"I did. She is a heretic and a danger. All her pain enlivens my spirit."

"You disgust me, Stephen," I inform him.

He lets out a roar of coarse laughter that crackles into the warm air and disperses outside the confines of the barge. People in smocks and work clothes are growing in number in front of our eyes on either bank as we move closer to Westminster. The sky is a clear blue as I gaze upwards. The oars dip in and out of the water with precise regularity. The sound of water splashing is all we hear for a few moments as all else around us is still and peaceful.

Stephen is a man of the church, but I find him cruel, unsympathetic and unyielding in his mistrust of people from all walks of life. The last few hours have brought me to a point where I can no longer continue in my present occupations. My future is uncertain.

"And at the end of it?" I wonder quietly.

"She is a ragged mess. A broken doll. Tomorrow she will crack wide open."

"No, Stephen," I say solemnly. "Her resolve is unbreakable. She will never confess. She will continue to protest her innocence even to death."

"Not if I have anything to do with it. I will break her if it's the last thing I do."

And I know now what I must do tomorrow.

SIR FRANCIS ENGLEFIELD'S DIARY

WHITEHALL AND ENGLEFIELD HOUSE, BERKSHIRE, MAY 1554

THE BARGE MOORS ALONG THE BANK AT WESTMINSTER LATE IN the afternoon. I step out and look around. I had not intended to return to London so soon; just two days in the country and I was feeling almost refreshed and invigorated. Now I am summoned back before I am ready to face the present circumstances. I turn away from the busy river with its constant stream of shipping and barges and walk through Westminster. Before going to Whitehall, I intend to find out why I was recalled so suddenly and, as the messenger came from Lord Paget, I walk to his house.

The servant shows me into Paget's privy chamber and brings wine and sweetmeats. Paget sweeps in looking hot and bothered and removes his doublet. It is an extremely hot but muggy day without sunshine or any relief from the blanket of mist and smoke that surrounds the city. He shakes my hand heartily and sinks into his high-backed chair.

"This weather is stifling," he complains.

"Bad enough in winter," I sympathise. "Unbearable in summer."

He pours wine and we both drink. My throat has been dry and somewhat irritated since arriving back in London due, no doubt, to the heavy atmosphere created by the mist and smoke. As my return to London was requested by Paget, I ask him what it is all about.

"I'm just the messenger," he states. "I know no more."

"Who wants me, William? You must know."

"The queen, Francis," he says chirpily. "You were always the favourite."

After attempting to squash that nonsense, I wonder why she wishes to see me back after such a short time away in the country. "No doubt she is pining for your company, Francis, and couldn't bear to let you stay away for long."

I caution him not to talk such nonsense but acquaint me, if he knows, with the reason for my recall, just as I was beginning to rest and feel invigorated by the fresh Berkshire air and my favourite countryside.

"I truly do not know, Francis," he assures me, "although I could hazard a guess."

"Do so, then."

"She seems much cheered by Parliament passing her bill for regal power. Not surprisingly, perhaps."

We both smile. The queen harried us all for many weeks to pass a bill that enshrines in law that queens hold power "as fully, wholly and absolutely as their male predecessors". After the pressure she exerted on all of us and her almost daily lectures in parliament to realise that as the queen regnant of England and Ireland, she must have, and demanded, full power and authority. She is understandably pleased at the bill passing through the chamber.

"No stopping her now," I say, grinning.

"No," he answers. "Do you know, Francis, only yesterday she was prancing about and making a speech about us all thinking she was a weak and feeble woman but assuring all who cared to listen that she had the heart and strength of a lion and would always do right for her country."

"Strong words."

"She means it, Francis."

"I'm sure. Time I presented myself, then."

On the walk down to Whitehall, my throat is again assaulted by a miasma of impure air. A dull, overcast day always makes the heavy atmosphere much worse. Even the white stone of the palace appears grey and sombre on such an afternoon. Inside, all is dark and oppressive and in need of some candlelight to brighten the darkness.

I finally find the queen in her morning privy chamber, where she seems to prefer to be no matter what time of the day or night. When I enter, she swiftly dispatches her ladies to another place and then looks askance at me. "Francis, you are late," she chides. "I expected you back here this morning."

"I received the summons only yesterday afternoon," I inform her.

"Well, I needed you," she complains. "You know you are a trusted adviser. And a friend."

She favours me with a penetrating look that is accusatory in expression, as though I had ill-used her. When I look closely at her I notice her pale complexion and anxious, red-rimmed eyes. The queen, I muse to myself, has a rather pinched look about her face which is not helped when she is vexed and frowns. As she is doing now. She says she is desirous of a serious conversation with me, so I prepare myself for her questions. Before settling, though, she changes her mind and asks me to accompany her to another chamber. We enter and she directs my attention to a large portrait hanging on the far wall.

"This is Philip," she says, brightening a little as she gazes at the portrait. "I haven't shown you previously, have I?"

"No."

"He is a fine, handsome, sturdy fellow."

"He is indeed."

"The man I intend to marry, as you know."

Her thoughts appear to wander and she walks slowly out

of the room, so I follow her at a distance. I hear her say that she has had enough resistance to marrying her prince and will broach no more, from anybody. Under any circumstances. I make no reply as I am uncertain how I am expected to respond but, as soon as we are returned to her morning chamber, she has become quite combative once again. She knows, she says, that I am not content. I came to her two days ago and asked for time away in the country but offered no reason for my application. Now I am back, and it is time for answers.

"So, what ails you, Francis?"

"I am not content, as you say," I tell her. "I feel that I should retire from most, if not all, of my public duties."

"I hope you don't," she says, looking alarmed. "What has brought this on, Francis?"

"I could talk about unrest in the country, the skirmishes between English church people and Catholics but the main problem, I think, is the ongoing persecution of your half-sister."

"I can relieve you of any further contact with that troublesome woman," she says in stark, clipped tones.

"Thank you, Your Majesty."

That is not everything though, is it? Not by a long way. She can see in my expression that other things are troubling me, and I can rely on her to change them. I am her most trusted adviser and a good friend and she cannot contemplate my leaving her court. Will I reconsider? She needs honest people she can trust by her side and she will not hold this little disagreement against me. Have I her support and loyalty still?

"Majesty, I am and will always be your most loyal and faithful servant," I say with conviction. "At present, though, I still feel I need time to consider my position."

She looks as though she is about to explode in anger and condemnation. Her eyes glint dangerously, and I feel rather

THE TITIAN PORTRAIT

uncomfortable. She glares at me for some time taking a long pause before speaking so that my discomfort increases.

"Take as long as you like, Francis," she says finally, surprising me. "Go back to Berkshire and your Catherine. I should not have recalled you so soon."

I bow down low and thank her profusely for her gracious generosity. I will always serve her loyally, even if I am unable to support specific projects. Ever since meeting her first when she was a young girl and I was knighted by her half-brother Edward VI, I have liked and respected her. Like all good Catholics, I learned early about her shameful treatment by her father and the dispatch of her poor mother, the Spanish Queen Catherine who did no wrong but was abandoned by Henry. Now I admire her strength, courage and determination as our first queen regnant, in her own right, supreme sovereign of England and Ireland. If her feud with her half-sister is ill advised I can, at least, understand why she fears so much; the very real threat of the Church of England supporters. They are many and varied. And the country at large is most discontented with her choice of a Spanish prince as her future husband.

I will retreat to my home in the country and reflect at leisure on my position. It will do me no harm if the queen respects my reasons and trusts my loyalty as I believe she truly does. I prepare to take my leave of her.

"One thing, Francis, before you depart?"

"Majesty?"

"How would you resolve the problem of Elizabeth?"

"I would release her, Your Majesty."

I await the outburst with trepidation, but it does not come. Instead of angry accusations of disloyalty and disappointment at my words she appears to be thinking deeply and weighing up my response in her mind. In charged silence.

"Which is, oddly enough, the advice I received from my prince, through ambassador Renard. He seems to think the greater threat comes from the Scottish Mary and that Elizabeth should be freed."

"I incline my head and raise an eyebrow but can make no reply."

"All right, Francis, leave it with me. I make no decision now."

I gaze out at the lake shimmering under a clear blue sky. It is good to just stand here in solitude and welcome silence and look ahead to only tree and bush and fresh green pastures. Good too, to feel only soft warm grass under my feet rather than the mud that seems to occupy London streets practically all the year round. Even in summer. No sounds of horses' hooves, clatter of heavy wagons and barrows or the street cries of merchants and their assistants rending the air. A distant tolling of church bells. That is something I welcome hearing, as now.

As I gaze around, it seems to me that I could indeed surrender most of my current duties, retire from court and council life and just function here in my native county of Berkshire as member for the area and magistrate. It seems I must have walked a good six or seven miles now, across fields, up hills and down dales, passing an occasional cottage of straw and wattle and an ancient stone church. Fresh air in my lungs is as good a tonic as any physician ever prescribed and the bird song all around is indeed, music to my ears.

I stroll back in leisurely fashion to Englefield House thinking, at this moment, that this life will suit me, and I will not miss the cut and thrust of parliament. At my leisure, too, as I do not expect a sudden recall to London on this occasion. The barge journey from town was long and tiresome yesterday although I appear to have recovered very quickly with the aid of a good night's sleep and fresh country food. As I gain access to the house as quietly as I can, I still manage to attract

THE TITIAN PORTRAIT

the attention of an alert servant who springs out of nowhere to open doors for me.

"Bring me wine and marchpane slices, please," I request. "And attend the wishes of Lady Catherine."

In the chamber, all is quiet and peaceful with Catherine engaged in embroidery and state papers, which I do not intend even to look at for several days, strewn across the table.

"I thought a walk meant a stroll down to the gates," Catherine chides. "Not a tour of the county."

"Have I been so long?" I enquire mildly.

"So long? I even thought you might have returned to London without a word."

I smile and pat her hand as I settle down next to her in my own high-backed chair. The servant brings the wine, marchpane and sweetmeats and lays it out in front of us. Catherine looks vigorous and healthy with her green eyes and long dark hair but most of all I am aware of her rosy cheeks, a sight rarely encountered in town unless it be applied by powder and paint. Her brightly coloured kirtle is another sight that is pleasing to the eye today. A cheerful fire burns brightly, too, although it is in readiness for a cooling evening rather than the present warm afternoon. Catherine, though, is becoming testy over the fact that I returned to London two days ago and then reappeared suddenly yesterday.

"Is all well with you and the queen?" she asks.

"Yes," I respond reflectively. "She is mindful of my concerns and worries."

"I'm sure she is," Catherine says with a knowing look which I do not find particularly to my taste.

I point out that the queen has much to occupy her mind and that of parliament just now. The recent street skirmishes between Catholics and protestants occupied her mind recently and putting down the more violent and aggressive groups has stretched the resources of her law-and-order stewards. I myself have been involved in handing out punishments to some of the worst offenders. Then there is the continuing problem with the Lady Elizabeth.

"Elizabeth is her father's daughter," Catherine suggests. "She will promote the new English church even to the point of death."

"Yes, that's what I'm afraid of."

"Well, you can't save her, Francis. Be assured of that."

"It's all coming to a head now," I continue. "Which is the main reason I needed to get away and rest."

Catherine smiles enigmatically. She pours more sweet wine into our crystal goblets and hands one to me. She thinks I spend too much time and effort in trying to please the queen and too little on my duties as the member for Berkshire. I point out gently that I cannot be in two places at the same time and if my duties tend to conflict on occasion, I must and will give my attention to queen and country.

"Fine words, Francis, fine words. Watch though that you do not get your hands burnt."

"Meaning what, precisely?"

"The queen may turn on you when you least expect it."

"That will not happen."

"Well, be cautious is all I say," she continues. "She has turned on others, as you well know. She executed Northumberland and Grey and the others who promoted young Jane as sovereign with, I am given to understand, a smile on her face. And she executed Jane, her own cousin, without compunction." I shake my head vigorously for I cannot agree with this assessment of Mary. I have always found her fair and just and willing to listen to sound advice. Catherine smiles with that knowing smile that can be quite irritating.

"Just have a care, Francis. That is all I say. I know how fond you are of her."

"Fond is not a word I find appropriate," I tell her with an

edge in my voice. "She is our queen, and I am merely a faithful servant."

"Well maybe you should direct your fidelity closer to home," she responds. "The queen will promote her own faith before ought else and push aside anyone who gets in her way. Keep a good head on your shoulders. And I mean that quite literally."

I find these words unacceptable and hurtful and caution Catherine to have a care. I remind her that I always put duty first as I am obliged to do in my position, but she is first in my thoughts and plans as my wife and companion. We live in the most troubled times and must find our way through the maze with as little agitation and confusion as possible. What the future has in store none of us may know but we must all work together to try to ensure a prosperous time ahead and cancel out the privations and horrors of the recent past. The late King Henry treated his elder daughter abominably and took her back to court only after she had been forced to renounce her religion against her will and take an oath of allegiance to the new church that she hated. If she is now going to great lengths to restore that religion in our country, who could blame her? As a staunch Catholic, not I, certainly. I have spent time in the Tower of London under guard myself but not during Mary's reign. She it was indeed that secured my release and welcomed me into her fold.

"Strong words, Francis," she says brightly. "You are a good politician, to be sure. But let us not disagree. I have planned something a little special for tonight."

We are to have supper in the large banqueting hall on this, my first full day back at home. What Catherine has arranged I do not know but she has a twinkle in her eye as she leads me down the long gallery to the hall. Our table has been arranged against the back wall and in front of us, a large area of the flagstone floor appears set up for an entertainment. Above, in the gallery, a company of musicians are already playing a jig on trumpet, sackbut, lute and viol. They wear colourful costumes in panels of red, white, blue and yellow. Their faces are radiant as they play, happily filling the large hall with music to brighten and cheer weary souls.

"So where did you find this motley crew?" I ask.

"Mostly from local farms and cottages," she says, grinning. "Organised by one of the estate stewards."

Next the arrival of food as the musicians slip into a stately air and slow down the tempo. In comes a large roasted boar, great legs of mutton, chicken and cherries, a delicacy favoured by Catherine, and assorted larks and pheasant. Onions, too, are provided and artichoke with a fresh loaf of pure white bread. A servant requests my desire and fills a plate as I feel quite hungry due to my lengthy walk earlier.

"Music to delight," I say, accepting another portion of roast pheasant, "and food to fill the empty belly. What more could I ask?"

"Well, you come home so infrequently now," Catherine comments with just a hint of reproach. "I thought a feast and entertainment was quite in order."

"Yes, thank you. 'Tis well received."

"More to come," she whispers mysteriously.

As I accept another plate of roasted boar and some soft, trimmed lark breast with onion, the musicians end their tune and slowly pick up their instruments and depart from the gallery. Suddenly there is pandemonium on the floor in front of our long table. A troupe of masque players in coloured costumes and hideous facial masks skip on and start to dance. Some, at the rear, play flutes and beat drums as the players begin their performance. It soon becomes apparent, as the masque unfolds, with many a ribald shriek and shout, that this is an enactment of the trial and execution of Sir Thomas Wyatt. My wife is beaming and she bursts out laughing as a figure with head swathed in fabric turns his back and produces a paper and glue model of a head, hideous in aspect and they all mime having it chopped off.

The troupe performs in mime a pageant whereby the lords and ladies, singing lustily, kick the head around the stones until it is a mass of mangled paper and glue. Catherine is laughing still, and she looks to me to check my mood. In truth it brings back memories I would rather forget of the actual event and the real head in a pile of straw soaked in blood. She has gone to much trouble and forethought to put on a special event for my homecoming and I cannot bring myself to censure her.

"Look how well they perform," Catherine murmurs. "And how they enjoy it."

I nod, not trusting my voice to betray my feelings.

Servants sweep in with a jelly of monstrous size, designed in bright colours in the shape of Englefield House. There are also plates laden with marchpane, sweet delicacies of fruit and sugar and various exotic sweetmeats.

"I can eat no more," I say, smiling.

"Oh, come now, Francis," Catherine protests, "you must have a little light jelly. I had it specially designed as our house and the cook has done so well."

I give way gracefully and in fact find the soft, fruity jelly an aid to digestion rather than a hindrance. Fresh, sweet French wine arrives at table and I drink more of that to help down the jelly. The monstrous masque has concluded, and the players troop out as the musicians return to the gallery and resume playing. We begin to feel mellow and warm as the jigs played are light and skippy and the huge fire is being banked up to keep out the later evening chill. Catherine turns to me and says that she hopes I found the food and entertainment to my liking.

"Indeed, yes."

"Of, course, I can never match the lavish and spectacular

entertainments the queen provides," she says wistfully. "I do fully realise that."

I pat her hand and refuse to be drawn into the contentious statement. Catherine smiles knowingly and focuses her attention on the musicians. The debris of the meal is cleared away and we are contented. When the musicians leave, they are given a large bag of coins.

It has been a pleasant day, though not without its shocks and surprises. When we mount the staircase to go to bed, I find that my bedchamber has been fitted out with extra, scented candles and a rather luxurious looking over-blanket.

We stand at the threshold.

"I trust you will be comfortable, Francis," Catherine whispers, looking in.

"I'm sure I shall," I confirm. "As I hope you will be."

"Yes," she murmurs. "And if you should wish to visit my bedchamber later, I can accommodate you."

I smile and say that the day has been long, and I am most like to fall asleep as soon as my head touches the soft, feathery pillow.

"Yes," she says briskly. "Goodnight, Francis." And she walks quickly down the corridor towards her own bedchamber.

SIR FRANCIS ENGLEFIELD'S DIARY

WHITEHALL PALACE, MAY 1554

The days spent at Englefield House were bright, invigorating and charged me both physically and mentally. What I had not expected was that after just four days I began to feel a sense of loss and detachment from my normal working life. I surprised myself by missing the cut and thrust of government work and my own position of privy councillor. The next few days after that I began to feel in limbo even as I enjoyed my native countryside and some unexpectedly fine spring weather. If Catherine guessed my feeling of isolation, she said nothing, and I did not attempt to enlighten her. And although grateful for a pleasant break from routine duty, I was not sorry when the time came to return to Westminster.

Now I gaze around the table at my fellow councillors and wonder, idly, what on earth I was so anxious to return to. The queen has already hinted that she can put my mind at rest regarding my thoughts of retiring from several duties. She spoke to me briefly before the present council meeting and plans, I am led to believe, to speak to me once again shortly.

"We can take this matter no further at present," she announces, "so you gentlemen are excused."

Several councillors look either bemused or annoyed, as though they think more discussion of the subject recently under review should continue. Bishop Gardiner clears his throat noisily and prepares to leave the chamber, standing up in readiness. The rest of us prepare to move but the queen indicates that I am to remain seated. They file out slowly and silently and I watch them go, my curiosity aroused.

"I trust you are well rested and invigorated," the queen says.

"Thank you, yes, Majesty, I am."

"That is good. You should know that we have been advised by my prince once again and are inclined to release the Lady Elizabeth from custody."

I nod and compose my expression to indicate contentment. She continues: "We are not altogether content regarding her current incarceration as we are advised that she has been given privileges that we never authorised. Moving her from the Bell Tower to state apartments was never my intention and even allowing her to walk freely along the walkway before that, I deplore. We are, however, further advised that she has been quite ill with stomach cramps and other diverse ailments so, being of a forgiving and generous nature, I intend to take no further action. Allied to that the intelligence from Ambassador Renard convinces me that Prince Philip is anxious that mercy should be shown to her and she is to be released immediately."

"Your Majesty is indeed wise as well as compassionate."

"Yes well, I know it is what you want. And we hope this removes any thoughts on your part to relinquish important aspects of your duties."

She is obviously in magnanimous mood and I do not wish to change that by leaving my situation in abeyance any further. I indicate that I am happy to continue in my present duties as her loyal and faithful servant. There is something else on her mind, however. I know her moods and expressions so well by now and wonder what is coming next.

"She is not to be given entire freedom, however. We have arranged for her transport to Woodstock where she will be held under house arrest under the close supervision of Sir Henry Bedingfield. He is a good servant to me and will keep her in close view."

Next, I am informed that the journey to Woodstock will be undertaken the following morning by barge to Richmond Palace by river and then on, the following days by road, stopping overnight at Windsor, West Wycombe and Rycote. She is to be escorted by Sir John Williams, Sir Leonard Chamberlain and Bedingfield. The journey should take four to five days. I nod and say that she will be well taken care of and watched. It is not quite what I expected or hoped for but is better than continued incarceration in the Tower.

"We shall be pleased if you will accompany her as far as Richmond by water and report back to me on her state of mind and behaviour."

"As you wish, Majesty."

She inclines her head and I look at her and realise she is not as content as she would have me believe. I know her so well and possibly too well for my own good. She is restless and cannot settle. She raps her fingers on the table in a slow, drum-like monotonous fashion. Finally, she tires of this pursuit and wanders over to the window. As she looks down, she commands my presence next to her and I walk over swiftly.

"Look at them, Francis," she says. "The bargemen, the carters, the farm workers, that beggar down there. That scruffy fellow playing the hurdy-gurdy across the street. They expect a king's leadership."

"So?" I ask, not sure what she is thinking.

"Well, they have got me, not a king but a princely queen."

Her outburst is sudden and unexpected. From relative

calm but disquiet she is now angry and inflamed. She thinks that the members of the Privy Council do not take her seriously or believe she can deliver the changes and reforms she plans. I can assure her of my belief and loyalty, and I do but it seems it is not that which is concerning her. It is the open disbelief in her abilities by councillors that she finds unacceptable.

"Take earlier this morning," she says. "They were all reluctant to push through a bill to improve our coinage, but I am determined to do it."

"You had my support," I remind her.

"Oh, I expect your support, but thank you, Francis, it is appreciated. It will be done, and I intend to increase the weight of gold and silver for our future coins."

When she is calmer and we are both seated, I try to change the subject by asking about the times for tomorrow's transport, but she will not be diverted.

"When will they learn, Francis, that it isn't just a set of words in a statute that queens hold power as fully and absolutely as their male predecessors?" she demands to know. "It means that I will exercise my full powers and push through any bill I think right and proper for the people of this realm."

"Quite right, Majesty. And you hold that power."

"I do. And while I am at it, I tell you, I will have our sea defences strengthened and I will have many new ships built. They'll give me a fierce argument on that, too."

It is early morning with just a faint white light breaking through to dawn. Mist enshrouds the Tower of London at this hour as the barges approach. A biting chill is in the air, too, even though we are late into the month of May. I shiver involuntarily as we moor, and Sir Henry Bedingfield alights.

"I'll just secure her release," he calls. "No need for you to move, Francis."

I have managed to persuade Henry that I should be best placed to travel in the leading barge with him as I have not, as yet, displeased the Lady Elizabeth in our previous meetings. Williams and Chamberlain travel behind us in the second barge. We are well equipped for all eventualities with a convoy of barges and more than 100 souls on board. So many soldiers might seem an extravagance but then there are all Elizabeth's advisers and servants to contend with. It is a considerable shock though, to see the lady as Bedingfield leads her out of the tower into the clear light of day after being locked in for the past two months.

She is pale and slim with a grey shade to her flesh, particularly her face. Her eyes appear dull and lifeless. Her hair, usually a vibrant shade of red, looks dull and unkempt. It is only her clothing, a dark blue gown and black kirtle, that gives her any kind of regal air.

I settle her down in the barge and try to convey a sense of sympathy by my bearing and attentions. She settles near the colourful side canopy of the vessel, which is luxuriously appointed and more like a queen's conveyance than a working boat.

"Breeze is picking up," I comment but she makes no reply. Indeed, her expression is bleak as she stares straight ahead. The crew manoeuvres the barge into a channel of the Thames where we can proceed, surrounded, as we are, by merchant shipping. I try again, asking if she is quite comfortable.

"A lamb surrounded by wolves; how can I be?"

"You will be strong again, Lady Elizabeth," I tell her. "You have inner strength."

"May God be with me to guide and sustain me. At this moment, I feel crushed."

Spray from the tide washes up to the side of our vessel and sways it slightly to port. The bitter breeze intensifies and I hope we stay dry for I feel a dampness in the air that suggests there is rain to follow. Bedingfield engages me in conversation, sitting on my left but he, too, is mainly concerned with the prospect of driving rain, never a comforting prospect on the river. Lady Elizabeth appears to be shaking slightly but whether from the inclement early morning weather or fear, I cannot tell.

"May I offer you my cloak for your shoulders?" I ask.

"I'm not cold," she tells me with a twisted smile. "You are considerate, Sir Francis, and I thank you. My shaking is occasioned by fear of the unknown. I feel the cold breath of an assassin stalking me."

"That will not happen," I assure her.

"You think not?"

"You are protected," I tell her. "A safe passage to Richmond Palace."

"And what then, Sir, what then?"

I am about to respond when the barge dips and sways suddenly causing us each to hold on to the nearest rail. Elizabeth remains stock still but does not attempt to steady herself. Bedingfield curses softly. Heavy merchant ships are passing us and the wake from many of them causes a swell in the water. Waves begin to rise and fall due to the amount of traffic and I am only glad that it is one-way and coming towards us. The European ships tend to arrive and trade at the city where we have just left.

"Mary would be quite content if an assassin's blade found my heart," Elizabeth says softly. "It would solve a problem."

"She is not so heartless, I can assure you," I tell her briskly.

"You do not know her, Sir, as I do."

"She just fears treachery and has faced it often," I decide to respond. "Now she knows you are innocent, so you need fear no more."

"So why am I condemned to country-palace imprisonment with a jailer outside my door?"

I cannot answer that one as I do not know myself. I tell her what I hope to be true that it will be very much a temporary arrangement. Queen Mary will have much on her mind to occupy her fully in the coming months and will most likely release Lady Elizabeth after her marriage. I ask her to be of good cheer.

"A strange creature indeed I would be, if I were to be of good cheer now."

"Why so?"

"Do you know what day this is, Sir Francis?"

"Saturday."

"More specifically, the 18th anniversary of my mother's execution."

"I'm sorry, I hadn't realised."

She shakes her head and smiles grimly. It is not for me to apologise; the day chosen to let her out of the Tower where her mother died was a twisted joke by her half-sister. It is just what Mary would do.

The threatened rain does not materialise. It becomes somewhat brighter as we pass through Westminster and I gaze idly at the turrets and towers of the palaces along the route. The breeze, though, has intensified and prevents warm weather from breaking through. We sail on past the green pastures on either side and the spring lambs jumping. The oarsmen pull hard in unison and glide us through the environs of Chelsea.

Richmond Palace is an impressive building, but it has not had the attention to decoration, furnishing and reconstruction that many similar structures have received. The corridors, galleries and many apartments have a bleak, cold hard look about them. On arrival Elizabeth gathers all her servants around her and spends an hour at prayer. I walk down to her chamber with Sir Henry, and we find her still at prayer. We walk back to Bedingfield's quarters.

"She has requested you occupy a bedchamber close by hers," he says stiffly. "Normally I would not agree to such but as you see she is pale and sickly and I do not want to be responsible for her health deteriorating further."

"Understandable," I agree.

"She appears to trust you but nobody else," he tells me, giving me a somewhat suspicious sideways glance.

"No reason to," I say casually. "Perhaps I have a kind face."

"Fie, get out of my sight, Francis."

The Lady Elizabeth looks worryingly unwell when I go to see her later. Her pale face has turned a ghastly grey with her eyes looking out bleakly at the world. What torment of the mind she must be suffering, I can scarcely imagine or begin to speculate. She has just ended her long period at prayer and her ladies are dispersing to their bedchambers. I ask if I can be of any further service to her.

"Stay close to me, Sir Francis."

I tell her I will, I am exceedingly close to her in my chamber.

"I fear this night."

"I'm sure there is no need," I say, I hope reassuringly. "Guards are posted in the grounds."

"But not against the enemy within."

"I am alert," I tell her, "and will remain so throughout this night."

She is shivering again so I offer her my cloak to place around her shoulders. She thanks me but declines my offer once again, telling me that no cloak can keep out the cold of the spectre of imminent death. I bid her good night and prepare to go to my own bedchamber.

"The ghosts will come to me tonight, in dreams," she murmurs softly. "My poor mother, bloody and headless, my father, arrogant, with bright attire and dripping with priceless jewels, the sores on his leg seeping pus and the black angel of death himself, wielding a bleeding dagger."

THE TITIAN PORTRAIT

"My lady, you must compose your mind to brighter thoughts to sleep well and soundly."

"You are a good man, Sir Francis," she tells me grimly. "Better by far than the others that interrogated me although they will corrupt you, too, with their insistence on their antichrist religion."

"I was born into the Church of Rome religion and never wavered from it voluntarily."

"Were you so? Ah well. Please stay close on this night until well past the dawn."

"You have my solemn word."

"I wish you were coming with us to Woodstock."

"I am recalled to court tomorrow," I say softly. "But Bedingfield is a good man. He will keep you safe."

"Good night, Sir Francis."

I bid her a safe night and a sound, restful sleep and retire to my bedchamber.

The rain pours down relentlessly and rattles on the roof above. The afternoon darkens under the onslaught and candles are lit to combat the gloom. Bishop Gardiner and Lord Arundel look bored and listless.

"How did she behave on the journey?" the queen asks, looking to me.

"Unwell, extremely nervous and frightened."

The queen frowns and clears her throat and cautions me not to be fooled. Gardiner grins and Lord Paulet looks bemused.

"That one is as strong as a lion and frightened of nothing on this earth," the queen says flatly.

"She is unwell, though," I say. "I can vouch for that."

"You are easily taken in, Francis," Gardiner says, twisting his fingers. Arundel smirks.

"I don't agree," I say testily.

The queen raises her hand and says we will not waste any more time on that troublesome woman. She is safely domiciled at Woodstock now and Bedingfield can be trusted to keep her under observation. She thinks that Elizabeth's illness and discomfort will evaporate as soon as she settles down at Woodstock and realises that nobody is taking any notice of her frivolities. And now to more serious and pressing business.

"Prince Philip is due here in England any time now although when exactly I cannot say," she states. "I want him made very welcome and preparations must be made well in advance for my wedding."

Her annoyance and shortness of temper is understandable. Philip was due here in February but did not arrive. Vast preparations were made but not as many as early this month when, once again, the queen waited anxiously to receive her prince, but he did not arrive. No explanation was forthcoming. I know that members of the Privy Council are harbouring thoughts that the Spanish prince has changed his mind and will not go through with the wedding. They would be well advised not to breathe a word of their suspicions within the queen's hearing.

Lord Paget asks how soon Her Majesty requires arrangements made. She suggests right away. It is quite possible that the prince may have to return to Spain on matters of state very quickly and it may be necessary to arrange the wedding within a week after his arrival. Lord Paget looks surprised and asks if that is possible.

"I depend on my councillors to make it possible," she replies swiftly.

"Time is against us," Paget opines gruffly.

"And much decoration and pageantry will be required," Arundel adds.

"Then I suggest, gentlemen, that you attend to it right

away," the queen says in a sharp tone that silences the chamber.

She offers no further time to discuss the matter, taking it that her wishes will be carried out. She reminds us all that the forthcoming marriage will be of great benefit to the realm generally in terms of new and increased trade with Spain. And all the countries allied with that important dominion.

QUEEN MARY'S JOURNAL

SALISBURY, JULY 1554

SUCH A DOWNPOUR OF RAIN, IT SEEMS FIT TO DROWN THE CITY. A deluge in July may not be unusual in this inconsistent climate but I could have wished for better near my wedding day. Outside, the rain beats down relentlessly on the walls of Salisbury Cathedral and I am pleased to have gained the shelter of the east hall of Wolvesley Castle. Here it is that our wedding banquet will be held, and preparations are already in hand. I must say that after spending several days in Southampton awaiting the arrival of my prince and then returning to London without so much as a glimpse of him, my patience began to wear exceedingly thin. When it happened a second time after I had travelled again to the city with my attendants, servants and close advisors only to find it a fruitless journey, I was in bad humour for several days.

Now he is here at last, finally, and I find myself in a state of excitement and anticipation quite unfitting for a sovereign queen of England. I must remain calm and dignified throughout at all costs.

Englefield has remained at my side at my request, although most of the others have been dispatched in various

THE TITIAN PORTRAIT

directions. He is always a most loyal and faithful friend, whose support I cherish.

"I hear a commotion outside," he murmurs softly.

"Then he is here."

"The moment has arrived."

"Ready?" he asks gently, with a smile.

"As I ever will be."

Sir Francis departs to greet the assembled courtiers, attendants and servants and escort the prince into my presence. I stand still, rigid, my heart fluttering like that of a young maiden and not feeling that my appearance is fitting to that of the Queen of England, Ireland and France. My expression is composed to look regal and calm even if I do not feel it. He enters.

I am not aware of the movement of various attendants and my own people all around me, even as they all depart in various directions and I am left facing my prince with only servants and guards at a respectable distance from us. He is everything my portrait conveyed to me and more besides. He is splendidly attired in brown doublet and hose, with many jewels and a mantle of cloth of gold trimmed in crimson velvet. His face is gloriously bronzed from the sun in his country and those eyes; bright, intense as he gazes at me with a smile forming on his lips.

"Your Majesty, I am your obedient servant," he says in Spanish, so I respond in his language. At first, though, I am unable to speak, only to return his radiant smile to the best of my ability.

"We kiss?"

"Is that usual in your country?"

"It is."

Before I am over the shock and expectation of his words, he has planted a brief kiss upon my cheek, and I feel my face burning, but with a pleasurable sensation. I am wearing a black dress of rich French cloth with sleeves of dark satin and lined with green taffeta and several pearls, but I feel positively underdressed by comparison with my prince. He is charming, though. I ask if he had a good journey from Spain and he tells me it was choppy at sea on occasion but with interludes of clement weather and overall, it was an enjoyable voyage. He hopes, sincerely that my journey from London to Salisbury was a pleasure to me and without incident.

"It was a good transport apart from the rain."

"Ah, your weather. The persistent rain."

"It is," I say softly, "much worse this year than usual."

"It is unfortunate," he continues. "It is unfair. A beautiful queen deserves warm sun and clear blue skies."

Now he is flattering me, but I am enjoying it immensely and do not wish him to stop. We settle down for our first meeting together and I call for sweet French wine and sweetmeats with biscuits. I am still so enamoured of him that I can scarcely think clearly, and I hope I do not embarrass myself by blushing like a young maid. Philip is 10 years my senior but, with his strong, chiselled features and youthful look, it would not be apparent to the casual observer. I have had applied to my own face the finest in paints and powders and hope that I still look young enough to please him. I feel I look at my best because I feel so vibrant and alive.

"You are my English rose," he says suddenly. "Are you not?"

"Am I?"

"But a strong and fearless queen of your realm."

"I hope and pray I am that, too."

"I see it in your eyes," he tells me tenderly and his own eyes are smiling. "Strength and resolve. Together we will make an excellent royal pairing."

He lays his hand over mine and I feel the familiar tingling run down my spine. Then I feel warm all over, including my face and pray that I am not blushing foolishly.

"We marry tomorrow," he breathes quietly.

"No, your Grace, in two days' time."

"Ah, you see," he murmurs, "I am in such hurry to marry my queen, I cannot wait."

I laugh and he obliges me with a smile. I tell him that preparations are going on at this moment in the cathedral, canopies and a long walkway are being erected. Attendants will wear his Spanish colours and the Bishop of Winchester will conduct our marriage ceremony.

"You do me great honour."

"As you do me, your Grace," I respond.

"Philip," he utters decisively. "When we two are together, in private, from this day forward, I am your Philip and you are my Mary. Is it not so?"

"Oh yes," I say, so enthusiastically that I do blush and regret that I should perhaps be showing more reserve and decorum.

It is getting late, but we continue talking in hushed, private whispers. For my part I would happily go on talking and getting to know this fine, strong man for several hours.

It will soon be time for prayers. The bells are ringing.

We wait under a canopy for the incessant rain to stop. Bells are chiming to announce the royal wedding. I will not walk even the short distance to the cathedral as rain falls, even if it means postponing the ceremony until tomorrow. A brief interlude occurs at last, but it is now over an hour since my prince entered the cathedral. He will not be pleased but my late arrival is inevitable. I smooth down my gown and turn, signalling with the briefest nod to the Marchioness of Winchester to pick up my train. My French style dress is pleasing to me and I feel I look my best in it. It is of rich, delicate cloth with sleeves embroidered on purple satin set with pearls. It is lined with purple taffeta. Over it, I wear a short sleeved partlet with a high collar and a white satin kirtle.

Slowly, regally, I begin the walk through the street to the cathedral. The marchioness holds my train aloft, assisted by the Lord Chamberlain and I am flanked on either side by two young bachelors. There are crowds all along the road waving and calling out good wishes, but it is not an occasion to respond. I keep my eyes straight ahead and walk on.

I enter through the west door of the cathedral with my noblewomen and walk very slowly down the nave on the raised platform until I reach the dais. I take my place solemnly under the canopy with only a fleeting glance at Philip on my left and then kneel down to pray. Stephen Gardiner, Bishop of Winchester and five other bishops climb up the five steps to the raised dais and stand centrally.

I wait patiently but looking on imperiously as I am not expecting or prepared to condone a delay.

Gardiner looks a little bemused and avoids looking straight at me as I face him with my unspoken question. Don Juan de Figueroa, a councillor of Philip's father, Charles V, steps forward to present Prince Philip with letters patent. The letters are handed to the bishop and he reads them out, first in Latin and then in English. It appears that Philip's father has bestowed on him the title and full rights of King of Naples.

My angry look evaporates immediately. Any other interruption to my marriage would merit harsh and speedy punishment but this fine gesture means that I am to marry a king and not a mere prince. If it does not, please me that it was announced in this dramatic fashion during my marriage, I am forced to concede that it was best for the people of my realm to hear it now. The ceremony proceeds.

Bishop Gardiner states that the treaty has been approved by Parliament and the realm of Spain has also given consent to the terms. He asks solemnly if anyone knows of any impediment to the marriage, either due to kinship or a preceding claim. There is a hush in the cathedral, a wall of imminent silence as we wait for the response. An echo of voices erupts suddenly and startlingly as the congregation answers that there is none. Gardiner then reads the papal dispensation from Julius III which allows us, as cousins, to marry. The bishop's voice, firm and resonant, rings out and echoes to the rafters of this old cathedral.

The Bishop asks who will give the queen away and the earls of Derby, Bedford and Pembroke step forward. The congregation shout out their support for their queen we exchange our vows. Philip then places a plain gold band and three handfuls of gold coins on the bishop's bible. He blesses them. Then my leading attendant, Lady Margaret Clifford, steps forward with the queen's purse and I place the gold in it.

Phillip and I kiss. His flesh is warm, and I feel the familiar tingle down my spine. His eyes gleam in the light.

I am filled with joy at this moment as we follow the bishop and take our places under the canopies on either side of the high altar. Gardiner celebrates High Mass with the other bishops acting as servers. Trumpets blare out bright and brassy piercing the air sonorously. Philip turns to me again and gives me the kiss of peace as the Garter King of Arms goes to the foot of the High Altar, along with the heralds and pronounces: "Philip and Mary, by the grace of God King and Queen of England, Naples, Jerusalem, Ireland and France, Archdukes of Austria, Dukes of Milan, Burgundy and Brabant, Counts of Habsburg, Flanders and Tyrol."

I receive biscuits and spiced wine. My sombre, official expression fades gradually as I look at my husband and we smile at each other. I am married and I am content.

A canopy is held up by the leading peers of England and is brought to the foot of the altar. I walk, hand in hand with Philip, under it and along the nave and out of the cathedral. We walk together to Wolvesey Castle and enter the East Hall.

Our wedding banquet has been arranged here and we make our way solemnly to the far end of the chamber to where a raised platform has been set up. We mount the steps and move to the royal table which is set with gold and silver plate. My chair is of the most ornate with rich carvings cut into the wood. We are under a canopy of state and, as I take my seat, I am impressed with the effort that has gone into our banquet. Philip sits down next to me and, further along our table, Bishop Gardiner installs himself.

"Impressive carving," Phillip says, running a finger along an edge of my chair.

"It is," I say but do I detect a slight cooling of manner in my husband? I know all the wall decorations and flags for ceremony have placed the emphasis on England and all things English but perhaps more attention should have been paid to the Spanish connection. This is, though, an English royal marriage designed for a queen and Philip will be more of a King Consort rather than a ruling monarch.

"Did you know of your father's gesture?" I ask quietly.

"I was aware."

"The timing of it surprised me," I tell him.

"Did you find it inappropriate?" he asks.

"Not really. I appreciate the honour he did us."

"Ah yes. I did, I confess, approach him on the matter some time ago to say I was not altogether happy marrying beneath a higher rank."

"Well, we are equal now," I say but it is disconcerting to notice that he looks vexed and makes no reply.

The hall is filling rapidly. A long table in front of us houses all the privy councillors and ambassadors. I catch the eye of Sir Francis and give the slenderest of inclines of the head. He smiles and returns the gesture. Two further long tables house the English and Spanish guests. On a dais at the other end of the hall, the musicians start to play, and bright music fills the hall. My mind begins to wander back to past events. It was

Charles V, Emperor and King of Spain who recommended his eldest son to me and proposed the marriage. I do sincerely hope it was not for political purposes alone and that Philip, whom I love dearly, will come to love me equally. This though, is no time for speculation so I shake out of my mood and prepare to enjoy the feast.

The food is sumptuous. Roasted swan, boar, beef and mutton form the main courses with onion and artichoke. Roast lark and pheasant are more to my taste and I eat these as Phillip does full justice to the large main joints. There are many courses and much choice. French wine of a good vintage is served. When we have both eaten our fill, we still need to contend with sweetmeats of great variety. Fruit pies and large, diverse jellies are served. I am reliably informed that we have consumed 30 different dishes served over four courses. We are replete.

Four heralds and a knight appear, and the knight makes a short speech in praise of me and the English monarchy, but he remembers to include and welcome Philip to our shores. Philip invites the councillors to drink a toast, which they do. While I am still capable, I drink a cup of wine to the health and honour of all our guests.

We all repair to a smaller hall where dancing, music and merrymaking continues. I begin to feel a little weary and Phillip and I retire to a small, private chamber where we can hear the music and dancing but have a measure of privacy.

Phillip is attentive to my needs and orders sweet, spiced wine to help my digestion. We toast each other silently.

"So how does it feel?" I ask.

"New responsibilities, is it not so? Yet this union will benefit both England and our vast dominions, will it not?"

"Yes, I suppose it will," I respond thoughtfully.

I want to ask if it does not mean much more than that, on a personal level. The glorious beginning of our life together, the consolidation of our love for each other and a lifetime of affection. Somehow, I am unable to frame the questions. He is saying something about assisting me in all my efforts to fully restore the country to the true and only faith, the Holy Roman Church. It is not what I want to hear on this day, however. I breathe a sigh.

"You are tired, yes?"

"A little faded. It has been a long day. Wonderful, though."

"Wonderful, yes. Your English ceremonial pomp and splendour is most impressive."

The time approaches when we feel the need of further privacy, so we leave the festivities early and move to a privy chamber set aside for our personal use. A light supper is served although I can only pick a few delicacies from the meal supplied. Phillip says he will leave me in the company of my ladies and join me later at the marriage bed. He kisses me, a light brush of his lips on mine.

My ladies are all attention and flattery, asking how I am feeling and telling me that I have made a good match so I must be incredibly happy to be wed to such a handsome and impressive prince. I thank Margaret Clifford for her close attention and fine performance of her duties on this day. She is my relative although always most diligent in her assistance to me as my main attendant.

My ladies assist me in disrobing in the bedchamber and putting on my night attire. They are all smiling contentedly as I prepare myself. Bishop Gardiner comes in and greets me cordially and I thank him for his good work in conducting the marriage ceremony. He solemnly blesses the marriage bed.

Philip enters and the bishop and my ladies depart. It is time. We climb into bed and it is all I ever imagined and desired. He is a careful, considerate and consummate lover. I am in a daze of love and affection. He showers me with kisses, and I return them hungrily, always wanting more and more. As our lovemaking concludes, my maidenhead is pierced and I am a woman complete, a wife and a lover. Phillip caresses my shoulders gently and bids me sleep soundly and peacefully. He is completely charming and affectionate, and I hope and pray our love will grow and blossom fruitfully. I can sleep contented.

QUEEN MARY'S DIARY

WHITEHALL PALACE AND HAMPTON COURT PALACE, AUGUST 1554

THE BARGE DIPS AND SWAYS IN THE CHOPPY WATERS OF THE Thames. A dull grey sky overhead promises further rain, which has been relentless this year. Philip stares ahead, his face impassive, and I am left with just a fine view of that impressive profile. We are approaching Westminster at last. There is a lot of traffic on the river, occasioning much rising and falling of crafts. I try to remain calm and seated in a dignified manner.

"They are waving to you, Philip," I tell him and smile encouragingly.

"They wave to their queen, more likely," he responds gravely.

"Oh, they see enough of me," I tell him. "It is their new king that sets the pulses racing."

There are many people in smocks and work clothes on either bank. I wave and am heartened to see a flurry of additional waving, some folks kneeling down as they face the barge. I know I have much public support and love even, and I thank God for the privilege. Today, though, I suspect, it is more for the new king. I nudge Phillip gently and he frowns involuntarily but he does wave then.

THE TITIAN PORTRAIT

"That wasn't so painful, was it?" I chide him.

"I am happy to acknowledge your subjects," he says, but in a cold voice. "I wish to be thought well of by them and to serve them as their king."

"As you will, Philip," I murmur, "as you will."

The barge, dipping somewhat and swaying perilously, finally comes to rest at the shore and I am pleased to experience the sudden stillness. Wind, occasioning choppy waters, an overcast sky and almost perpetual rain. What have we done to deserve such a horrible climate in August? I make no move to leave the barge as I await patiently for my conveyance to arrive. Phillip is very still and quiet. When the litter arrives, he helps me into it and walks by my side as we proceed to Whitehall. I am wearing new jewels he has given to me as gifts, and they give me much pleasure. I wish he looked less intense and happier than he does because I love my husband and all I want to do is to please him.

At Whitehall, he surprises me by announcing his intention to start work on state business immediately. There is little he can do for my government and, in any event, he has no power to make decisions there. But, as he points out, he has work in connection with Spain and several dominions under his stewardship. A large chamber has been set up as his office with furniture, paper, ink and quills. I know he must dictate many letters to his attendants, but I had hoped he would wait until tomorrow at least.

"I have urgent letters of state to attend to," he tells me.

"Oh well, if they are of such urgency," I say irritably.

"The dangers that surround our countries on all sides do not stop for our marriage," he responds coldly.

"I did not suppose they did," I reply, equally coldly.

"Forgive me," he blurts out, with a charming smile that melts my heart immediately. "I did not wish to speak harshly to you."

"Let us speak of it no more," I respond, squeezing his hand lovingly in mine.

"I will see you at supper."

"Yes, of course."

And he is gone, leaving me feeling bereft and lacking his love. My ladies rally round me and Margaret offers to comfort me by swapping stories of errant husbands. I decline her offer graciously.

I sit in the window alcove and presently Jane approaches and curtsies. I invite her to sit next to me.

"I love him so much, Jane," I tell her softly.

"And he loves you," she replies airily. "I'm sure he does."

"I do hope so. I need his love."

"And you deserve it," she whispers urgently.

He appears tired and listless when I see him later and I fear he has perhaps been working too hard. I ask how his work progressed and he tells me he has written a large pile of letters and dispatched the ambassador abroad to deal with the most pressing matters immediately. At supper, he is quiet, almost silent. My attempts to stimulate conversation are only half successful. I remember how pleased he was to see me when we first met and how full of conversation he was then. Now, after our wedding and return to London, he appears to be constrained and mostly quiet. I know how to raise his passion, though, and tonight, in the bedchamber, we will continue what we started so successfully in Winchester.

We sail down the Thames towards Hampton Court Palace. Philip has never seen it but, I am sure he will love it. His affection for lavish, grand buildings knows no bounds and he has already told me much about his favourites in Spain. The barge cuts through the clear water with ease, sending up a little white spray but maintaining a smooth passage. We are enjoying a brief respite from the seemingly endless rain with a clear day, not overbright but mercifully dry. Silver fish can be seen jumping in the river near the bank.

As we glide along, I notice a citizen in a horse-drawn cart on the left bank. He would appear to be maintaining roughly the same speed as my barge but as he disappears behind a row of trees, I lose sight of him. Phillip sits next to me looking thoughtful. I ask what is on his mind and after hesitating he says he has been studying my first statute of repeal. Religious legislation passed during the reign of my half-brother Edward has now been repealed. The church is now governed by the doctrine set out in the Act of the Six Articles of 1539. The church is now restored to the position it had in the last year of my father's reign. We are starting to convert back to a Roman Catholic nation.

"Are my councillors not working fast enough for you, Philip?" I ask.

"The Latin Mass is restored," he concedes, looking thoughtful.

Sunlight bursts through the clouds suddenly and unexpectedly, glinting dazzlingly on the surface of the water as we glide along. We are moving round a bend in the river that is wide and expansive. The green pastures and trees on either side have more of a pleasant glow than I have seen for some time now.

"So what troubles you, then?"

"We still have married priests," he murmurs, frowning.

"That is being attended to," I say.

"Is it so? I understand many are still practising."

I shake my head. I want to receive his love and affection and he has mine unreservedly. But he has been in this country only a little over 10 days and he is already attempting to influence state affairs. I am not happy with this although I am reluctant to chastise my prince.

"Those priests already married have been ordered to leave

their families," I tell him gently. "And they may only continue their roles in the church if they do so."

"I would wish to see the process speeded up," he replies in a quiet voice.

"I think, Phillip," I respond, quietly but firmly, "we may safely leave that in the capable hands of my Lord Bishop Gardiner."

"I do not seek to interfere," he tells me. "I only offer to help if I can, as your king and consort."

"You may talk with Gardiner," I say, wishing to grant him some small part in affairs. "However, I caution you not to attempt to override his decisions."

"As you wish," he replies coldly, and I am saddened that there is a hint of a disagreement between me and my husband. He means so much to me as my companion and lover.

I place my hand over his in an attempt to bring back warmth and friendship into our relations. I tell him he will love Hampton Court Palace and we will be happy there together, as we will wherever we dwell. The oarsmen are slowing down their rhythmic strokes through the water as we near our destination. It is clouding over once again.

I am happy here at Hampton Court. I love the vast, colourful gardens, the great tiltyard where my father enjoyed his jousting, with its four great towers from which visitors watched the proceedings, the cavernous banqueting hall and the huge kitchens where the smell of roasting boar, ox or beef is ever floating out invitingly and the many rooms, not least my personal privy chamber and lavish bedchamber. The early years spent here with my mother and father when I was a small girl and my parent's only child are memories of happy hours that do not fade or die. I was a quiet, often clumsy child, not given to speaking much unless spoken to but my mother ensured my fine education and learning of musical instruments even if she made sure to convince Henry that it was all initiated by him as befitting his daughter and princess of the realm.

The place is always crammed with hundreds of people when we arrive, so it is pleasant to seek the sanctuary of my privy chamber and suite of private rooms. Here only people whom I wish or need to see gain access; my door guards see to that. I enter with Philip and we ask for wine and beer to be sent in. He seems to be acquiring a taste for our English beer or perhaps he is being polite.

"It has an odd taste, somewhere between strong and mild ale but curiously tepid," he says, sampling it.

"You will get used to it, Philip," I tell him, laughing.

Something else is on his mind; I am already beginning to pick up on his moods from his expressions.

"The heresy laws," he says, turning to face me.

"They are being put in place," I offer cautiously.

"And will they be acted upon swiftly?" he enquires, still looking at me attentively.

"That is the law of this country now."

"I ask merely to be informed," he responds hurriedly. 'Is it not so?"

I tell him he need have no worries on that score. My parliament agrees for the most part; one of the few matters all the members seem to agree upon. Offenders will be apprehended and brought swiftly to trial.

I take hold of his hand as we go down to dinner. He eats much and with relish, unable to resist the various meat roasts laid out. I peck delicately at a plate of chicken and cherries but can manage little more. We finish with a few sweetmeats and wash it all down with mead. Most of the meal, though, I spend looking on contentedly as Philip eats his fill. He seems to be restless as we return to the privy chamber.

"I am desiring to wander round this magnificent palace," he tells me. "At my leisure."

"Of course," I agree. "I can accompany you."

"No, no. you will be bored," he answers. "You have seen it all many times, is it not so? Besides, at the conclusion, I must go to work on state papers and will go straight to my new office."

"Well, if that is your desire," I murmur, disappointed. "I'll send attendants."

"Just one, Mary, to show the way. I'll take a few of my Spanish noblemen along."

I settle down in an alcove seat by the window where I can see the Thames flowing peacefully past. I had hoped that Phillip would accept the English noblemen and attendants I assigned to him, but he always seems to prefer to have his Spanish retinue around him when we are separated. It is not to my liking, but I must, I suppose, give him time to adjust to our ways and practices.

I send for Sir Francis Englefield and he arrives promptly. He is looking most refined and handsome in a new doublet and hose of a delicate shade of blue with purple velvet trimmings.

"There is much to vex me at this time, Francis," I tell him when he is settled down.

"If I can assist," he offers.

Important matters of state are pressing, and I do not know which to deal with first. Allied to that, my parliament is far from agreed on certain points and the appropriate action to be taken and cannot reach an accommodation. I am troubled about the number of priests that still have wives and appear reluctant to part from them, but they must do so. The heresy laws must be put into full operation and, in particular, I am concerned about Thomas Cranmer, the lately removed Archbishop of Canterbury who was taken from office and is currently languishing in an Oxford prison cell. In addition to

THE TITIAN PORTRAIT

of all this, Philip, my husband, is already pressing me for faster action and it is not his place to do so.

"Where to start?" Francis wonders out loud.

"Come along, Francis, you are my most trusted adviser."

"Cranmer, then. As you press me."

The former Archbishop of Canterbury. A surly, sinister man whom I have never liked and who has been preaching the services of the English Church since my father set him off in that direction. A man who denies the sacraments, advises people not to acknowledge the saints and who keeps a wife. Not that he has seen much of her as he has been residing in Bocardo Prison since his trial last year. He was found guilty of sedition and sentenced to death. Before sentence, however, he faces a second trial on heresy charges.

"Parliament has dragged its feet on this man's fate," I complain. "They cannot agree."

"Then you must instruct them, Majesty."

"Yes. And the only instruction I can give is to carry out the sentence. If the heresy law is passed."

"Death by burning," Francis says looking grim indeed.

"That would be the sentence under English law."

"What if," Francis begins, tentatively. "What if he should recant and accept the authority of the king and queen and recognises the Bishop of Rome as head of the church?"

"That would put a different light upon the subject," I concede.

"And then," Francis continues, still looking apprehensive and a little tentative, "would you consider showing him mercy?"

"Let us not get ahead of ourselves, Francis," I say, considering my answer carefully. "One step at a time."

He looks somewhat confused and regards me in a questioning manner. I will not go further into this matter now, with him, or indeed with anybody. Cranmer has much to answer for and I am more aware of that than anybody on earth. Now is not the time though, to consider the man's sins or virtues. I direct his attention to the problem of priests with wives and the growing pressure from the church here and in Rome, to restore the monasteries to the monks and friars who lost them when my father began his beastly new religion and appointed himself head of the church, next to God.

"The people who were given those lands and properties will fight tooth and nail to keep them," Francis says. "And with much sympathy from most of the population."

"Which is why," I agree, "I cannot return them."

It is not easy juggling with a population half of whom are Catholic and half, approximately, who follow King Henry's reformed Church of England. It is, though, something I must attempt to do daily. I sigh and look out of the window at the river flowing past peacefully and feel the need of fresh air.

"As to the thorny issue of your husband, the king..." Francis begins but I cut him short.

"The afternoon improves," I state. "Let us have a rest, Francis, and walk through the gardens."

We walk casually through the well-structured gardens, flowers and herbs floating out sweet scents on the still air of a grey but dry and warm day. A small troop of guards and attendants follow behind us at a discreet distance, some armed with pikes. We stroll at a leisurely pace right down to the river and begin to walk along the bank. A farm worker in a white smock comes towards us unexpectedly and drops down to his knees immediately. I am still surprised at times like these at where and who I am.

When did the slight, clumsy and rather tongue-tied girl change into a warrior? It must surely have been at the accumulated slights inflicted on me over the years and the blatant attempt by Northumberland to put Jane Grey on the throne and deny me my birth right.

"His majesty will attend parliaments, with you, as he should," Francis is saying, "but he will not be able to initiate or change laws. Parliament will advise him regularly on that point, you may depend."

"Yes," I reply. "And if he is unwilling to accept their strictures?"

"Ah, then, I'm afraid, Majesty, they will refer him directly to you for final arbitration."

"Yes, of course," I say, smiling grimly. "As I thought. And I will uphold parliament's full authority.'

A snow-white swan glides past us on the river as the slightest of gentle breezes picks up.

"I don't want him upset, though, Francis. I couldn't bear that."

QUEEN MARY'S DIARY

HAMPTON COURT PALACE AND WHITEHALL PALACE, AUTUMN 1554

THE LEAVES OF RED AND BROWN PILE UP. FIELDS AND PASTURES take on a warm, grey-green aspect if the weather remains dry, as now. Even pale sunshine has been known as the driving rain of winter and summer alike recede and dry ground and fields return for a time. The tiltyard is deserted, with only the flags and heraldic posts looking worn and deserted. Trees gradually shed all their vast foliage and begin to take on a bleak, black, twisted aspect of many intertwining branches. Flowers fade and die and it seems a long time until fresh green shoots will arrive in spring.

To walk through the grounds and extensive gardens of Hampton Court at this time of year is pleasant and refreshing indeed. The deer run freely under blue-tinged skies and pheasants strut along with nonchalant ease. Fish jump in the pond of the sunken Dutch Garden. Ornamental and blazing with colourful flowers in summer, it looks somewhat bedraggled in autumn but is still, somehow, pleasing to the eye with only the decorated stonework surrounding it.

Down by the Thames, the river runs smoothly now, unencumbered at last by waters disturbed by rain and heavy winds or the blocks of ice clogging it in winter. When I take walks, I always return to the fish-pond where fish are free for now, waiting to become served up as part of the dinner and supper tables. It was one of my father's better and more intelligent ideas to have it built and regularly stocked with fish.

With a break in the endless downpours, more craft take to the river, small boats and private barges of moderate size. I eat more fish and birds in autumn, although why I do not know. As Philip tucks in voraciously to boar, ox, beef and mutton, I pick delicately at pheasant, lark, blackbird, woodcock and partridge. The lean, white meat suits my palette well at dinner and supper alike.

"Reginald Pole is to return to these shores, then," Philip says.

"Who told you that?" I ask as a second helping of partridge is served to me.

"The word is out, is it not so?"

Philip is attacking a side of roasted beef with relish. He has onions with it and cabbage and some English ale of which he is becoming rather fond. White bread, too.

"Renard, your ambassador," I murmur knowingly.

"Surely no secret," Phillip protests. "He is a good man. A staunch supporter of the faith. He will aid the complete restoration of the Roman church in this land."

He has been away a long time, these many years. He defied Henry's demands to take the oath of allegiance and would not accept my father as head of the church. Had he not gone over to Rome when he did, Henry would have removed his head and spiked it. I have not deliberately kept news of his impending return to England from Philip, I have merely not discussed it with anybody. Only a few councillors are aware.

In my privy chamber I am alone and lonely except for such of my ladies with whom I choose to converse and sometimes I leave them to their embroidery and do not talk to anybody. It is not my desire. I would wish that Philip chose to spend more time in private with me, but he is always busy with state papers and sending out letters abroad. It is why I choose to walk the grounds often with only my courtiers and attendants behind me, soaking up the pleasing late summery weather we enjoy for the moment.

The river is fairly bubbling, with pale sunlight glinting on the surface of the water and silver fish jumping on the other side, near the bank. Crafts of small or medium size sail past us sending up a whitewash of spray in their wake. The fields and pastures have that green and dry look so appealing to my gaze.

"In two days from now, I return to Flanders," Philip says, shattering my peaceful mood instantly, although I doubt that was his intention.

"Surely not?" I respond. "We have been together so short a time."

"Affairs of state," he informs me.

"Send an emissary," I suggest.

"Not easy," he responds, shaking his head.

"Please, Philip," I appeal. I cannot bear to lose him so soon after our wedding. I have such plans for our future together. He requests that I leave it with him, that he can make no promises now but will make the necessary representations. I thank him and try, unsuccessfully, to concentrate on enjoying the countryside.

Westminster does not have that healthy glow of autumn colours. Too many fires from too many houses send up noxious fumes and poison the atmosphere. Fog and smoke float through the air. The roads are marked with cracks and even small craters from too many heavy carts passing by. The surfaces of roads, where surfaces exist, are slimy with horse dung and the piss and excrement flung out of windows constantly. As Queen of England and Ireland, though, I am obliged to spend much time here.

My list of items to be given attention and resolved as

quickly as possible leaves Gardiner, in his role as Chancellor, advising me that I may be asking the impossible. None of the councillors look confident that such actions can be taken. I want our coinage upgraded imminently. I wish to see new coins with my head and Philip's engraved on them. I want Cranmer's second trial brought forward and I dispatch councillors to visit him in prison and attempt to persuade him to renounce his English religion. I want preparations put into place to welcome Reginald Pole back home to assist in returning us fully to the Holy Roman Church.

"And return of the monasteries to the church?" Arundel asks.

"I can't do that my Lord," I inform him. "I need to keep the English nobles content or a new uprising will occur, doing much severe damage."

"Or even topple our king and queen from the throne," adds Paulet.

"Exactly," I agree.

"We need to proceed cautiously, Majesty," Gardiner suggests.

"Yes," I agree. "Which is why I intend to return those monasteries held currently by the crown. But only those."

"And Elizabeth?" Sir Francis Englefield wonders.

"Safely billeted at Woodstock," I respond. "Where she will remain."

Philip has been quiet and said little. Only an occasional nod of the head at my pronouncements, giving me silent support. For that I am grateful. If he intends to support me and not try to introduce new bills and legislation in Parliament, it will make life easier. The trouble is it does not coincide with what he says to me in the privy chamber. Does he seek to influence English law by pressing me to introduce it? I sincerely hope not. I will not worry about it now, though. My immediate concern now is to get through business in the next week and return swiftly to the peace and tranquillity of Hampton Court.

Menstruation has ceased and I have felt rather sick on several mornings. Can it be true? A pregnancy now would be wonderful for Phillip and me and would give us the heir we need so desperately to preserve the line of the Tudors into the next reign. I can hardly believe it. What I must do though is try to separate the frequent ailments I am subjected to and all the aches and pains I go through regularly.

I am sickly in my body on many a long day and night. I have never enjoyed good health. Now I have other little irritations to disturb my equilibrium such as a sickness most mornings and a heaviness in my breasts and nipples. If these do indicate a pregnancy, however, I shall bear them with fortitude and gratitude even and a complaint will never escape from my lips.

My physician is most thorough. He examines me closely, pokes and prods me and wishes to know about the most intimate of private functions.

"How is your appetite, Majesty?"

"I eat well generally," I say. "A desire for pears just lately, I confess."

"Fruit will do you no harm," he concludes, "although do eat plenty of good meat at dinner. You need to keep your strength up."

"For what purpose specifically?"

"If you are eating for two rather than one, you need all your strength."

I feel a warm glow inside as it appears that I am not mistaken and I am, really, going to have a child. For the moment, all my usual ailments seem to evaporate and leave me thinking only about sore nipples and a distended belly. Philip has postponed his trip to Flanders twice but warned

THE TITIAN PORTRAIT

me only yesterday that he must now make the trip. Now I have news that will make it easier to persuade him to stay here.

"I will make up a special potion for you," the doctor tells me.

"It is true then," I ask cheerfully, "I am to be with child?"

"It would appear so," he agrees and offers his congratulations.

Like myself, Phillip has taken to walking through the extensive grounds of Hampton Court but often on a whim and alone whereas I would prefer to join him and have us enjoy the moderate late-autumn weather together, as a couple. When I chide him about this, he informs me that after work in his office he frequently needs to clear his head and a walk alone allows him to think things through satisfactorily.

I find him by the Dutch pond, watching the fish as I myself often do. He appears surprised to see me and even a little vexed. Affairs in France, our mutual enemy, have been troubling him lately and made his temper somewhat short. He reminds me regularly that he should be in Flanders and cannot postpone the trip much longer. I invite him to sit with me on a stone bench, close to the pond.

"Are you sure, Mary?" he enquires.

"As sure as I can be," I reply, a little harshly. "And my physician has agreed."

"Then that is good news indeed. Is it not so?"

"Our baby, our child," I confirm, mood changing back instantly to delight. "An heir and, with luck, a son."

He nods his head slowly.

"You will not leave for Flanders now, will you, Philip?" I ask. "I need you by my side."

"No, Mary, I will not leave. My place is here."

Suddenly all around me appears to take on an enhanced, warm glow. The multitude of fallen leaves being swept up by servants around us as we talk, take on a more vivid shade of gold and brown. The stonework of buildings appears brighter, clearer. The dull, warm day more welcoming. The sky, blue.

"Are you pleased, really pleased?" I ask, my eyes pleading for a positive answer.

"Indeed, I am," he says, and his smile is infectious.

He tells me gently that I must take great care of myself and not do anything untoward. I must not exert myself for the time being until it is time to go into confinement. He kisses me very lightly on the lips, but it is enough to give me that familiar tingle.

"I would urge you," he says solemnly, "to seek one more opinion from a different physician." He pauses. "To confirm, for peace of mind."

"Yes," I respond thoughtfully. "That I will certainly do."

LADY ELIZABETH'S WOODSTOCK NOTEBOOK

WOODSTOCK LODGE, AUTUMN 1554

THE CEILING, A CRISSCROSSED PATTERN OF ORNATELY CARVED wood in a hideous shade of deep blue with red and gold inserts. Seen from below when looking up, it is a fascinating example of carved woodwork, painstakingly created over, one suspects, many years. Or, alternatively, carved and constructed by a small army of workmen, in concert, all aware of the builder's intention and put in place in a relatively short space of time. Useless to speculate, really, for nobody now is likely to know or care.

How many hours in total now I have lain on my prison bed, for prison I must call it, and stared at this horrible ceiling? I neither know nor really care. The chamber is not so big that I can vary much my walking round it and, apart from sitting endlessly on the only good chair provided, all I can do is lie on the bed and stare. And in this supine position, all I can see is the ceiling.

I rise at last and walk over to the window. From here can just see the trees in the forest, the old hunting ground. It is a pleasing sight indeed but the more I stare, the more I desire the opportunity to get out and walk through that forest. That

I can never do. The heavy door unlocking and opening intrudes on my thoughts, but I do not look in that direction.

"A turn in the gardens?"

He knows I would never refuse for it is the only escape, however brief, from four enclosing walls.

"I'm ready."

Sir Henry Bedingfield is a big man, of heavy build with a red face, sensuous lips and an unkempt beard. His eyes seem altogether too little for his large, fleshy face and they are small and piercing.

He is an unattractive man, to be sure, but clean and well-dressed mainly, which is more than I can say for the guards assigned to watch me. When one of those people escorts me and watches me when I walk in the gardens, I keep my distance, if only to avoid the unpleasant odours from their bodies.

"Come along, then."

I turn at last away from the window and face him.

It is a dull but mercifully a dry day and the grass is moist but fresh underfoot. I walk out and wander slowly round the same familiar landmarks. The burly guard with the dark skin and black hair stands almost completely still outside the door to the gatehouse.

"To what do I owe the honour of your presence as my escort?" I ask with barely disguised sarcasm.

"I like to ensure that you are comfortable and in good health."

Good health? I have felt unwell since arriving with no variation. The back pains persist and I feel nausea and sickness all day and every day. I last felt reasonably healthy the day before I was arrested and taken to the Tower of London. Every day that passes, I wonder if it is the day the assassin's knife will find my heart. They are efficient here at keeping me inside, but I doubt they would make any effort to keep a hired killer out.

"Why am I here in the gatehouse, Sir Henry?" I ask. "Why not the main Woodstock Lodge building?"

"You wouldn't thank me for such a domain," he replies grimly. "The place is in such dilapidated state of repair it would feel like living in a bleak prison cell."

"Would it surprise you to know I see my present lodgings in such a light?"

He smiles. "You reside in luxury by comparison."

"Well, I'll never know," I inform him, "because I never get to see anything beyond the gatehouse."

"You have space and to spare," he asserts. "And your own small chapel."

That is my one and only welcome haven. A place to retreat and pray, which I do, prodigiously. How it came to be built into the gatehouse I have no idea, but I thank God for it every day. I exercise now by continued walking, which I practise by increasing my pace. Despite his heavy build, Sir Henry keeps up with me, but he need not trouble himself, really. One brief signal from his stubby hand and guards would come rushing and restrain me instantly.

"How long must I be kept a virtual prisoner here sir?" I ask irritably.

"Only until you renounce the English Church religion and return to the church of Rome."

"Is that all?"

"And admit that you were part of the conspiracy to overthrow the queen and become queen yourself."

"A conspiracy I knew absolutely nothing about," I tell him, for the hundredth time. "And, for your information, Sir, I could never return to the Roman church because I was never, ever, part of it."

"Then embrace it, Lady Elizabeth, embrace it now."

"I'd rather embrace a poisonous viper."

He laughs and asks me if I am ready to return to my chamber. I say that I am not and would like a little extra time walking alone down to the flower garden yonder and he surprises me by consenting and walking back to the building to speak to his guard. The fountain in the courtyard is spraying clear fresh water into the little pond as I walk past. It would be an attractive sight if I had not already seen it hundreds of times before. Although, in truth, today is a special day as I have been allowed to walk the length of the courtyard without a guard at my elbow.

I reach only halfway back along the courtyard before a burly guard comes rushing down the path to escort me. Locked up again inside the gatehouse, I reflect on Bedingfield's words. If they are waiting for me to confess involvement in Wyatt's plot or to renounce my religion, I will be here until hell freezes. They will not need to wait that long, however. Mary will arrange for an assassin to gain entry.

I try to ignore the carved heads of saints and other items associated with the Catholic Church in the chapel. It is the one place of peace where I can linger in silent solitude, praying.

Bedingfield paces the floor of my chamber impatiently, as I sit very still and remain calm. He tells me that I have been informed repeatedly that my reading will be limited. I am allowed a book of religious anecdotes and precious little else. As to visitors, I can have very few and only those approved by the queen.

"You had two last week," Bedingfield claims.

"Two lords of the Privy Council to question and bully me yet again," I complain. "Hardly visitors pleasing to my eyes."

"Then tell them what they want to hear," he suggests, "and they will become more friendly."

"That is something I will never do," I inform him.

He shakes his head in exasperation. "You have an important visitor later today," he informs me.

THE TITIAN PORTRAIT

"Another privy councillor?" I ask in disgust. "I can do without that."

"One you know well," he tells me, grinning. "And do not dislike."

I ask who but know in advance he is not going to tell me. He likes to play these silly games, presumably to amuse himself. He does not amuse me, however. He is right, though. I am not displeased to see my visitor as he is let in by the gaoler and moves towards the window where I stand.

"Is it a pleasant view from here?"

"It is, Sir Francis, but so appealing it only makes me desire my freedom more to go there and explore fully."

The view takes in the forest with a dense collection of trees, and I can also see part of the old hunting lodge where my father used to come so frequently. The stonework of the palace is clothed in antiquity, a building that dates back to King Henry I. He it was that had wild animals in the walled pasture; lions, tigers and exotic creatures such as peacocks. A few peacocks are still to be seen walking around today, but stags and deer predominate.

"Are you well treated here?" he asks solicitously.

"I am well fed and watered and Bedingfield is not a bad man," I say quietly. "But he deprives me of such comforts as books and writing paper and I have only limited access to the garden and grounds. The queen has instructed him, and he will do exactly as she requests. I am a prisoner without a cell."

"Write to the queen," Englefield suggests.

"I have done," I inform him. "There was no reply."

"Write again. Tell her you are loyal to her and always have been and have never known of any plot to remove her. Remind her of your royal blood. Make yourself humble. She is your sister, after all."

"Half-sister."

"Blood is thicker than water, Lady Elizabeth."

"Would that be the same blood that destroyed her mother and later killed mine on the block?"

He shakes his head and walks away from the window to sit at the small table where I eat my meals. After a short time, I turn away myself and go over to join him at the table. He sighs deeply before speaking.

"Write another letter, I urge you. I think the queen will come round in time. You have an unlikely friend in an unlikely place."

"And that would be who?"

"Philip, the king. He has, I happen to know, already advised her to bring you back to court."

I thank him for his consideration and good offices. As a staunch Roman Catholic, he has no reason to help or be considerate towards me. Also, he is a friend of Mary's and her councillor. I really do not know who to trust and who not. He has a kindly face, though, and I do, instinctively, think he is a good man. I hope I am not mistaken.

"Why would he do that, Sir Francis?"

"He fears the influence of Mary, the Scottish Queen. He sees no threat from you."

"And I represent none."

I still have much reason to fear for my life here, in what is now a remote and overgrown lodge. The gatehouse maybe the most well-preserved building on a crumbling estate but I still feel unsafe.

"The guards may detain you, but they will also keep you safe," he tells me.

"Can they keep me safe from being poisoned?" I enquire.

"That will not happen," he tries to assure me.

His assurances continue and I am aware that he is genuine in his attempts to ease my fears. He is not successful, but I appreciate his kindness and tell him so. As he prepares to return to London, his attendants gather outside and his horse is led round, fed and refreshed. He bids me farewell and asks me to be of stout heart and in good cheer. He is about to open the door and depart.

"I hear that Cardinal Reginald Pole is due to return to these shores," I say quietly.

He swivels round immediately, and I can see from his expression that my words have struck home.

"How on earth did you hear that?" he wishes to know.

"I still have some posts that filter through to me," I inform him with a wide smile.

"I don't know how," he tells me, genuinely puzzled. "Nothing is settled yet, though."

"Oh, he will come," I state confidently. "Bringing his retinue of Roman Catholic bishops and reforming ways and I shall have even more enemies to worry about."

"Live for today Lady Elizabeth," he murmurs softly. "And trust in the queen's good intentions."

"I should rather trust a ravening tiger. I shall write that second letter, though, Sir Francis."

QUEEN MARY'S PRIVATE JOURNAL

HAMPTON COURT AND WHITEHALL, AUTUMN AND WINTER 1554

THE CONFINEMENT BEDCHAMBER IS MUSTY AND COLD FROM LONG disuse. Even the tapestries on the walls look faded and neglected. I move to the window to open it and let in a burst of chill, fresh air. Down below, a dozen gardeners go about their clearing work.

"Best if you don't stand too close to the window, Majesty," Jane whispers behind me.

"A cold wind is blowing up," Margaret adds.

"No need to cosset me so," I tell them, smiling. "I won't blow away in the wind."

They are both silent, looking chastised. I walk around, checking on the sparse furniture and the solid flooring. The bed looks well made up and fresh, just about the only item that is in this large, cold room. I look to the windows that let in much daylight and reflect that, when I enter here, there will be large drapes up and no light will penetrate. The darkness will be broken only by a few candles. I might just be able to make out the shapes of a few knights and other figures in the tapestries and the pictures on the walls.

"How long is it since a royal birth occurred in this chamber?" I ask.

"Your brother Edward," Margaret says.

"Half-brother," I correct her. "Yes," I add reflectively, "born to Queen Jane Seymour, all of 17 years ago."

I snap out of my reverie and say that I want this chamber cleaned and tidied from top to bottom immediately. It may be in line for attention by various attendants and servants to be done but I will not wait. It must be done thoroughly and done now.

"And in a few months from now, a son, or…" Jane begins, breaking off abruptly.

"You may say 'or daughter', Jane," I reassure her. "I think I have proved that a woman can reign effectively already. The days of destroying our faith and slaughtering queens for lack of a son are over."

I find Philip standing by the fountain, instructing a courtier. He dismisses the man promptly but looks less than pleased to see me. "You should not be out here in the cold, Mary," he chides me.

"I am well enough," I tell him, pulling my heavy cape around my shoulders. "I am only a few weeks pregnant and not feeling any ill effects yet."

"I'll escort you back to your chamber," he says decisively.

I am not sure I want to be treated like a small child or a woman who has no mind of her own but conversely, I do enjoy having Philip so attentive and concerned about me. It makes a refreshing change as his attitude towards me has been less than loving in the past few weeks and I crave any indication of his love and affection. I do not know what I would do without him now. In my chamber, I assure him I am feeling well, apart from a little nausea and sickness first thing in the mornings. He need not fuss as otherwise I even feel somewhat livelier and rejuvenated, most probably because the news of a forthcoming baby delights me and strengthens the chances of continuing the Tudor line.

"The arrival is imminent," I tell Philip.

"Pole?"

"I'm informed by messenger that he landed on time at Dover."

"And he progresses safely through England."

"He does. Everything else is in place, at long last," I say with a sigh. "I've written to him requesting that he come not as the Pope's legate but as cardinal and ambassador. That request may not be granted, however."

"At least the attainder against him has been reversed by parliament."

"And a merry dance parliament has led me on that," I say ruefully. "I've harried them and pressed them but at last, thanks be to God, it is done. He is now free of all the charges against him that my father put forward."

"Will he know?" Philip asks.

"Yes indeed. I have dispatched Tunstall, bishop of Durham and the Earl of Shrewsbury to meet him at Gravesend and there they will present him with letters under the great seal, certifying repeal of all laws against him in the reigns of Henry and my half-brother. From Gravesend he will sail up the Thames in my barge with his silver cross fixed on the prow."

"You authorised that, is it so?" Phillip wonders, surprised.

"I did. Nothing has been left to chance."

And that was not all. As soon as he arrived at Dover in a royal yacht, I had arranged that he be greeted by Anthony Browne, Viscount Montague, the bishop of Ely and other noblemen, where Browne would hand him a letter from me, with a few additional words from Philip, thanking him for coming before proceeding to Canterbury where he would be greeted with a fine oration from the archdeacon. I can only hope and pray that everything goes as smoothly and accurately as it was planned.

"In two days, he arrives at Whitehall, where we meet and greet him."

Philip frowns. Surely, in my present, delicate condition, it is better if I stay here at Hampton Court, in comfort, as he greets the cardinal on my behalf as my consort.

I shake my head in disbelief. "Do you seriously imagine, Philip, that after spending all this time and after endless letters to Cardinal Pole, seeking his advice, requesting his invaluable help in restoring us to favour with the church of Rome, that I would allow you to deputise and fail to greet him myself?"

"I seek only your welfare and comfort in your present delicate condition, is it not so?"

"Delicate condition? God's bones, I am but a few weeks pregnant, not six months."

The diplomacy and negotiations have been endless. The letters flying hither and thither and Renard being whisked all around the globe. Even the very thorny question of the restoration of monastery lands being returned to the Roman church was tackled head on and I was in the very centre of it all. Most, other than those that I will return as crown properties, will not be returned and we have Cardinal Pole to thank for that, requesting a papal disposition. It cannot have been easy.

I have worked ceaselessly on this homecoming of the cardinal, up at dawn, late to bed, and if Philip thinks I will sit back and let him enjoy the reconciliation and greetings at Whitehall, he is very wrong.

Philip sits in the window seat and glares into a place in the far distance. As a pampered prince of many dominions and lately created king of Naples along with consort of this realm he is not used to anybody asserting themselves in defiance of his pronouncements, least of all a woman. I settle down next to him but do not speak. He turns and glares at me. I hold his gaze steadily.

"We sail up to Westminster tomorrow morning, then," he suggests quietly.

"If you think that the opportune time," I reply demurely.

"It would be well."

So all is resolved at last.

Tonight, I will do everything I possibly can to make him happy in the bedchamber.

The barge dips down under a heavy swell caused by a passing ship. Spray shoots up and spreads out, a few drops reaching our faces and dampening mine. An attendant appears in front of me holding up a shield to protect me from further splashing. As the barge dips frequently on our progress to Westminster, I begin to regret not moving back to Whitehall earlier and settling in. A light wind is picking up and swirling around us, containing the chill bite of oncoming winter.

"Papal legate, then?" Philip asks.

"It would seem so," I reply. "He comes to us as the Pope's chosen counsel."

"He will be of great assistance."

"You think so?"

"Rome want us fully restored," Philip suggests.

If they do, then Cardinal Pole is the right man to do it. I have sought his advice frequently on spiritual matters and procedure. I have sent several bishops to be consecrated, although it is never easy communicating with somebody abroad. He has been in Rome or in various parts of Europe on the Pope's business for many years now. It saddens me that neither our country nor our church is fully reconciled to Rome. Pole will get things moving.

We greet the cardinal in the Presence Chamber at Whitehall Palace. He is a slight figure, not as I expected he would look, and he seems older, too. Although physically unimpressive, there is a positive aura of authority and command in his presence. He has a long grey beard and, when close to him, I am aware of dark, piercing eyes that appear to look right through me.

"Queen Mary, it is good to meet face to face," he tells me and then he greets Philip. Turning back to me, he adds: "You may not remember but you were an exceedingly small girl when I last saw you."

I shake my head. Much has occurred since he left these shores, still in possession of a head that he would surely have been parted from, had he stayed. Anyone who told Henry he had no right to appoint himself head of the church, next to God, could not expect to remain in this world for long. He left these shores as a scholar and returns, now, as a cardinal and the Pope's envoy.

We settle down on a raised dais under a canopy. The cardinal looks tired and somewhat weary of body. Doubtless the long journey from Europe and the slow progress through England from Dover to London has taken its toll.

"There is much to do," he says solemnly but his eyes light up as he speaks.

"Much indeed," I agree. "But with your help, Cardinal…" I leave my sentence unfinished.

"Together we must restore the lost glory of this kingdom."

Philip and I assure him that is our true desire, and we will work tirelessly to achieve it.

"Full reconciliation with Rome."

"As to the restoration of the monasteries," I begin but he holds up the palm of his hand to halt me.

"You need have no worry on that matter, Your Majesty. I understand, indeed that His Holiness understands that the lords and nobles holding those lands and tending them would not give them up without considerable bloodshed and rebellion. And nobody wants that. There is no requirement to return monastery buildings or land and there never will be."

"Ah, that is good," I say.

"As to the matter of heresy," the cardinal continues, "that is more fraught with danger."

"If anyone is found guilty of heresy," Philip says, "English law requires that they burn at the stake."

"Yes, I am aware. But oftentimes, it is wise to proceed with much caution."

"I can never condone it," I tell the cardinal.

"Nor should you, Majesty," he responds, smiling. "Other directions may sometimes be looked to for good, wise advantage."

"You mean long imprisonment, Cardinal?" I ask.

"Possibly. Although each case should be approached entirely on its merits."

I bridle a little, raise an eyebrow and say that I am determined to stamp out rebellion and uprisings by the followers of the English church. The heresy laws, now newly restored, will be used to prosecute those who speak evil concerning God and the holy Roman church and, if found guilty, our laws require that they burn at the stake. Philip appears a little uncomfortable at my words, but I know he agrees with my thoughts.

"I do not seek to undermine your just use of the laws of England," the cardinal says. "If I speak in terms of moderation, it is merely with the understanding that there will always be those whose views are opposed to ours. In the long term, attempts to get heretics to recant and earn absolution must, surely, be the aim of wise councillors."

"Do you speak of followers of the English Church, Sir?" I ask, surprised.

"To all good men and true," he responds. "We will restore the Catholic Church fully in this country, Majesty, but we must all live side by side with those of other persuasions. Would you have them all executed?"

"Of course not."

"Then all I advocate is moderation towards all men even

while we uphold the true religion for all who follow it. Those who do not follow our church must live in peace, provided they do not speak out against it or break the law."

"That is essentially what I believe," I tell him doubtfully. I will no longer tolerate heresy in any form, and I will always stamp out uprisings but, I do not say this, and I will not pursue the point at this, our first meeting.

"Then we are in agreement," he says, dark-blue eyes twinkling. "You have in the region of almost half the population of England who follow the new English church founded by Henry, your late father, and their views and beliefs will not be changed overnight."

"Perhaps never, is it not so?" Philip offers.

"Perhaps never," the cardinal pronounces solemnly. "We must surely all learn to live together."

"A bleak outlook," I murmur sadly. "Not the living but the heathen, antichrist church."

"God will guide us to the correct, righteous path," the cardinal continues solemnly, "as he always has and always will."

We can only agree with that, Philip nodding enthusiastically and I accepting it graciously. Cardinal Pole is not exactly what I had expected. From distance, he can be seen as a staunch, crusading Catholic, his object in life to convert all sinners and disbelievers to the faith. Meeting face to face, I find a man of humility who advocates caution and moderation, in all things. Is this the man who lectured Henry on the evil of appointing himself as head of the English church? With age, he must surely have mellowed.

"As to the wider issues facing us," Pole was saying, "I intend to begin work tomorrow and carry on until we have restored this nation to greatness again, under God's eye and in his church. God shows special grace to a repentant nation and this, I pray, will proceed as I forecast. I wish to grant absolution to sinners, not death and damnation."

As the lords and dignitaries depart, Bishop Gardiner, my chancellor, prepares to escort the cardinal to Lambeth Palace, where he will reside for a time.

"Not too heavy-handed with my pronouncements, was I?" the cardinal asks with what looks like a twinkle in his eye.

"Of course not," Philip says, and I incline my head.

"You speak with wisdom, authority and humility," Gardiner informs him.

"A potent mix indeed," the cardinal says, laughing at his own humour.

"I look forward to your sermons, Sir," Gardiner continues.

"Your Majesty?" he asks, seemingly to be sure he has my full support.

"You will set us back on the righteous road, Cardinal Pole," I tell him. "Of that I have no doubt whatsoever."

QUEEN MARY'S DIARY

WHITEHALL AND HAMPTON COURT, WINTER 1554

IF MY LADIES-IN-WAITING SEEM ESPECIALLY INDUSTRIOUS THIS morning, it is not without merit on their part. Much excitement has been generated by the cardinal's sermons and his celebration of high mass at St Paul's Cathedral. Busily embroidering or sewing, they sit in my privy chamber amid piles of fabrics of all hues as their talk varies from admiration of the cardinal's early work by the most pious to a debate upon who is the most handsome man at court from the most frivolous. When Philip comes in unexpectedly, I feel inclined to say that they need debate no further, the winner has just entered the chamber.

"I regret it," Philip is saying. "But the early arrival of this man from Spain precludes my presence at prayers."

"If you must remain with him," I respond, "so be it. I'll pray alone."

"I'm so sorry," Philip says, and he looks as though he means it.

"A prime candidate?" I hear Anne Bassett say as she suppresses a giggle.

"Might even be the winner," Gertrude Blount opines, grinning.

Philip is an easy winner in any competition for the best-looking man at court but I do not take kindly to my ladies discussing his looks so blatantly. I fix both Anne and the Marchioness with a reproving glare. Anne blushes but Gertrude has the audacity to wink at me. Catherine Brydges is giggling now although Jane Dormer, to her credit, looks uncomfortable.

"I will see you at supper tonight," Philip tells me.

"You had better ensure that you do," I inform him starkly.

He departs swiftly as a rustle of clothing, giggling and chatter erupts from the ladies. I look around and wonder what sort of motley crew I have assembled around me as my "ladies". Lady Margaret Douglas, Dorothy Boughton and Mabel Browne have not been blessed with what might be termed feminine beauty, to state the case mildly. Anne Bassett and Jane Dormer have pleasant, attractive faces, though, if not exactly pretty in the best sense of the word. Only Magdalen Dacre, who is tall and has long, straw-coloured yellow hair is truly pretty. And speaking of Magdalen, I did note the way she looked at Philip as he walked out. That young lady would be well advised to watch her step very carefully in future or she will have me to deal with.

"In truth, we could do with some more handsome men around court," Gertrude pronounces. "I despair of most of them."

"You're too fussy by half," Anne Basset tells her with a grin.

"Do you think you might direct your observations to more pressing matters?" I enquire. "Important changes are going on around us and all you ladies can do is discuss male attributes."

"What should we discuss then, Mary?" Catherine asks.

"The good work being carried out by Cardinal Pole," I tell them.

"I hear that he intends to introduce a programme of

education and further training for all priests, helping them to communicate with all citizens," Jane says, helping me to change the subject effectively.

The discussion of Pole's early dedication to restoration of our Roman church and his ideas for improvement is discussed in some depth but the ladies show by their responses and facial expressions that they are far more interested in male appearance and frivolous matters generally. The arrival of Francis Englefield is a welcome distraction and I dispatch them to their chambers as I wish to hear in private what he has to say.

Francis looks gaunt and grim; indeed, I suspect he has been on an errand I set for him that was distasteful to his sensibilities. I greet him cordially enough and bid him be seated near me in a high-backed chair. I ask first about the cardinal, which will make for more agreeable conversation than the second matter.

"He continues his good work unabated," Francis informs me. "At times he looks weary and pale of face but when he mounts the pulpit, he seems to take on an aura of invincibility."

I smile. When he received the two houses of convocation at Lambeth, he dispensed absolution for all their perjuries, schisms and heresies. This will be to restore the Pope's supremacy. In this and other matters of supreme importance, the cardinal does, indeed, take on a special aura.

"Two heretics appealed to him and were given a penance each and absolved," Francis tells me, "as soon as they recanted."

"I'm not surprised," I admit. "The cardinal is happy to show mercy if he feels sinners are fully repentant."

"Do you not think…" Francis begins but appears unsure how to proceed.

"Say it, Francis," I command. "Say it."

"Well, could you not show mercy yourself on occasions, Your Majesty?"

"You fail to understand, Francis," I begin grimly. "If I show weakness to followers of the Church of England, the poison will spread like wildfire. I will be seen as a weak and foolish woman who has no authority and, in all probability, someone who has no right to be on the throne of England."

"I disagree," he tells me. "You are seen as a strong, spirited sovereign who, for the moment, is extremely popular with the majority of the people."

"For the moment, Francis?"

"There is much unrest in the country," he proceeds. "As you are doubtless aware."

As, of course, I am. I know it stems from the unpopularity of Philip, my king, my husband and the love of my life, with many commoners. I was told most of the country was against my marrying a foreigner and one from Spain specifically. Even my own councillors, including my Chancellor and Bishop of Winchester, Stephen Gardiner, tried to persuade me not to go through with the marriage. I am told my popularity diminishes by the day and the people are enamoured of that troublesome woman, Elizabeth whom I now hesitate to acknowledge as a relative.

"Do the people not understand," I ask, "that the alliance with Spain keeps us safe from the threat of French or indeed any other invasion?"

"Most of them lack the education to understand anything to do with war and potential invasion," he asserts.

I wave him away as if dismissing the subject as too banal to discuss further. Then I remind him gently that there is the other errand on which I dispatched him today. His face clouds over and he pauses before speaking.

"I arrived early at Tyburn this morning," he says with a grim expression.

He pauses again and I wait, without speaking, knowing he will proceed in his own time.

"There was the usual ragged mob there, in particular a woman with pockmarked face and straggly hair, carrying a small child. There were several working men in grey smocks and a few women. A toothless woman kept swearing and cursing and yelling out that the man was innocent. Then a particularly savage group of young men arrived and stood there, chanting words to the effect that they wanted to see the burning now and what was the delay. Two officials were piling large balks of timber around the stake.

"Finally, the guards marched him out, a pathetic figure in a long grey robe, a bald head and a blank, rigid white face that looked as if he had lost all ability to move his muscles. The eyes were the worst of all; they never moved or flickered as far as I could tell but you could see the blind terror there."

"Did you stay to the end, Francis?" I ask, noticing his discomfort.

"Oh yes, Majesty, as was my duty."

"You could have refused, Francis. Or asked that somebody else be assigned."

He shakes his head and tells me he knows that I depend on him for the important matters, and he is always pleased to do my bidding, whatever it may be. I do not believe him but say nothing.

"Then they strapped him in and lit the fire almost immediately. The flames leapt up, crackling and spitting and I looked at his face as he opened his mouth to scream but no sound came out. Maybe his body was caught in a spasm or something, although you could see the terror in his eyes increase."

Francis pauses and shakes his head before continuing.

"Then the fierceness of the heat embraced us all and I could see the flames burning his robe, turning it black and his face had little boils of heat appearing and then a woman fainted in the crowd and had to be removed. The face was becoming blackened, but I couldn't get the sight of his eyes out of my mind and…"

"All right, Francis," I say quietly. "So sentence was carried out. I needed to know."

"Don't you want to know how it ended?" he continues. "The body turning black and then the liquid yellow fat, the bones, the fire burning out slowly and leaving a stream of vile sludge, the awful stench and…"

"That's enough," I command.

"Yes, I'm sorry."

"No, you're not," I tell him. "You didn't want to go but you went because you were commanded."

"I am loyal," he whispers.

"Indeed you are, Francis. I have to do many things I would rather not but have no choice."

"What next?" he asks apprehensively.

"A change of scene, I'm thinking."

"Yes," he murmurs, as though resigned to inevitable reprimand and punishment.

"I believe a few days' rest in Berkshire with Catherine will do you the most good," I tell him.

A fast if slightly choppy journey down the Thames to Hampton Court. A clear sky but cold and a light breeze picking up again to lick our faces. I am always pleased to speed away from Whitehall to the palace and grounds where I feel most at ease. And most at home. It will be good to get back as I have not been feeling well at all for the past four days. My stomach is swelling and it feels a little painful. Philip says it is what I must expect as I am pregnant, and I will have worse discomfort before all is done. My head aches and I suffer from nausea in the mornings. But it will all be worthwhile if I deliver a healthy baby boy.

The wind is picking up sharply.

"We'll be back soon," I say optimistically.

Philip has been attentive to my needs and fussing around, although, as it is all most recent on his part, I suspect he is more concerned about his future son and heir than me. He was showing concern that I was so busy with the government and affairs of state and might, in his words, do myself some harm.

"Rest, lots of rest for you Mary," he murmurs softly as the wind drops for an instant.

"Prayer first," I tell him, to catch up where I have neglected lately.

"Stay with your ladies," he suggests. "Leave all state affairs to others."

The water of the Thames looks black and bleak. It will not surprise me if it ices over in midwinter this year. The cold weather has come down suddenly this week like a freezing blanket. As we approach Hampton Court the barge slows down and the starboard-side oars rest.

In the chapel, I pray for health, strength and God's blessing to help me reign. I tell the rosary beads gently in my hands. My belly is extended quite visibly now, and I feel a gentle nagging pain that I hope is not an ill omen. My physician has made up a new potion for me, which I must take again.

My ladies receive me and make me comfortable with cushions. Margaret sends for spiced wine and sweetmeats then Magdalen pours the drink out for me and hands me the cup. Jane asks me solicitously if I am comfortable and asks about Philip.

"He was in his privy chamber as soon as we landed," I reply, "meeting up with his Spanish diplomats."

"Such a busy man," Margaret breathes, as though she admires him.

"Perhaps too busy," Gertrude suggests.

"He has several kingdoms to concern him, not just one," I tell her icily.

"Of course, I meant no offence," Gertrude hastily asserts. "I just thought it would be pleasant if he were able to spend more time with you, Majesty."

"Well, he doesn't," I tell her coldly.

"More spiced wine, Your Majesty?" Magdalen asks in her pure, sweet, gentle voice.

They mean well, all my ladies, but what I really need is more personal attention and affection from Philip, my husband.

LADY MAGDALEN DACRE'S DIARY

HAMPTON COURT, WINTER 1554

BRUSHING MY HAIR OUT IS ALWAYS A PLEASANT DIVERSION during the long hours when there appears to be little else to do. I take my time, often sacrificing most of dinner time to get it done and enjoying every minute. When I feel fingers running gently through my hair at the back I smile and wonder which of my companions is having a joke with me.

"Would you like to take over and brush it all out?" I ask quietly.

There is no reply, which I find strange, but the fingers continue to caress my hair sensuously. I turn around, puzzled and I am shocked to find Philip, the king, his hand in my hair and a smile on his face. I pull away, out of his grip and turn to face him.

"What are you doing, Your Grace?" I ask, startled still. "You should not be in here."

"I saw you there and your bright yellow hair fascinated me," he answers. "I just had to touch it."

"Please don't," I say. "Please go."

He does not go but moves towards me and attempts an embrace, which I struggle hard to escape. He is gripping me round my shoulders and pulling me towards him with much strength and I panic a little. I seize a staff by my hand and use it to whack him hard across the back, twice. He lets go of me and steps back.

"How unfriendly you are, Magdalen," he complains. "How stiff and unresponsive."

"Please leave now," I say, trembling a little.

"Do not fret, little one," he commands. "I will not hurt you."

"You should leave, Sir," I repeat. "Now."

"Time for dinner in the great hall," he says, smiling broadly. "Do not leave it too late, little one." And he strides out purposefully.

It takes me some time to regain my composure. I finish brushing and go to my dinner.

I still feel strange and a little shaky now. I sew steadily as my companions do around me and begin to wonder if I dreamed it all. The queen is singing Philip's praises and the others are listening attentively and commenting where appropriate.

"Sometimes I think he works far too hard," she is saying. "I rarely get him out of his office at night before suppertime."

"You would like it if he spent more time at leisure, though?" Margaret suggests.

"I would, 'tis true," the queen answers. "It can't be done, though. That father of his, the emperor, makes too many demands of him."

"It is the price you pay, Majesty, for having such an important prince as your king and husband," Jane is saying, and the others nod or shake their heads in sympathy.

"You would not exchange him for a lesser man though," Anne Bassett offers.

"Indeed I would not," the queen says emphatically.

"Maybe, when the baby is born," Anne continues, "he will try to find more time with you both."

"For that day, I hope and pray it will be so," the queen agrees.

They all laugh, except me, and gradually everybody resumes their silent sewing. The queen is looking at me intensely and I feel myself blushing.

"You are extremely quiet, Magdalen," the queen says. "What say you?"

"I-I feel sure Anne is right," I stutter, "and he will find more time when the baby comes. I often wonder what it is like to be married." I do not know why I added those last few words.

"Your time will come. young Magdalen," the queen promises me. "Your time will surely come."

Not once, twice but three times. He creeps up behind me in absolute silence and starts running his stubby fingers through my hair. I used the staff again on the first occasion, but he just laughed and called me a wild child. One he could tame. Some things, though, are completely unexpected.

"It's from an ancient Spanish family. All dead now."

"It's beautiful," I say, astonished.

"And it's yours."

I gaze at the pearls and the setting. Such an item I have never received from anybody in my life. I cannot accept it and I tell him so excitedly, all the time thinking about it and how good it would look if I wore it. He just repeats that it is mine and he wishes me to have it, so I had better make up my mind and place it in my privy purse.

Today a diamond pendant. Small, but exquisite.

A mistake is showing one of the pearls to Anne Bassett and Jane Dormer while the queen and the others are at prayer and we are finishing an embroidery task. Anne is open-mouthed in astonishment and wonders where it originated. I tell her Spain and then she is suspicious.

"He insisted I accept," I say sulkily. "He wouldn't take no for an answer."

"Do you have any notion of the danger you have put yourself in?" Anne asks and the expression on Jane's face is a picture. "Possibly to us as well."

"He pursues me," I state indignantly. "I'm not to blame."

"You are just a brief diversion to him," Jane states. "But if the queen finds out, you'll be in the Tower before nightfall."

"And without your young head by Saturday," Anne adds, as I shudder.

"You won't betray me?" I plead, eyes widening.

"We dare not," Jane says as Anne nods agreement. "We are all safer knowing nothing and having seen and heard nothing."

They advise and then plead with me to keep away from Philip, run a mile any time and every time I see him. It is good advice and I assure them I will heed it.

I walk slowly and carefully along this unfamiliar corridor. With only one candle in my hand and no servant to call upon, I feel in danger already. It is pitch-black and the shadows on the walls all around me as I proceed are frightening. They seem like ghosts come to haunt me and warn me of Purgatory to come.

At the door to the designated chamber an armed guard is positioned. He gives me a penetrating glance before opening the door for me to enter. He closes it heavily behind me and I feel tense all over as I think the sound would wake the dead. In the chamber, it is brightly lit with candles and a huge fire burns warmly.

"Is he safe?" I ask, nodding towards the guard outside the door.

Philip smiles. "Ah, Pedro. A loyal Spanish servant of mine

these 10 years," he assures me. "Even the queen would not be admitted if she appeared outside the door."

"Speaking of the queen," I say softly, "Where does she think you are just now?"

"In my bedchamber. We do not share a bed since she became with child."

"How convenient for you."

"She is sound asleep. She took her sleeping potion and went straight off."

He puts his finger to my lips as though to say no more talking for now. He leads me to the bed and pulls aside the heavy drapes. He sits me down on the soft feathers and sits facing me. He kisses me on the lips, gently, sensuously.

"What do you want of me?" I ask.

"You know what I want, My Lady," he tells me. "I want to lie with you and slip into your cunt."

"Why me?"

"Because you are a delightful little creature and I wish to make love to you and only you."

"Why not make love to the queen? She is your wife and the love of your life."

"She is old, Magdalen," he complains. "She is wrinkled and not too pleasing to the eye."

"So why did you marry her?" I want to know.

"It was an excellent alliance of two great nations," he tells me. "It should keep the might of France and Italy from making war. And it was what my father, the emperor, wanted."

"Is that the only reason you married?" I ask, shocked.

"No," he muses, thoughtfully. "I liked her well enough when we met and since then we have had moments of intimacy."

"But not enough to stay faithful," I say sadly.

He tells me I am young and do not understand the ways of princes. To fight for and protect his country is his wish and he will always put that first. Now he has a new country to fight for and protect and he will do his duty. Always. As long as he has breath in his body.

"And I must have beautiful women around me, always," he states, and he reaches out and clasps me by my arms and draws me close to him.

"Am I beautiful, Sir?" I ask quietly.

"You know you are."

I am swept along by a sudden flurry of flattery mixed with desire. I close my eyes and enter a world of passion.

SIR FRANCIS ENGLEFIELD'S DIARY

ENGLEFIELD HOUSE, BERKSHIRE, EARLY SPRING 1555

PALE SUNLIGHT DANCES ON THE RIVER SURFACE BUT IT IS COLD today. I pull the heavy cape around me tightly, covering my doublet. My fishing line is still out but no sign of a bite all morning. I look to Benson, my estate manager, and he has an optimistic expression on his face. I try to feel the same myself, but it is not easy. I feel I am in the right place at the right time but still my mind is not easy. I am far away now but I still see images of a burned man every time I close my eyes and even when I look towards the grey-blue sky. Or an axe coming down, blade flashing in a sudden burst of light. Two more died before I left London but mercifully, I did not witness either.

"He's biting, Sir. Hold hard."

Can Benson have seen a fish before I even felt a pull on my line? He is right, though, and slowly, with his careful guidance, I finally manage to land it. A good-sized silver fish but of what sort I have no idea.

"A goodly fish," Benson says. "He'll make a fine supper."

"He's yours, Benson," I tell him. "For you and Mrs Benson."

"Why, thank ye very much, Sir. You are most kind."

I must have spent a good three hours here but at least I finally got a catch. Looking at the fish, now dead and being loaded into Benson's water-filled bucket, I begin to feel the pangs of hunger.

Catherine has arranged for a dinner of lark, pheasant, partridge and a fish course. Some beef as well, of course, but I soon find I am not as hungry as I thought I would be and pick at the various courses as delicately as a maid. The pheasant is soft, white and tender, so I concentrate on that. The flute player and the lutenist play softly on the balcony, as instructed.

"Are you past your spell in the doldrums yet?" Catherine enquires.

"Not yet," I tell her. "I haven't got the mud of London off my boots yet."

"What is it that is ailing you really, Francis?" she asks, looking concerned.

I give her a brief summary of all that has occurred in the last month but do not mention the horrors in any detail. I tell her that I have been involved in the arrest and trials of certain prominent clergymen such as the bishops John Hooper, John Bradford and John Rogers. The Chancellor, Bishop Gardiner, was instrumental in pursuing and prosecuting all three.

"The heresy trials?"

"Well, yes. Gardiner it was that pressed the queen to reinstate the heresy laws."

"And those bishops were burned at the stake?"

All three of them, I tell her. Others, too, are being added to the list almost daily. There is no defence and little hope of survival for anybody openly supporting the new English church. Catherine's intense glare and knitted brow indicate that she is most unhappy with the situation.

"You should get out of it, Francis," she blurts out suddenly. "Come back here to Berkshire and live quietly as a local magistrate. Where you are, you are in danger."

THE TITIAN PORTRAIT

"I'm not in personal danger," I tell her quietly. "I just find it difficult living with all the hate, death and destruction all around the court."

"Leave it to Gardiner," Catherine says. "He thrives on persecuting and killing people. Always has."

"It's not entirely his fault," I admit.

"Who then? The queen?"

"Yes, precisely, the queen."

Catherine is genuinely shocked to hear that the execution of those found guilty of heresy are condemned to death on the direct orders of Her Majesty Queen Mary. After taking in the unexpected news, she says she expects the queen is supported vigorously by Cardinal Pole.

"No, not so," I protest. "He makes no pronouncements whatsoever and stays in the background, concentrating purely on church matters."

"Well, you should stay in the background, too," she says haughtily.

When supper is finished and the musicians have departed, all is quiet in our privy apartment. The fire has burned down low to a bright-red glow and sends out fierce heat. The flickering candles send dancing patterns across the panes in the windows. Around the hot fire in high-backed chairs, all seems peaceful as Catherine and I sit, sipping brandy wine. A scent of lavender, Catherine's favourite, fills the room. All appears settled but a current of discontent stirs the air.

"I can't abandon her," I say quietly. "She depends on my advice and support."

"Times are changing," Catherine asserts. "The queen was popular when she asserted her right as next in line to the throne, fought for it and secured it. When an ill-timed rebellion started, she made a rousing speech at the Guildhall and received overwhelming support. But it was never just a bunch of ill-advised rebels and commons that followed the new church, it was almost half the population and now they are discontented. Burning heretics will cause huge resentment and hatred. Can you not see that Francis?"

"I see it, but I also see that the queen's priority is the full reinstatement of the Catholic faith in this country, something we must all support."

"At any price?"

"I sincerely hope not," I offer wearily. "Although I must confess, I see the stamping out of heresy as necessary. And I support a full return to Catholicism."

"As indeed do I," she agrees, "but I fear the queen goes too far."

"And who will tell her so?"

"Not you, Francis, not you. Leave it to others."

The fire burns low, and the heat diminishes to a comforting warmth. The brandy wine does its job and I begin to feel mellow and much less agitated. Catherine, too, I suspect; she smiles and her bright eyes glow in the candlelight. She says softly that she knows I will not abandon the queen and she will never persuade me, but she just urges caution, great caution in my future support.

"Then there is Elizabeth," I continue at length. "A strong presence and, in the queen's eyes, a permanent threat to stability."

"She is much loved by the people," Catherine points out. "They say she is cheered from the streets when she passes, and people fall on their knees in front of her litter."

"Well, they won't be doing much cheering now," I respond. "Not while she continues a virtual prisoner at Woodstock."

"For how long, though?"

"That," I say with a smile, "is one beacon of light on the horizon. I have long tried to persuade the queen to release Elizabeth and now I am told by the king that he sees no danger from her, either, and will attempt to persuade his wife to release her."

"I hope she comes to no harm," Catherine replies. "The people would never forgive Mary if she executed her half-sister."

"I am confident it won't come to that."

I remain unreconciled to Catherine's persuasions and, although she has accepted that, now I still feel there is much tension between us generally. We are both tired, however, and proceed to the bedchambers. My room has been regally appointed in my absence and soft, new, feathery pillows supplied. Catherine asks quietly if I will be comfortable as she dismisses the servants. I nod in acquiescence.

"Then again, we have the marriage bed in my chamber," she whispers softly.

"So we do," I agree cheerfully.

"Which always appears somewhat too big for little me, alone."

"Then I suggest we return it to its correct function."

"Yes, good idea," she breathes enthusiastically. "Come along, Francis."

LADY ELIZABETH'S DIARY

➣

HAMPTON COURT, SPRING 1555

I WEARY OF JOUSTING VERBALLY WITH SIR HENRY BEDINGFIELD, which is my only diversion held here as captive. I am allowed to walk the grounds alone occasionally, which is a distraction from being continually watched. I often walk the far length of the gardens and round the side of the main building. If I stay out of sight too long however the guards come running and I am politely asked to return to the gatehouse. Today I feel particularly bored and lonely, even though my servants come and go to serve me food and wine.

"A moment of your time, Lady Elizabeth," Bedingfield requests.

"All my time is at your disposal, Sir," I reply. "By force, not by favour."

He smirks and Is obviously up to something, but I do not wish to bandy words with him today. I am tired of his silly games.

"You won't want to miss this," he tells me, still grinning.

"Go on then, surprise me."

He takes his time, just to irritate me further. He walks over to the window and glances out and murmurs something about the new green shoots coming out. I say all seasons are beginning to look the same to me, imprisoned with only a dull fellow like him to speak to occasionally.

"You are recalled to court," he announces pompously and pauses to let the surprise sink in. "To Hampton Court. By order of Her Gracious Majesty Queen Mary."

"Is this your idea of a joke, you miserable tormentor?" I respond. It is safe to say that our relations have deteriorated considerably during my detention.

"We leave tomorrow morning, early," he replies tartly and strides out of the room, offended.

Somehow, I do not believe a word of it. I have been incarcerated for so long now that I have begun to believe I shall never again know freedom of movement. I think about it long and hard, though. All day long and through the night, wondering. Bedingfield does not come near me again. I have upset the poor fool. A guard lets me out to walk the grounds before suppertime but keeps a close watch on my movements.

The day is fair, the carriage bumps and dips along the roads, full of unseen potholes. Unseen, that is, until the wheels dip into them and jolt our bodies mightily.

"At first you will be under guard still," Bedingfield informs me.

"Ah, I see. Not so much freedom as further imprisonment at Hampton Court?"

"Merely a preliminary precaution," he murmurs as the carriage grinds onwards.

"In case I go mad on arrival and attempt to assassinate the queen with my bare hands?" I ask.

He shakes his head from side to side as though impatient with an obstinate child but makes no reply. I begin to look around me on the journey, however, and feel just a little spark of hope in my breast. Our convoy is large with many guards, attendants and servants filling our carriages. Near Oxford, the people are out in great numbers just as though they had received advance news of our procession. They wave to me, a sea of smiling, happy faces and quite a few kneel down as we pass. I wave back heartily and fix a smile on my face that stays there. These people still see me as Princess Elizabeth; they have not accepted the false charge of illegitimacy.

I wear a plain black gown and a pale blue kirtle, nothing showy or ostentatious. I wish to look well- presented but not overdressed. In the villages, there are few people abroad, but it is good to note that they recognise me and pay their respects.

In Rotherfield Greys, near Henley, the house, Greys Court, stands regal and bathed in sudden sunlight. It is a fine old building that has stood now for more than 200 years. Sir Francis Knollys is away in Germany, I believe, but it will be good to see my cousin, Lady Catherine Knollys, the daughter of Mary Boleyn, my poor late mother's sister.

"It is a joy to see you again, Elizabeth," she says, her eyes lighting up and genuine pleasure suffusing her face.

"And so it is for me, Catherine," I respond, and we embrace.

Even here, in an old friend's house where we spend the night, nothing has changed. I am assigned a spacious, comfortable bedchamber but will have two guards posted outside the door all night long. I will have my own servant close by but also one of Bedingfield's. At least it will be luxury compared to the Gatehouse at Woodstock. After supper, as Catherine and I settle down to talk in her beautiful small reception chamber. The Bedingfield guards have the decency to stay in the hall outside.

"I'm so sorry you've been subjected to this ghastly treatment, Elizabeth," she tells me, grimacing.

"My good half-sister never could bring herself to trust

me," I say wearily. "But I will come through to fight another day."

"Indeed you will," she responds. But do I detect a lack of conviction in her voice?

"Mary should be ashamed of herself," she continues.

"Well, I am recalled to court at last," I tell her. "I may be free before too long now. And my courtiers inform me she is with child so she will want to gloat about that. And delight in informing me that I will never be queen. Unless, of course, I outlive her unborn child."

Catherine smiles. I tell her it is wonderful to spend a night in her delightful house, although I am sorry to have missed Francis. Enough about me. How is she faring?

"I miss him, of course," she muses. "He found it expedient to go to Germany. He is too well known for his support of the English church and his antipathy towards Catholicism."

"Yes," I sympathise, "it is a cross many of us have to bear."

"I was brought up to believe the Church of Rome represented the Antichrist," Catherine is murmuring sadly.

"I know," I whisper. "Do not let any of this unruly mob hear you say it, though."

We link arms and walk upstairs, parting company only at our various bedchambers. After being kept in isolation for so long it is a pleasure to spend a night at Greys Court.

The roads down to Surrey are long and winding and rain impedes our progress. Few people are abroad as we head down towards Hampton Court Palace but those whom we do see wave excitedly. On arrival, I am shocked to find we are taken in at the rear door and I am taken, under guard, to my chamber.

"Still a prisoner," I say to Bedingfield.

"Things will change gradually," he tells me.

. . .

I have been here for almost three days and seen nobody but attendants and servants. I dine alone in a chamber set up for me. My accommodation is comfortable, indeed luxurious in the extreme compared to the privations of Woodstock. I send requests to have a meeting with the queen but receive no response. She will not invite me to her privy chamber nor come to me in mine. I do have a visitor, though.

"I trust you are comfortable and well looked-after, Lady Elizabeth?" the king asks.

"Yes, Your Majesty," I almost stumble over my words, so surprised am I by his sudden, unheralded appearance.

He sits and invites me to do likewise. He tells me he has studied my progress from London to Woodstock and discussed it frequently with his wife, the queen. He requests that I remain patient and try to make the best of my situation here. He will personally ensure that all comforts are provided for me.

"I have frequently requested permission to speak to the queen," I tell him, "but she refuses to see me. Why?"

He smiles and I am made aware of light blue eyes that are, I must admit, quite captivating and a handsome face that looks bronzed and healthy. Unlike my own pale pallor.

"If you will be good enough to leave it in my hands," he says, "I will endeavour to make an arrangement."

"I've written three letters and sent direct requests," I tell him in a surly manner. "Nothing makes any difference."

"My apologies," he responds graciously. "She has been most unwell and uncomfortable physically, due to a painful and far-from-straightforward pregnancy."

"Ah, I did not realise that," I tell him, contrite. "Then it is I who should apologise."

"It has been a difficult time," he is saying quietly. "Much unrest in the country, dissident factions spreading alarm and the threat of rebellion and treason."

"Yes."

"One does not know whom to trust and whom to fear, is it not so?" he asks, and his smile is warm and enough to melt many a maiden's heart. Fortunately, I am made of sterner stuff and, although young, not likely to be charmed by a handsome face and a charming manner.

"Well, she has no need to fear disloyalty from me," I tell him briskly. "And never will have, while I breathe."

"No, no, that is understood," he continues. "I ask only your continued patience, Lady Elizabeth."

"Can you secure a meeting for us, Your Majesty?" I ask more quietly.

"My powers of persuasion are not infinite," he goes on, with that seductive, intimate expression and charm that I imagine he employs when talking to all women. "One will do his very best, though."

I am only very slightly cheered and barely optimistic about his visit although it is good to know that I have an unexpected friend in Philip and not another enemy. The time appears to drag unbearably from day to day when I still do not know where I stand and the queen still resists a meeting. In desperation, I ask to see members of the council.

"You should ask the queen's pardon, admit to past wrongdoing and beg her forgiveness," Stephen Gardiner, the Lord Chancellor tells me pompously.

"But I haven't done anything wrong, My Lord," I say wearily. When will it ever end?

"In her eyes, you have," he continues, not really listening to me.

"What say you, Sir Francis?" I ask, seeking one friendly voice.

"Declare loyalty, ask forgiveness," he replies. "It's the only way, I'm afraid, Lady Elizabeth."

"Although you must admit wrongdoing, too," Gardiner adds spitefully.

I become exceedingly angry. "I will not ask forgiveness for

what I have not done," I repeat. "I do not want mercy. I want justice and the law. I would rather remain a prisoner for ever than admit to crimes I have never committed."

The councillors look dismayed, which does not cheer me. Gardiner shakes his head and looks at me as though he would like to strangle me with his bare hands. Even Sir Francis looks peeved and unfriendly.

And so it continues. If I am not still a prisoner, I am still not yet free. My comfortable apartment in the prince's wing of the palace affords me gracious living in the style to which I am accustomed, even if I have been falsely robbed of my title of princess. My bed is soft and with feathered cushions, along with many lovely covers and pillows. The drapes around the bed are damask of high quality and prettily tasselled. I have high-backed chairs and a table and even the luxury of writing paper and quills.

Subtlety is introduced into my imprisonment. I can walk freely in the grounds and sit by the fishpond or the fountain or visit the tennis grounds. The guards are always there, however, their presence constantly felt even if they are seldom seen. My freedom of movement is really an illusion, and I am aware that if I stray beyond a certain point or attempt to leave the precincts of the palace, I shall be stopped rudely in my tracks. One time I did try to walk down to the river but before I could proceed further a guard, unarmed but rough of appearance, stood in front of me. He appeared as if from nowhere.

"Please proceed back towards the palace, My Lady," he said with ill-concealed menace.

I sit in my chamber with my books and drink spiced wine, eat sweetmeats and wait patiently for bedtime. The days pass, long and wearying. Only one visitor returns in over a week.

"Philip is persuasive on your behalf," Sir Francis informs me.

"Is he, now?" I ask. "I see no signs of change."

THE TITIAN PORTRAIT

"I, too, have made representations on your behalf," he continues, "although the king is considerably more persuasive than I."

"Let us pray that he is ultimately successful," I murmur.

"Be of good cheer, Lady Elizabeth," he advises. "She loves him dearly and will do anything for him."

I am totally unprepared when it finally happens. Well into the evening, past 10, and I am advised that the queen will see me. She has sent her Mistress of the Robes, Susan Clarencieux, to escort me. Susan greets me in a pleasant-enough manner, but she is, nevertheless, quite stiff and formal.

"Come with me, Lady Elizabeth," she instructs coldly and not another word do I hear from her until we reach the queen's privy chamber. The room is dark, and it takes me some time for my eyes to get used to it. The queen is over on the extreme right-hand side of the room, just beyond the bed drapes and in semi darkness. Candles are lit but they are sparsely distributed throughout the chamber so overall it is an eerie effect as I step in. Something impels me to throw myself on the floor in front of her and blurt out loudly that I am an innocent woman.

"Come forward," the queen says, "and sit by me."

I do as she bids, and I get the impression there is somebody else in the chamber, someone hidden on the bed behind the drawn drapes, perhaps. It may be my imagination, though.

"No need for elaborate displays of emotion," I hear her continue. "You've made yourself abundantly clear in past messages."

"I just want to make it clear that I'm innocent of all charges and assure you that I am your most loyal and obedient subject," I tell her earnestly.

In the weak light, I can hardly make out her features,

although I do detect that she is smiling. As my eyes gradually become used to the light, I notice her lined face and a look of weariness. She is wrapped in heavy ermine drapes that seem to enclose her, to parcel her up somehow.

"It has been a long time since we talked together, you and I," she is saying.

"It has, yes."

She is silent for a short time and continues to stare at me as though I were a stranger. When she speaks, it is like an avoidance of the subject in hand and a sudden deviation.

"Are you quite comfortable in your apartments?"

"I am, yes, thank you."

"They were all clamouring for your execution, the councillors," she suddenly begins saying, in a rush. "I felt it safer to keep you locked up. For your own ultimate safety."

"That's not true," I blurt out. "You wanted me dead, everybody knows."

"That is a lie," she shouts. "How dare you speak to me like that?"

I apologise. I have no option. I tell her that I have been under strain in prison and restrained in other places and feel in peril. She almost sneers as she wonders what happened to being her most loyal and obedient subject. I try to assure her that I am, but I hate injustice and feel I have been unjustly treated.

She nods and surprises me by saying she understands. Mistakes and misunderstandings have occurred.

"I myself have been in some pain and often great discomfort during my pregnancy," she is saying. "I soon go into isolation for the final months."

I attempt a smile, not overly successfully, and wish her a good birth, a son, if it is God's wish.

"It will be good for the realm," she is saying, her voice suddenly brighter, more optimistic. "A son or daughter to continue the Tudor line."

"Yes," I say, teeth clenched.

"And you will be his aunt Elizabeth," she is saying brightly now. "As prince and doubtless as king if you outlive me, which I feel you are bound to do, being younger and of much more robust build than I."

What she is really saying, beneath the surface, is that she is ensuring that I will never be Queen of England, even though at present I am next in line in the succession. She is digging at me where she knows it will hurt most for, although I would be loyal and true to any future king or queen she might produce, I could never accept their Roman Catholic continuation.

"My loyalty as a subject will never be in question," I say. "To you or any future king or queen."

"We should not quarrel or fall out," she says, with another sudden change of tack. "We have a tie of blood and both of us have been badly used by those who should have put our welfare first."

"You speak truly indeed, Your Majesty," I agree.

"Our father, his ministers and advisers."

"And others."

"And others, yes."

She is looking quite contented in the gloom, but her dreary pallor is not good. I have the uneasy feeling again, more intense this time, that somebody is hidden behind the bed curtains. It is an eerie, uncomfortable feeling. Now she is looking at me quite interrogatively and I sense a question coming.

"How is your health, Elizabeth?"

"I've had my problems," I answer honestly. "Back and belly pains with cramps. I am in reasonably good health now, though."

"That is good. I am pleased to hear it."

"Thank you, Majesty, you are gracious."

"We should," she begins imperiously, "draw a heavy black

line under events of the past two years and begin again to live in harmony."

"That would be my fervent wish," I tell her.

I am thinking that it will be difficult indeed, if not impossible, to forget the privations and humiliations recently bestowed on me but I keep my own counsel and hope that this is the dawning of an era of peace and goodwill. I am feeling a wave of optimism and hope now but will not count my chickens before they are hatched.

"I lift all restrictions on your movements from this day forward," she says with a smile.

"Thank you, Your Majesty."

"And your full retinue of servants and attendants will be returned to be at your disposal," she adds, appearing to take pleasure in her own generosity.

I manage to smile naturally and without strain. I thank her again.

"A return to court, and not before time," she is saying. "Best probably if you stay at court for a while but you will be free to return to Hatfield shortly after my confinement ends."

Hatfield House is my home, the place where I feel most comfortable and alive. I long to see my old chambers and favourite nooks and crannies and sit under the big oak tree on warm summer days. Last night I thought I would never see the place again in my lifetime. To have Kat Ashley and all my favourite servants back is another reason for hope for the future.

The queen bids me good night and pleasant dreams and I return the good wishes. She summons Susan with a little bell and Susan escorts me back to my apartments. As we leave and the door is closed behind us, I stop and attempt to adjust my kirtle. Yes, I was right, I am sure, I hear very faintly, a male voice. Philip, the king, was listening behind the drapes.

QUEEN MARY'S DIARY

HAMPTON COURT PALACE, AUTUMN AND WINTER 1555

Sickness almost every morning, cramps and pains in my belly and a constant feeling of nausea. Strange are the ways of a woman's suffering during pregnancy but I must remain calm and diligent. If all this discomfort is God's will, then I must bear it. The rewards later will be greater. I find I want to eat pears all the time and the crop this year was not so good. Some pears are stored for me, but the pile is getting smaller.

I want to just sit back on clement days and watch the world outside the casement, but I cannot do so. Affairs of state occupy most of my waking hours and I am locked into my office. When Philip joins me to deal with affairs of state together, that is when I am most content. Mostly, though, he is to be found in his privy office dealing with affairs from distant lands or making representations on behalf of his father, the emperor. Just now I am assailed by councillors from all sides advising me that they have been hounded to beg and seek mercy for the many citizens, mainly clergymen, under sentence of death for heresy.

I cannot do it. Heresy and blasphemy against God are the one unforgivable sin that I will never pardon. I might, at times, under certain circumstances, forgive it against my person but never God. I have papers in front of me of another 15 men and two women found guilty. I can and will authorise the execution, at the stake, of all of them, even though it pains me to do it. Sir Francis and others have recommended leniency and even Cardinal Pole indicated that there were circumstances where he would grant absolution with a penance. My business though is that of the state and the people and the stability of every citizen so I will not hesitate in my duty.

Cardinal Pole visits and we spend a pleasant hour in the chapel praying for myself, my baby and the world in general. He is a calming influence on me and God's representative on this green earth of England.

My ladies work tirelessly, knitting, sewing and embroidering baby clothes. Gertrude, Anne and Mabel are industrious in this respect and forever holding up carefully fabricated items of fabric for my inspection. Jane Dormer is slower and not the swiftest needlewoman you would ever encounter but she is thorough, working diligently to finish items of clothing, even if she misses her meals. Even young Magdalen has produced something soft and fancy, made with her own hands and she is less a needlewoman than Jane.

I worry though about my pregnancy and the bad symptoms I have been going through. Every symptom I have experienced I have thought it unique to me as I have never observed it in others.

"It is quite normal to experience sickness in the mornings," Doctor Owen assures me.

"A friend of mine, Lady Margaret," I tell him, "had no such experience."

Owen smiles and shakes his head. "Not all pregnancies are the same, Your Majesty. Far from it."

"Well, it is confusing," I complain. "I get stomach cramps, too."

He frowns and shakes his head. That is not usual, he

thinks, unless, of course, it is a particularly active baby kicking in my belly.

"Perhaps that is it," I tell him joyfully. "In fact, I'm fairly sure I felt a strong kick just a moment ago."

In my privy chamber though, alone, when the ladies have all departed and it is a dull day, I do, sometimes, almost despair. I walk over to the casement and gaze out towards the river. Tugs, barges and an occasional large ship drift past as the rain beats down and drums noisily against the window. This is a time when I begin to have black thoughts. What if the baby were born dead or I were not to survive the birth? What if the pain and sometimes churning in my belly were not a baby kicking but some other cause? It is when these thoughts come, unbidden and unwanted, that I feel most pain.

Today I move over to the window and sit on the floor, under it, drawing up my legs to my chin. I can sit like this, quite still, for long periods of time, just mouthing an occasional silent prayer and crossing myself. Nobody is allowed in the privy chamber at these times of contemplation, that is understood. Only Philip may enter at any time and rouse me if I appear to be in a stupor.

I have been sitting here on the floor, legs drawn up to my chin, shivering a little, for more than two hours. It is much longer than usual but I feel I need to stay here, still and unmoving, seeking peace and solitude. I hear bells in the distance chiming, but I close most of it out, listening only for the quiet and the stillness of the chamber.

"What are you doing, Mary? Why are you in this position?"

He lifts me up gently, persuasively, in his strong male arms as I tell him I find it restful and peaceful in my present condition. Philip shakes his head and tells me I may get cramp or even catch a cold. It is not good for me, in any way.

"A walk in the grounds, slowly," he tells me, "will do you far more good."

"Will you walk with me?" I enquire anxiously.

"For a short time," he answers. "I have much state business to conduct."

Fortunately, it is one of those perfect late-autumn days; dry, warm, misty with pale sunshine occasionally breaking through. I can only walk slowly and a little painfully, my legs aching from long inactivity but as it is one of the rare times when Philip is with me, I am content and only anxious that we spend some considerable time together. He is patient with my lethargy, considerate and his very presence close to me is a tonic that I welcome, unexpected as it surely is.

The fountain, bubbling pleasantly with the water gushing down into the pond below makes me feel calmer, exhilarated. Coming out here alone, though, would not be the same and I need his strong arm to support me.

"How are you feeling generally?" he enquires.

"Not too bad," I assure him. "Just a minimum of belly ache and cramp."

"That is not good," he says, frowning.

"Doctor Owen tells me it is natural enough," I protest. "The baby kicking."

"If that is all it is," he says doubtfully.

All too soon he says he must leave me and will walk me back slowly to my privy chamber. I plead for longer with him, but he is adamant that state affairs will not wait, and I ask him to send Jane Dormer down to walk me back. Meanwhile, I will rest on a stone seat and watch the birds flying. A peacock has strayed and provides a colourful spectacle as he walks slowly past, some feet away from where I sit.

I ask Jane to take me to my confinement bedchamber to see what it is like now. Inside, it is dusky and indeed dusty, although servants are busily cleaning and dusting as we enter. The heavy drape curtains are up now and enclose the room in darkness, excepting a few well-placed burning candles. The tapestries are colourful and depict stirring views of knights in armour and peaceful rural scenes. The bed is large and strewn around it are many feather cushions.

"I must enter here soon," I murmur, not so much to Jane but to myself.

"We will make you comfortable, Mary," she tells me optimistically.

"Two months in solitude," I ruminate.

At supper, Philip tells me he is worried that I spend long hours alone, sitting in an uncomfortable position, which is not good for the baby or for me. I assure him that most of my time is spent on state business, signing authorities for government, executions and other matters. It is only on the few black days when I feel low in spirits that I seek the solitude I occasionally need.

"I will ask Doctor Owen to visit you more frequently," he says. "And every day as you enter confinement."

"I appreciate your concern, Philip," I tell him, "more than you know. I am strong, though. All will be well."

"I am keeping a weather eye on Elizabeth, too," he states. "She is now moving about freely and I am sure she no longer poses any threat."

"That is good," I tell him.

"Any threat to our shores now," he continues, "comes from the French and, by association, Mary, the Queen of Scotland and her French prince. The alliance of our countries, England and Spain, however, will ensure the safety of the realm."

I have ordered a cradle of the finest craftsmanship and required a nursery to be prepared. I go to look at these on the day before I am due to start my confinement. Margaret and Jane accompany me to the nursery where everything appears to have been arranged to my satisfaction. There are gifts for the baby piled high and, over by the casement, a large wooden cradle.

"Beautiful carving," I say, running my finger along the side.

"The carpenter has done well," Jane agrees.

Margaret just looks on but says nothing. She looks apprehensive, though.

On my desk there are piles of cards announcing the birth of my baby, with all the details filled in apart from the child's name and the birth date. I walk slowly back to my privy chamber, holding my extended belly in both hands and breathing evenly.

"As far as I can tell, all is well," Doctor Owen says.

"As far as you can tell," I repeat. "Is there a doubt?"

"No," he says hastily, noting my alarmed reaction. He puts his hands around the protuberance that is now my belly and prods very gently. "I would recommend much rest, Your Majesty."

"I'll get plenty of that tomorrow," I tell him. "My confinement starts."

"Yes, of course."

As it turns out. I spend much of the day at prayer. I pray for God's guidance in serving my country.

In my office, I take up papers concerning the trials and heresy of five further clergymen and await the arrival of Sir Francis Englefield. When we have gone through some minor government business and resolved it, I pick up the sheaf of papers relating to the heresy. What is being done? I ask. He looks puzzled but we are not amused at his evasion.

"All these men were found guilty," I say icily.

"Yes."

"And sentenced to death?"

"Yes, but…"

"But what, Francis?"

THE TITIAN PORTRAIT

"Several councillors wondered if there might be mercy shown?" His face is almost pleading.

I shake my head wearily. I tell him I do not want to incur the wrath of God and wonder if he does. He does not.

"The sentences must be carried out. Now. Do you understand?"

"Yes, Your Majesty."

Before I enter the confinement chamber, I must speak with Philip, however busy he may be. This is my final day of freedom for six weeks. He is busy in his office on urgent continental problems, I am told by the messenger I dispatched, but this is unacceptable. I send the messenger back, informing Philip that he is required to come to me. That one word makes all the difference, but I use it sparingly. The problem, as always, is that when I need to be angry with Philip and chastise him, he always arrives looking handsome and wonderfully fresh and melts my heart instantly.

"My last day," I remind him. "Tomorrow we are parted."

"I'll always be near," he responds irritatingly.

He looks so good today, with his reddish-brown doublet and with his beard trimmed to a fine point just under his chin. The pale blue eyes are regarding me with humour, I am thinking.

"I want you with me, Philip, not near," I tell him.

"Men are not allowed in the confinement room," he says. "Is it not so?"

"You are my husband," I remind him. "I want you to promise to visit me at least every two days."

He shakes his head in an irritatingly vague way that suggests he is not sure he can comply. He will do his best, though work in relation to Spain and his other colonies is pressing at this moment. We will have supper together and that is the last I will see of him for some time. I sleep alone since the advance of my pregnancy. I cannot bear it. I ask him if he is happy with me and he replies that all is well at present and we will soon be three; him, our baby and me. I tell him that I love him and think about him all the time, but I want him to love and be considerate towards me. Can he promise to do that?

"Of course," he tells me. "We are a partnership, in love and in the binding together of our countries."

I think he cares more about the binding of countries than he does about me, but I do not say so. I tell him that I shall miss him every hour that I spend in confinement.

"Just concentrate on the birth of our baby," he tells me solemnly. "Eat well and keep warm for this is a cold, wet and dull place we live in. I miss the Spanish plains and the hot sun on my face."

I suddenly burst into tears at this statement and find that I am crying uncontrollably for some minutes. He makes a half-hearted attempt to console me, but a Spanish courtier sends an urgent message for his attention and he must leave me to weep alone.

The scent of lavender floats through the air in the bedchamber. Candles flicker night and day as the heavy window drapes are drawn tightly across the casement and do not let in so much as a thin shaft of daylight. Fresh, unrecognised faces are all around me as new nurses, midwives and women to clean have been brought in. Jane sits by my bedside and reads to me or talks to me as the mood takes me. The others move in, out and around the chamber with their encouraging smiles and bright talk but Jane is consistently there for me, always.

"Doctor Owen said he thought my belly should be bigger by now," I say, a worried frown darkening my features.

"Don't fret," she advises. "He is a cautious man but thoroughly capable and he will see you through."

Time is passing very slowly, agonisingly so at times. I have been in isolation so long that I expected the baby to have come by now. Doctor Owen looks serious, an instant concern for me.

"Any sign of the baby kicking, Your Majesty?"

"Not lately," I say. "A few weeks back he did."

He calls the midwife over and then they both take turns to feel my stomach gently. Then they step back and retire to a dark corner of the chamber, where I can see they are having an urgent conversation. I feel panic and reach out for Jane's hand.

"Something's wrong," I tell her.

"No, no," she replies. "They are discussing the best treatment for you."

The midwife returns with some liquid in a cup, which she bids me drink. It tastes sour and unpleasant, but I drink it all down dutifully. She retreats and Doctor Owen returns.

"What is it, Doctor?" I ask anxiously. "What is wrong?"

"Nothing at all," he tells me with a reassuring smile. "Baby is rather late arriving, but God will send him at the appropriate time. I am going to make up a special potion for you. It may make you feel extra drowsy, though; nothing to worry about."

"It's an omen," I tell Jane, as the doctor departs.

"An omen?"

"God will not allow my baby to be born," I tell her, "until all heretics are executed. Contact Francis Englefield for me, Jane, and ask him to let me know when the men sentenced are dead."

She seems confused but, when I press her again, she agrees to take my message immediately.

The strong potion has indeed made me drowsy. I lie back on the big bed, pillows raised so that I can look out over the entire great chamber. I see my ladies sitting in a group near the bed talking in whispers. I think I may have been asleep for several hours but although I am now wide awake my head seems giddy and I cannot seem to focus on anything in the room clearly. The candles burn brightly and appear to dim all other items around them. I hear Magdalen's tinkling laugh burst out and then the room reverts back to eerie silence. I do not know if it is day or night. I drift off to sleep again and have no idea for how long.

When I awake, there are fewer people in the room. Most of the nurses and extra women brought in to assist the birth have gone. I still feel drowsy and unable to speak for the moment. but I am aware of voices around me. My ladies speak softly, probably thinking I still sleep and cannot hear them.

"It will be an exceedingly small baby indeed," Anne Bassett is saying.

"Her belly hasn't increased in size for two weeks," Margaret affirms.

There is a general murmur of assent, difficult to hear but just audible. Jane wonders if the physician's potions are doing the job well enough and someone else I cannot quite identify agrees.

Then they are silent for a while and I try to think clearly but my head will not let me concentrate on anything. Gertrude Blount is saying something indistinct that I cannot quite make out.

"In my experience… belly twice the size."

"One can't apply hard-and-fast rules," Dorothy Boughton is saying.

"The rumour at the time was," Mabel Browne is saying, "that the countess had a baby so small it resembled a monkey in shape and size."

"Some even insisted she had given birth to a small monkey," Anne continues and there is a ripple of laughter from the women.

In the silence that follows I feel most uncomfortable. Then my mood shifts to panic. What if something has gone wrong? I try hard to clear my head and focus my mind by attempting

THE TITIAN PORTRAIT

steady breathing. Doctor Owen advised it whenever I felt discomfort.

"Names?" Anne Bassett is saying. "Oh, Philip if it's a boy, I'll wager on that."

"Well, it certainly won't be Henry," Gertrude asserts.

"Or Edward, I'll wager," from Mabel.

"Nor Elizabeth or Anne if it's a girl," somebody says, I cannot quite make out who, but laughter follows.

I find my feeble voice at last and cry out that my lips are parched, and I need to drink. They all jump up at once, but Jane is with me first and is soon applying water to my dry lips from a pitcher by the bed.

"Thank you, Jane," I whisper in a gravelly voice, "but now I need something fit to drink. Fetch sweet wine for me."

Doctor Owen is approaching my bed, but his expression is grim, and it immediately turns my insides to jelly. He has something to say to me but is reluctant in the extreme to say it. I have seen that same expression on hundreds of faces in the past year as they sought to speak with me. I try to look straight at him in an enquiring manner that will encourage his openness.

"A private word, Your Majesty," he breathes nervously.

I wave at my ladies who are hovering close to my bed and they retreat to the rear of the bedchamber. Owen says he has discussed his examination of my stomach yesterday with the midwife.

"I regret very much that we have both reached the same conclusion," he says. "There is no increase in size of your stomach in nearly three weeks and it does suggest that your pregnancy may not be active."

"Of course, it is active," I say, angry but alarmed. "The baby is late arriving, that is all."

"Well, you may be right, of course," Owen agrees

subserviently. "Perhaps though, Your Majesty, you should consider the possibility that you may have been experiencing a false pregnancy. I'm very, very sorry."

"Don't be sorry," I snap. "The baby will arrive by next week at the latest. You'll see."

He nods, accepts my word and withdraws from my presence, advising, as he goes, that I keep warm and drink plenty of water. My hands inevitably go down to my belly under the bedcovers and I feel the flesh, exploring it. It seems a little sore and is not as distended as it was. That is a cause for some concern.

I persuade myself that the doctor cannot be right. Of course, I am pregnant and the baby must be on the way now. My menstrual cycle may be erratic, but I never stop completely for more than eight weeks. The doctor is being cautious, that is what it is. If a doubt enters my mind, I suppress it instantly and try to cheer myself up.

"Spiced wine, Jane," I call out. "Bring me spiced wine."

"Doctor Owen says you shouldn't have it," Jane murmurs nervously.

"My decision," I say curtly, "not his. Spiced wine, please."

After I have supped well of the wine, I start to feel more confident and expect the babe to appear in a day or two. I invite Jane to sit with me, by the bed. I am weary and it has been a long and worryingly enclosed time in this tomb-like bedchamber, dark velvet drapes closing in on me and not enough light from the candles to brighten the gloom. When I ask for more to be lit, they tell me the physician forbids it. He says too much light is damaging to my eyes and may even affect the baby's health.

"Is all well, Mary?" Jane asks, looking most wide-eyed and concerned.

"It is," I respond. "Baby is extremely late arriving. Doctor Owen advised me to be ready any time now."

"He looked very worried," Jane ventures cautiously.

"Yes, he was a little bit concerned. He likes to be especially safe," I tell her. "Over-fussy, really, but all in my best interests."

Jane smiles doubtfully and nods her head.

The lethargy that can creep over one as week after week passes and nothing significant occurs can be overwhelming. The very casement windows, black-draped, seem to be closing in on me, overhanging and about to smother me in my bed. Suddenly the quiet of the chamber erupts into a loud shout as young Magdalen bursts in. The other ladies all turn on her as one and bid her be silent. Does she not realise where she is?

"Pandemonium has broken out in London town," she says, toning down her loud voice but barely able to control her excitement. "Messengers report bells ringing, bonfires lit and people dancing in the street."

"For what reason?" I demand to know, my tone austere.

"Notices outside churches and other buildings," Magdalen replies, suppressing a giggle, "that you have given birth to a healthy baby boy, Your Majesty."

"What nonsense," I respond irritably. "The baby has not arrived yet."

"They think it has," Magdalen cannot stop herself saying and has to suppress another giggle.

"Go and compose yourself in your bedchamber," I instruct Magdalen. "And do not return until you have done so."

As she slinks away, contrite, I give orders for messengers to ride swiftly to the city and place notices informing all that the royal baby has not arrived yet and when he does everybody will be duly informed of the birth. My ladies fuss around me and attempt to calm me down, although I am much disturbed. Wine is brought and I drink heartily and hope desperately that my baby will come quickly now and bring this long-awaited event to a happy and joyful conclusion.

QUEEN MARY'S PRIVATE JOURNAL

HAMPTON COURT AND OATLANDS, SUMMER 1555

I sit up in bed, cushions heaped up behind my head and stare resolutely at the tapestry hanging on the far wall of the chamber. My ladies are all present, but few come close to me for fear I may snap at them. Only Jane, loyal and faithful as well as a friend, keeps approaching from time to time to ensure I do not want for anything. The ladies are correct. I am irritable and often bad-tempered, but I am sorely tried. Although it is now well past the nine months' period, I am not yet delivered of my baby. It seems I have offended God in some way, and he keeps me waiting. Philip has visited only once in all the long weeks I have been incarcerated here and on that occasion he would talk only about the baby and when I might expect him and also told me that he must return to Spain on urgent business before the New Year.

Only Doctor Owen and another physician are in this chamber regularly and they begin to offend me.

"I beg your indulgence, Majesty," Owen bleats. "But I must ask you to reconsider."

"Reconsider, Sir?"

"Your stomach is receding," he tells me. "You do not have

a baby, Madam, and there is no further reason to stay in this chamber."

"You overstep yourself, Doctor," I say. "God will inform me when my baby is due and why he is late."

I instruct him to leave me in peace and he shakes his head and departs. I put my hands down to my belly and run my fingers over the extended flesh. The bump is still there, although smaller now. An exceedingly small baby will require extra care, tenderness and attention. He, or she if female, will receive that care from me, Philip and my ladies. If two doctors pronounced me pregnant and I have missed menstrual function for more than nine months, there must be a baby. Doctor Owen is failing in his duty and has been misled by certain outward signs that only a pregnant woman can understand.

The days stretch on endlessly, dark and dreary and no sign yet from God to advise me why I must wait so long. It is a hot afternoon and an unseasonal fire burns in the grate. I have the only visitor I really want to see. Philip comes in, sends all the ladies out of the bedchamber and comes over to me.

"Philip, you are here at last," I murmur, finally content.

He takes my hand in his and his pale blue eyes sparkle in the reflected light from the fire as he speaks.

"I've come to take you back to your privy apartment," he tells me softly, his face stern.

"I can't leave," I say, suddenly alarmed.

Without speaking, he lifts back the bedcovers and gently places my hands on my belly. I feel the flesh and gradually come to realise that my belly is almost flat and there is no longer any large bump.

"There is no baby," he says sadly. "You must realise that?"

"No baby," I repeat. "No baby?" and I burst into tears. He comforts me and I bury my face in his chest and weep. I pull back from his hold. "It is God's punishment because I have not burned all the heretics yet."

"Dry your eyes," he requests gently. "And I'll take you back to the comfort of your apartments."

He tells everybody waiting outside the chamber to leave but sends word that he wants Jane and Susan to return. I do not want to see anybody except him, Philip, and I tell him so.

"They will help you to dress," he says quietly.

At first, my eyes cannot adjust to the bright light. After so many weeks in the dark, blackened bedchamber everything around me now appears overbright, glinting, flashing, piercing my eyeballs. I have to walk slowly round my privy chamber, at first shielding my eyes from the window's glare. They have dressed me in a sombre grey and brown gown and a neutral-coloured kirtle, but they could just have put a sack over my head, and I would have made no protest. When Philip led me out of the confinement chamber, I had reached my lowest ebb.

Now I sit in my favourite velvet-upholstered high-backed chair. I am comfortable but I have no desire to carry on living. I was sure that I would give birth to a fine baby and we would be assured of a son and heir, the next great Tudor king. Now I feel robbed, assaulted and just about exhausted. Not from physical exertion but from loss, a loss as deep and painful as if I had given birth and the baby had died or been born dead.

I stare out of the window at a clear blue sky, but it still hurts my eyes. Philip left me here alone but promised he would return within the hour. I wait patiently for he is the only one who might, in time, bring me back to a desire to continue living. The door opens slowly, the heavy timber frame creaking somewhat but I am disappointed to see it is not Philip but Jane, come to see if she can assist me in any way.

"Not really, Jane, I feel as low as a snake," I tell her.

"I'm so sorry," she says, looking genuinely sympathetic. "Time will heal, slowly."

"I doubt that. I am humiliated. How could I have been so wrong?"

"You couldn't possibly know," she tries to convince me. "The physicians all got it wrong. They are to blame for all your pain."

I send her away with thanks for her concern, but I really want to be alone until Philip returns. I must appeal to him for his support and help now that I need it more than ever. A noble or even a common person can go away and hide in corners or seek refuge far away from anybody when tragedy strikes but a queen of England has no such luxury. I must carry on, no matter what I feel and no matter how much I have suffered.

With Philip by my side, in meetings of the privy council and at state functions, I may just about manage to preserve some dignity but without him I shall be lost. I must urgently request him to abandon plans to return to Spain and his other territories for the immediate future. I shall need him here more than ever. I am the queen of England and Ireland and he is my king consort. When he returns, much later than promised, I am reduced to a silent, lone figure, seated as still as the dead and staring straight ahead.

"Tomorrow, If the weather be fine," he tells me, "I should like to walk with you in the palace grounds."

"No," I say firmly. "I cannot stay here, Philip."

"But you love Hampton Court. Is it not so?"

"I do indeed," I tell him sorrowfully. "But not now. Not after all I have been through. I must get away."

"Ah, I see. To put it out of mind."

"That I can never do," I advise him. "But a place with no sad memories is what I seek for now."

"Where to, then?"

"I have thought about it, sitting here," I inform him. "I

think to Weybridge, to the Palace of Oatlands. It is smaller and quieter and quite peaceful in that part of Surrey." There, I think to myself, I shall be out of the public eye for a short time at least and in relative peace to contemplate and prepare myself for the inevitable return to Whitehall and public duties. "That would be a good place."

"I will make the necessary arrangements," he tells me. "Right away."

He makes to depart but I restrain him with my hand on his arm and urgency in my voice. I tell him that I need him by my side more than ever at this difficult time and I urge him to stay with me in the coming months and support me in all essential duties until I am over the first flush of grief and suffering.

"You need rest and peace," he states brightly, smiling. "Let us not discuss any plan of action for now. Time enough on the morrow."

"But I will have your full support and help?" I enquire desperately.

"Always," he states.

Even though my heart is full of grief and sorrow, the considerations of queen and country do seep unbidden into my brain. The things I must do that have been festering slowly in my mind the past several months are coming into focus in my thoughts, whether I want them or not. As our royal barge slides gently through the waters of the Thames towards Surrey's shores, I am silent, staring ahead under the canopy, not looking at Philip but glad of his presence next to me, observing the rise and fall of the oars as the boatmen whisk us along under a grey sky but on a mercifully dry summer day.

I shall continue my efforts to reorganise the militia. I shall expand and increase our navy and add considerably to the number of new ships. I shall revise our coinage. I shall continue to authorise the execution of heretics. There is no

THE TITIAN PORTRAIT

place for those people, nobles, clergy or commons who defy God's true Christian church. All these things I will do and more.

But now, at this moment, I am stricken with grief for my unborn baby, and I will take a few days' rest from affairs of state.

Although much smaller than Hampton Court, I find Oatlands expansive enough for great comfort and always welcoming. Entering the largest of the three main courtyards, I immediately feel at home. It could be said that the place is a haven, a refuge where I can retreat when all goes awry but in any case it is home when I need it to be. As now, on a warm summer day as I sit again in the window alcove. It is simply a different alcove in a different building.

Philip is in an adjacent building in conference with his Spanish attendants and has been for some hours. He tells me regularly that there is much to do in the land of his birth, and he really should be there now. I always reply that there is much to do here in our English parliament, and I need him by my side. Somehow, I feel he is slipping away from me even when he is right next to me and it gives me a hollow feeling inside.

Jane comes in to ask if she can do anything for me. She is exceedingly good and most patient. Several ladies have approached and I just send them away, pleading to be left in solitude.

"Stay with me a moment, Jane," I ask. She is the only one I care to have near me at this sad time.

She takes her seat in silence, picking up instantly on my mood of sadness and reflection and pours sweet wine for me, which I sip slowly.

"I saw the king just now," she tells me. "He told me he will be with you very shortly."

"He did?" I ask, perhaps a little too eagerly. I do not want them all to know how much I depend on him and yearn for his company, but it is useless to try to disguise my true feelings. They all know the love I have for him and how lonely I feel when he is far away. Why do I deceive myself?

Jane asks if I mind if she continues with some embroidery, she has been working on. I wave my hand to signify permission and she continues with her work silently, occasionally looking up to check whether or not I need more wine. When Philip comes in, she excuses herself and slips away silently. She has fulfilled her purpose admirably even though we have exchanged very few words.

"A walk through the walled garden and beyond?" Philip suggests.

"Would you not prefer to stay here, quietly?" I enquire.

"No, no. Fresh air, fresh late-summer air," he replies, smiling.

We walk briskly through the inner court, past the tall corner towers and move around, past the old manor house and where the moat used to be. We move through the outer court, passing the kitchen block and the kitchen garden, which has the remains of the vegetable crop, unpicked. After venturing into a field and returning to the shielded, walled garden, we sit on a stone seat. Philip is frowning.

"What is it, Philip?" I ask, concerned. "You are not feverish?"

"No, my health is excellent," he replies, sounding awkward. "It is another matter."

"Tell me," I say gently. "I can tell all is not well."

"I must return to Spain," he is saying, and the words cut through me like a knife. "My father's health is failing fast, and I have many problems that must be dealt with in the Low Countries."

"Not now, Philip," I say, desperately. "I need you more than ever, having just lost our baby."

THE TITIAN PORTRAIT

"There never was a baby, Mary," he says slowly. "I share your bitter disappointment but now I must return to outstanding work on the Continent. I have put it off several times due to your pregnancy, or as we thought, but now…"

"Please," I ask pleadingly, "send your most able generals, your best councillors but do not leave me alone, I beg you."

He is not listening to me, I can tell. He has decided that he must go and is determined to do so. I begin to weep, and he bids me dry my tears, it is inevitable that he returns first to Spain and then to other countries. The rumours are that his father, the emperor, is thinking of retiring very soon due to his ill health and he, Philip, must be ready to take the reins in hand and assume the responsibility. A baby would have made a difference, he concedes, but now he must comply with his father's urgent request.

I tell him anxiously that we can live together and produce another baby, a true one, a prince and heir; there is still time. But even as I speak, I am dimly aware of the desperation in my voice.

"It cannot be, Mary," he tells me, frowning. "I regret I must return. I will ask Jane to look after you and see you have every comfort, every desire. She is your favourite lady, is it not so?"

"I want only you by my side," I murmur with great despondency and feeling a sadness that is unbearable. "I need you Philip, my love."

"I have asked Cardinal Pole to look after you in my absence," he continues. "And I have his promise."

In my privy chamber I sit stock still, staring at the casement and watching the late afternoon daylight slowly fade and die. Soon comes the darkness.

SIR FRANCIS ENGLEFIELD'S DIARY

WHITEHALL, AUTUMN 1555

NEVER BEFORE HAVE I SEEN QUEEN MARY LOOK SO DESOLATE and forlorn. She is always dressed in finery of the best taste and quality, always regal in appearance whenever she is seen outside the palace grounds, so this was something completely unexpected. Standing by the embarkation point at Greenwich with her court followers at a respectable distance behind her, she seemed at one point to be holding the king's sleeve and trying to prevent him from moving away from her. I was quite close, so I saw that anguish in her eyes and her pleading look. Fortunate indeed that the nearest members of the public had been kept back at a safe distance. To see the queen's distress, close up might well lead to revolt or fear.

Then it was over, quite suddenly. The king kissed her, said a few brief words and then he was gone, striding forward briskly to board his ship. From my vantage point I could see the queen's face, but I quickly avoided her gaze, turning to face away until she had composed herself.

I approach her privy chamber apprehensively, with caution, having no idea what I might expect on this day. As I enter, I am relieved to see that she is dressed in her finest; a blue damask gown, laced with velvet and sparkling with jewels.

"I have an assignment for you, Francis," she greets me. "Fairly straightforward."

"Thank you, Majesty," I murmur, watching her carefully. Her face is pale and rather lined and she appears tired, listless. Fortunately, her appearance and manner are much improved from the day of departure at Greenwich.

"The trial of Cranmer, the Archbishop of Canterbury, begins in Oxford."

"Ah."

"I have Doctor Martin and Doctor Storey, my proctors, in attendance as my official observers but I want you to go and let me know exactly what happens."

"Surely the proctors will report thoroughly," I suggest politely.

"Yes," she responds irritably. "With lots of legal phrasing and mumbo-jumbo. You can just watch and make notes and let me know everything that transpires. Everything."

The queen puts a lot of emphasis on that last word. She stares at me intently and I begin to feel uncomfortable. Although her appearance is much improved from the day at Greenwich, I do find her mind to be confused and disturbed. I quickly agree to do her bidding.

"Cranmer's trial has been too long coming," she says, looking anguished again. "That man has a lot to answer for, a whole lot. He it was, as archbishop, who assisted greatly in having my father's marriage annulled and my mother's life ruined. He it was, too, who paved the way for Henry's marriage to that Boleyn woman. And officiated. Oh yes, Francis, that man has a great deal to answer for."

I enter the University Church of St Mary the Virgin in Oxford and walk slowly down the aisle. A high scaffold, decorated lavishly with a cloth of state, is standing at the eastern end of the church in front of the high altar. Slowly I proceed, my shoes clacking on the stone flooring, sending an odd echo reverberating around the grey stone walls. Many people are seated, waiting expectantly and I am aware awkwardly of my late arrival. Seated on the specially erected scaffold are James Brooks, the Bishop of Gloucester, the Pope's representative and, below him, the queen's two proctors.

An ominous silence, the air almost charged with venom, is apparent as I sit in the stillness and allow my gaze to roam around this fine old church. It has certainly known better, happier times for prayer but also, perhaps, other tragedies. The colourful stained-glass windows are suddenly illuminated by a shaft of autumn sunshine from outside. The echo continues and multiplies as I hear footsteps approaching.

Cranmer is brought down the aisle by three burly warders. He wears a long black gown with a hood on each shoulder. His face is gaunt, and he sports a long white beard. He carries a white staff which he taps ominously in front of him as he walks to the dais. It is noticeable that he does not doff his cap to any of the commissioners present. A commissioner calls him forward and tells him that he has been brought here to answer charges.

"Appear here, Thomas Cranmer, Archbishop of Canterbury, and answer to all that is laid to your charge. That is to say for blasphemy, incontinency and heresy."

He is brought forward, on to the scaffold and asked to make answer to the bishop of Gloucester. There is a short gasp around the church as Cranmer doffs his cap to the queen's proctors but refuses to do so to Bishop Brooks. The bishop asks him loudly, why he does not respect him.

"I have taken oath never to submit to the Bishop of Rome's authority in this realm. I did so advisedly and will by God's grace keep to it and will commit nothing, by either sign or token that might be interpreted as accepting Rome's authority."

The Bishop of Gloucester addresses the congregation, explaining that it is the queen's desire that Archbishop Cranmer be tried by court of law for blasphemy and heresy, but my attention is diverted to Cranmer who is shaking his head and muttering grotesquely although it is impossible to make out his words. Then Cranmer clears his throat noisily and gets to his feet and addresses the bishop.

"My lord, I do not acknowledge this session, nor you, my unlawful judge. Neither would I have come here except I was brought here as a prisoner. Therefore, I openly renounce you as my judge and I will not make any meaningful answer."

There is quite a buzz of murmurs, coughs and expletives of surprise emanating from those present in the church. I know I shall be required to report back all the details of this trial to the queen, much of which will not be covered by her proctors. Cranmer's outbursts and defiance though, are only going to exasperate her even more. I dare not tell her less than everything that occurs, though.

Cranmer has sunk to his knees now and is reciting the Lord's Prayer. He finishes, stands up and recites the Creed. Dr Martin steps forward to question, him and the two men glare at each other.

"Can you tell me," Martin asks, "who you think is the supreme head of the Church of England?"

"Christ is head of this member, as he is of the whole body of the universal church."

"I asked about the head of the church on earth," Martin persists.

"Only Christ."

"Then why did you make King Henry the supreme head?"

"For Christ only is the head of his church, and of the faith and religion of the same," Cranmer answers in a strong resonant voice that echoes through the building. "The king is head and governor of his people, which are the visible church. There was never other thing meant by the king's title."

The bishop listens carefully but appears agitated and dissatisfied. He orders Cranmer to appear in Rome, within fourscore days, to answer the Pope. Cranmer nods briefly and then says he will do as instructed and he is taken out by the guards to return to his prison cell. I exchange a few brief words with the proctors and then take my leave to begin the journey back to London. My thoughts as I travel are that the man appears strong with his loud resonant answers to questions and the intense glare he bestows on questioners, but I did notice that his shoulders were shaking uncontrollably throughout the interrogation.

I may be dressed in my fine new tunic and colourful breeches, but I feel less than composed. If the corridors of Whitehall are dark and forbidding, it is not just the inclement weather outside these walls that are to blame. I will tell the queen everything I can recall but why do I have a nagging feeling that it will not be acceptable?

She is dressed quite severely in mostly black and grey but with a brightly coloured kirtle. Her jewels sparkle fiercely as though in defiance of her sombre dress. It is, though, her face that causes most concern. It is lined and wrinkled now more than I can ever recall in the past and her eyes are dull, lacking lustre. Even her hair seems straggly and somewhat lifeless. I do, however, manage to keep my expression bland and speak with clarity as I run carefully through the events at the University Church in Oxford.

"As crafty as a barrel of monkeys," the queen hisses, "and much nastier."

"He spoke loudly, clearly, I thought, but was still rather

nervous and uncomfortable," I tell her. "His shoulders were shaking somewhat."

"I would have shaken the teeth out of his head," she replies, "had I been there."

"But he was most evasive about appointing your father as supreme head of the English church."

"Of course he was," she replies, her voice rising perceptibly. "He did everything Henry asked him to do without compunction and now he'll do anything to save his own slimy skin."

I describe the exact words used by Cranmer and his interrogator as closely as I remember them. I also mention the looks of disbelief on the faces of Martin and the bishop representing the Pope.

"He has, though," I finish, "been ordered to go to Rome and answer to the Pope."

"He won't go, he won't go," the queen says with heat. "That slimy toad will not go anywhere near Rome, be assured."

"He agreed to go."

"What that creature says he will do and what he actually does are two different things," she says, having visible trouble in keeping still, her regal stance threatened by her own strong feelings.

She makes a concerted effort to control her emotion and, after a brief pause, invites me to be seated. She does not wish to appear displeased with me; I have done my duty and served her well, as usual. She orders spiced wine and clinks her goblet with mine before drinking. I take a drink and savour the hot liquid as it refreshes my dry throat. She is calm and composed now, every inch the queen, as usual. It is impressive to watch her take control again and become the regal monarch.

"I will never forgive that beast for what he did to my mother and to me," she tells me quietly now.

"I can understand your feelings," I tell her.

"Can you, Francis? I doubt you can, truly. He annulled the marriage with never a thought for the rights and wrongs of the matter. And he cleared a smooth straightforward path for the marriage to Boleyn and performed the ceremony. I will never rest until he burns."

"Many will call for his pardon," I say tentatively. "Especially if he recants."

"Oh, they will, be assured," she replies calmly. "I will be inundated with cries for mercy. And he will recant to save his miserable skin. I shall never weaken in my resolve, though."

I do not respond, feeling it wise to keep my own counsel and not risk her ire. Having imparted all the news from what I have witnessed and discussed it with her, I feel my duty is done and ask to be excused. As I begin to move towards the door and my departure, the queen stops me in my tracks.

"One other thing, Francis," she says stridently. "I will never accept or be referred to as the supreme head of the church."

SIR FRANCIS ENGLEFIELD'S JOURNAL

ENGLEFIELD HOUSE, BERKSHIRE, AUTUMN 1555

A MAGNIFICENT FEAST, SERVED BY WHAT I SHOULD REGARD AS the best-trained squad of servants in Berkshire. Sir Thomas White and his wife Joan are always good hosts and, indeed, close friends of both Catherine and me, even though he spends far more time in London these days than I do. It is a pleasure, though, when we are both on home ground and can meet up. Even Catherine looks bright-eyed and interested in the conversation round the dinner table.

"More pheasant, Francis?" our host enquires. "It is from our own estate."

I accept a little more as it is delicious, but Catherine had shaken her head in refusal when invited to indulge in another plateful. She does, however, accept a small amount of delicately spiced chicken.

"So what is the queen's position currently?" Thomas asks.

"Believe it or not," I respond, "she talks of burning all heretics by the end of the year, just as though she had hardly even started."

"And we are talking in hundreds already?" Thomas enquires.

"Going on for a hundred," I agree.

Sir Thomas shakes his head and gives his opinion that the situation is serious. Catherine agrees and tells him she has been saying that for months now. I try to explain, as carefully as I can, that the queen is in a delicate state at this moment. Shaken both physically and in her mind about losing her baby she seriously thinks it is God's punishment for not executing all heretics. Add to this she is desperately lonely now that Philip, the king, has departed for Europe. Her love for him knows no bounds and at this moment, she feels completely lost.

"Well, she certainly has her champion in you, Francis," Thomas says in a mixture of wonder and surprise.

"She can do no wrong in Francis's eyes," Catherine murmurs and we all turn to look at her.

"Oh, she can and does," I contradict her. "The problem is dealing with it when she does wrong."

"A delicate balance, I'm thinking," Joan ventures.

The table is cleared and dessert is served. Catherine is particularly fond of the custard-based Florentines and we are refreshed by our host with a fine display of jellies, fruit, tarts, gingerbread and marzipan sweets. We all find we have a sweet tooth and begin eating again in earnest. I take a little marzipan cake and some fruit as I am slowing down after the lavish first courses.

"The thing is, burning all those people stirs up so much hatred among the populace," Thomas muses quietly. "And not just the followers of Henry's church. Catholics, too, have seen too much bloodshed to live comfortably with it."

"Just what I have been saying," Catherine contributes, glancing accusingly at me. "Think what it could lead to."

"Another revolt," Thomas says soberly. "And a really well-planned one could topple Mary from the throne."

"Could it ever come to that?" Joan asks her husband, and all our eyes are on him.

"Who knows?" he replies. "Who could have foreseen the

THE TITIAN PORTRAIT

attempt to put Jane Grey on the throne or the later Wyatt rebellion?"

"We live in such dangerous times," Catherine contributes.

I shake my head and tell Thomas that I think Queen Mary has the country in her grip and she is still quite popular with most citizens. She is successfully restoring the country to Catholicism. Heretics must die, it is now English law, and I support her in that. And she can be persuaded to do right; she has now, finally, made peace with her sister Elizabeth. Thomas looks sceptical as we all revert to the silent enjoyment of sweetmeats, finishing with a large and elaborate jelly of many colours and shapes that is quite delicious.

As the ladies retire to their privy chamber, I accept a measure of spiced Madeira wine that Thomas recommends, and I find is much to my taste. Thomas wonders whether or not support for so many burnings is the right way to advance.

"I take your point," I tell him. "Many advisers, myself included, have tried to instil the policy of pressing clergy to recant and offering absolution with a penance. Cardinal Pole himself has led the way in this respect."

"But does the queen listen, Francis?" he asks. "Does she listen?"

"Heresy is much on her troubled mind," I admit.

Thomas shakes his head again and calls for more Madeira wine. I sip it slowly and luxuriously, anxious to keep a clear head.

"Philip has much to answer for," Thomas suggests. "If he had stayed with her, he would have been a stabilising influence."

"Indeed. She is adrift without him."

"One other matter, Francis," he begins, looking most serious. "If the queen should be toppled or if she should die from failing health, Elizabeth would be queen and you would find she is no longer any friend of yours."

I had not thought too much about that, but he is right, of course.

It is so peaceful and pleasant in the Englefield church that I will often linger, sometimes for an hour even, after my prayers. I am not alone today as Catherine sits in a pew on the front row gazing at the high altar. The cold of the grey stone walls and floors are transmuted by late afternoon sunshine outside, seeping in under the heavy door and blazing through the colours of the stained-glass windows. I say a final, private prayer and cross myself.

"The weather is good for a brisk walk now," I say. "Are you inclined for one?"

"Yes, down towards the farm," she answers, "and back up the hill behind."

We walk slowly, taking in the scenery around us and filling our lungs with clean, fresh country air. It is such pleasure to me as most of my waking hours are spent breathing in foul, dust-filled air, accompanied by the stench of human and horse excrement, piss and other foul waters. I mention this to Catherine, speaking my thoughts out loud and she pulls a face.

"You know the remedy well enough, Francis," she tells me. "Come back home to Berkshire."

"What would I do with myself all day?" I enquire.

"Local business, run the estate yourself with help from your manager. Magistrate duties. You could even retain your membership of parliament and concentrate your efforts on local matters only."

It sounds so easy when she says it off the cuff, just like that. As I keep reminding her, though, it is not so easy. Last year I was appointed master of the court of wards and liveries. The queen's revenues have already improved considerably since I watched over them and will, I forecast, continue to do so. I have had to examine a property dispute between the Duchess of Suffolk and the Baron Willoughby. I have had bills committed to me and carried them up to the House of Lords. Most bizarre of all, I was ordered to search for John Dee, the astrologer and mathematician and was required to examine him on charges of witchcraft and heresy. Even on the thorny question of which monastic lands should be returned to the church, the queen sought my advice rather than that of the bishops such as Gardiner. I explain the importance the queen places on just a few of these matters and how she needs my advice.

"Yes, that's all very well and fine, Francis," she says, "but if you were not there, she would soon find somebody else."

"Not necessarily as competent, though," I tell her immodestly.

"And so it goes on."

"The queen does need me," I continue. "I am one of the few advisers she trusts implicitly, and there are not many."

The afternoon fades down quickly now that we are late in the autumn season. The sun has long faded, and the breeze has a wintry bite suddenly. We walk back briskly to Englefield House, our movement adding warmth to our cold bodies until we once again gain access to the manor house and stand in front of the roaring fire in the grate. Catherine settles down near the fire and I join her, but I am aware that she is not content. "What is It?" I ask, desperate to create a happy atmosphere on my all-too-brief visit home.

"I feel that you are slipping away from me, Francis," she says honestly.

"That's not true."

"You are the queen's man, Francis," she says sadly, "not mine."

I point out that my work is important but separate in my

mind and, from my home life, and my marriage. Catherine smiles crookedly and says that it is not that simple. She is the one left at home, alone, as I am away in London all year round.

"As you do the queen's bidding," she adds, "I sit and fester."

"You are lonely," I blurt out which does not go down well as it sounds as though it has only just occurred to me.

"So you noticed, Francis," she says, with sarcasm. "You noticed."

I move closer to the warmth of the fire and reach out to take Catherine's hand in mine.

"I have the answer," I tell her. "I will purchase a small town house in the City of London. Then you may spend as many months in London as you desire."

Her expression is bleak, and she looks more as though I have landed a blow on her than made an offer to ease loneliness.

"That isn't what I want," she tells me sadly. "Do you think I desire to spend much of my life in the stink and muck of London?"

"What then?" I ask quietly.

"I want you here, Francis," she states grimly. "In our home."

"You know that's not possible."

There is an atmosphere of unresolved emotion as we go into the banqueting hall for supper. The gallery is silent as Catherine has not employed any musicians on this occasion. The only sounds are those of the servants preparing our table covers and implements with which to eat. Then they bring in the roasted boar, beef, mutton and all the accoutrements and we begin to eat silently. Some light conversation ensues as the meal progresses but the tension in the hall is almost visible.

SIR FRANCIS ENGLEFIELD'S DIARY

WHITEHALL AND WESTMINSTER, LONDON, AUTUMN 1555

THE QUEEN IS LISTLESS IN HER PRIVY CHAMBER AT WHITEHALL. I hand her papers that she signs quickly, automatically, without even glancing at the contents. She is well attired indeed, dressed in her finest with an array of jewels that would brighten and gleam in the lowest dungeon. Only her face betrays her mood, lined and world-weary as she continues to grieve deeply for the baby that never was. But mostly for Philip, the king whom she misses, it would seem, every moment of every day.

"Do you go to see my Lord Chancellor on his sickbed?" she asks, quietly turning over a vessel of colourful venetian glass in her hands.

"I do," I respond. "I had not realised he was so ill."

"Nearing death, I am reliably informed," she replies, voice little more than a sad whisper.

"Surely not?"

"I spoke to his physician yesterday," she continues. "Best make haste, Francis, before it be too late."

I am not really prepared for the sight that greets me at Bishop Gardiner's home. Everywhere is in darkness, blinds and shutters drawn. I am taken to his bedchamber by a weeping servant who makes a conscious effort to control the sounds of sorrow she is making when we reach the room.

Stephen Gardiner's face is as white as a sheet and his eyes are sunken. He is propped up with cushions behind his head but appears very fragile indeed. He looks up at me as I enter and his face contorts as he tries, not altogether successfully, to smile.

"Francis, I am glad you're here," he whispers, croaking somewhat. "Just the man I wish to see. Draw up a stool near the bed."

I do as he bids me, apologising as I sit for not visiting sooner. I had no idea he was ill. I look at him closely and see a frail man, nothing like the large-as-life, blustering, forceful cleric I am so used to.

"I am dying, Francis," he tells me. "I have little time left."

"Surely not," I protest. "The physicians…"

"Can do nothing more. I demanded complete honesty and I received it."

I protest that they cannot be sure, only God has that sure knowledge, but he repeats his twisted smile and assures me that he is trying as we speak to make his peace and is ready to face God.

"As ready as I can ever be. Listen to me, Francis, take heed. I have made my confession to Bishop Bonner, but I speak to you as a friend and colleague. I am plagued with guilt and remorse for I have sinned with great magnitude. God may forgive me for he welcomes all sinners that repent. It is within the last year that I most regret my actions. I sought and instigated the burning of many heretics, but I see now, too late, that Cardinal Pole was right to recommend the constant attempts to persuade them to recant and gain absolution. It is not for us mere mortals to take lives. Only God has that right."

I tell him that I think I understand but he waves my words away, feebly flapping his hand in my direction. He tells he

THE TITIAN PORTRAIT

that he now regrets, bitterly, that he assisted Archbishop Cranmer is declaring Henry's marriage to Catherine null and void. He also regrets vindicating Henry's new title as supreme head of the Church of England. Of course, he is pleased to say that he did help to prepare the Six Articles that reaffirmed the traditional Catholic doctrine on transubstantiation, clerical celibacy and the vow of chastity.

"Backwards and forwards," he continues agonisingly, "going with King Henry's wishes and later returning to the true faith under the queen's command. I was a changeling in my religion and protected myself by following on in whichever way the wind was blowing."

"You are too hard on yourself, Stephen," I tell him. "None of us is without sin."

His breathing becomes laboured, and I ask him to rest and not speak for a while. I call for a nurse who brings him a soft liquid potion and he gradually becomes calmer and less restless.

"Try to persuade the queen to put much pressure on heretics to recant," he suggests. "You have the queen's ear."

"My influence is minimal," I tell him.

"It is stronger than you know. And when you next see the Lady Elizabeth, ask her to forgive me for my relentless interrogation and menacing behaviour."

That is something that I can and will, willingly, do. I tell him that the queen has much respect for him as her chancellor and as her Bishop of Winchester. He it was who officiated at her coronation and performed the ceremony at her wedding to Philip. She is for ever in his debt. He must rest now and get some sleep and tomorrow he may feel better and will slowly recover from his malady. He shakes his head irritably and tells me I do not understand. He is suffering, he tells me, from jaundice and dropsy and is doomed. He is silent for a short time except for laboured breathing so I do not speak or disturb his rest. I notice that his skin is wrinkled and has a yellow pallor that I am only now aware of.

"There is more that I would tell you," he whispers.

"Then you should take your time and speak slowly," I advise.

"You helped with the prosecution, trial and sentence of Bishop Hooper, Francis, did you not?"

"I did."

"As of course, did I. Lord Chandos came to me and described the death of bishop Hooper," he continues. "His description was so graphic that I gasped, although I doubt that he even noticed."

"Chandos is not one of God's most gentle or compassionate souls."

"Indeed. His words burnt into my soul, though, and caused me to repent."

Gardiner breaths deeply once again, sinks his head into his cushions and calls for more of the potion to ease his troubled throat. I hold the liquid to his lips, and he drinks slowly, painfully.

"Chandos reported to me, in great detail of Bishop Hooper's arrival in Gloucester, where he had been granted one last, small privilege and allowed to sleep in the house of a gentleman the night before his execution. He was led down next morning past about 7,000 people to just beyond the elm tree next to the College of Priests where he himself used to preach."

"So many?" I ask, incredulous.

"According to Chandos, yes, that many. Anyway, he told me that the bishop was calm, dignified, smiled towards the people and prepared to meet his maker. He was asked if he wished to recant before going on but refused. So they tied him to the stake and, according to Chandos, he refused a neck brace that might have hastened his end. They put a metal strap round his middle, though, and lit the fire.

THE TITIAN PORTRAIT

"Now the terrible part of this, Francis, is that it was a windy morning, and the flames would not rise above the bishop's waist level and they had not enough reeds and faggots to stir the fire. The fire burnt the man's nether regions and he uttered not a sound even when his face was blackened, and his hair scorched. After time had passed, agonisingly, he called out: 'For God's love, let me have more fire.' More faggots arrived and were put to the fire, but the wind was fierce and only burnt his lower extremities until his bowels fell out. Now this is only a brief description of all that Chandos told to me, Francis, but you may see the horror of it all. A third fire was lit, more faggots applied to the flames and the bishop cried out: 'Lord Jesus have mercy upon me. Lord Jesus receive my spirit.' He spoke no more. According to Chandos his lips blackened, his tongue swelled and although he could not speak, his lips moved as he beat his chest and one of his arms dropped off. Fat, blood and water dripped out of the fingers of his other hand before the fire leapt up at last and finally consumed him."

Stephen leans back on his cushions and gasps for breath as I put my hand on his arm gently.

"It took almost an hour to kill him," the bishop wheezes and then coughs.

"That is the most horrible thing I've heard in my life," I say. "And I have witnessed a burning at Tyburn."

"They do things differently in Gloucester, apparently," he whispers, breathing noisily.

He is fading fast, though, and perhaps not fully conscious of all he is saying. He asks for more potion and I apply it to his parched lips once more. His eyes close after drinking and I think perhaps life has left his body, but he opens them suddenly with a gasp of breath.

"Erravi cum Petro, sed non flevi cum Petro," he whispers hoarsely and then, looking straight at me repeats the words in

English: "Like Peter I have erred, but unlike Peter I have not wept."

And those were the last words uttered by Stephen Gardiner, Bishop of Winchester, I am reliably informed. He died a short time after I left the chamber.

QUEEN MARY'S PRIVATE JOURNAL

WHITEHALL, WINTER 1555

AFTER A MORNING OF LISTENING TO MY LADIES CHATTERING aimlessly, even foolishly, about the various men at court, I feel even more miserable than I did upon waking up this morning. Someone, I think it was Ann as I scarcely remember any conversations in detail, mentioned the king. She described his manners and deportment as excellent and was about to become lyrical about his looks when I silenced her swiftly with the threat of dismissing her from my household if she persisted. That silenced her completely and she uttered not one syllable more all morning. Most of the others were quiet, too, after that and when I announced that I was feeling low in mood and their inane chatter was pulling me down further, silence ensued. I like silence these days; it is less hard to bear than conversation. My private thoughts are in turmoil and have been these past three weeks.

In my privy chamber and alone I have no such problem. I can sit for hours and not speak to anybody. That way, the pain is easier to bear. If it were not for urgent business of state, I would spend even more hours in quiet isolation. Except for commands to servants for whatever I require, all is silence. And silence can be golden to me at present. When Francis

Englefield arrives and wishes to converse with me, I agree but reluctantly and only because he is the least offensive to my sight of everybody around me.

"Would a potion from the physician be acceptable?" he asks.

"Why, do I look as if I need one?"

"Frankly yes," he replies, "if I may be forgiven for saying so."

"You are not forgiven," I tell him irritably. "You are rude and impolite and speak out of turn."

He apologises and says he spoke only out of concern for my health. He thought I looked rather tired and weary, probably from too much work as he knows I am relentless in pursuing my duties, even to my own detriment. I tell him his subservient attempts at flattery are abhorrent to me and he may take himself out of my sight. He may not go too far away though as I may need to speak with him again.

I call for a looking glass when he is out of the room. When I look into it, I am appalled to see how drawn and wrinkled I have become. I am tired, too, from lack of sleep. It is a blessing that my Philip is not here to see me now although I miss him every minute of every day. When I eventually feel ready to recall Englefield, I ask him how things go with the government and the privy council. I have not been to the house for some time now.

"Nicholas Heath is settling in well as Lord Chancellor," he says blandly.

"Yes, he should do well," I agree. "I think Gardiner was better although I never really liked the man."

"He was most repentant on his deathbed," Francis muses softly.

"So, he should have been," I respond. "I have never known such a turncoat."

Francis smiles. "Going whichever way, the wind was blowing, as he put it himself."

THE TITIAN PORTRAIT

I relent and invite him to sit next to me. There is sweet wine on the table and I invite him to recharge my vessel and pour one for himself. As he does so, I recall that I never asked about the last conversation Francis had with Gardiner. Perhaps he would like to enlighten me?

"Mostly he was concerned about heretics," he proceeds, sounding tentative. "He felt more efforts should be made to acquire recantation."

"Heretics deserve no mercy or consideration," I say. "They are evil, an insult to God and the queen. I will rid this land of every last one of them before I am done."

"But if they recant, do you absolve them, Majesty?" he asks.

"You are treading dangerous ground again, Francis," I warn. "I told you that Cranmer would not go to Rome and I was right. As it happens, the Pope settled his fate for him by stripping him of the title of Archbishop of Canterbury and confirming that his sentence should go ahead. I see no good reason to postpone that sentence of death. Bishops Latimer and Ridley died at the stake and Cranmer was taken along to watch. The same fate awaits him, and it will not be long now."

I tell him, more gently now, that I will do everything in my power to strengthen our resources, increase the number of ships for our navy, restore our coinage and everything else outstanding to parliamentarians but the one thing I will never agree to is to show mercy to heretics.

"You know that Cranmer wrote to me," I say, trying to control the agitation I am feeling. "He had the audacity to suggest I refuse to accept the authority of the Church of Rome. I couldn't read the letter. I regarded it as a sin to receive it and to read it."

"You know what was in it, though, Majesty?" Francis asks, playing with fire again.

"Only the gist of it," I explain. "Cardinal Pole told me when I passed it to him to reply to that creature."

"That will infuriate him beyond measure," Francis says, smiling. "Having Pole reply to a letter he sent to you."

"Exactly what I had in mind," I tell him.

Alone again, I feel no better this time. Worse, if the truth be told. Although I indulge in long hours on my own to work through the misery and loneliness of my recent losses, there comes a time, on occasion, when I need other voices around me. When I am surrounded by my ladies, I cannot claim that I find any of their conversations stimulating. Or even interesting. But they do question me endlessly.

"How fares His Majesty in the Netherlands?" Anne Basset enquires.

"Well, he is now responsible for the entire area," I reply. "Now that the emperor has resigned them to him."

"As if he didn't have enough to do," Anne continues. "With the recent addition of Naples and Sicily."

"Exactly, Anne," I agree irritably. "No wonder he is kept away from his queen and these shores for so long."

It is not something I wish to discuss further so I tell them I wish to be alone for a while to contemplate and consider some of the problems of parliament. None of them believes me but it makes no difference; the time has come again for isolation. I walk slowly down the long corridor that leads to my special chamber. I enter and note that the substantial fire I requested has been built up satisfactorily. I move over to the window and look out on ice-encrusted window ledges and a frozen pond beneath my chamber. The snow has settled well, creating a white shroud over the land and inadvertently adding light in the palace.

Then I look up at the real reason I have come here, the portrait of my prince, in all his glory, posing for the artist

Titian and looking so fine, so confident and so very impressive. I call a servant over and ask for more candles to be brought and lighted. The chamber is quite bright with light from the afternoon winter sun and the blazing white snow. It is merely an extra source of illumination to focus on my precious portrait. Sometimes I even find myself talking to him through his picture on the wall. I reprimand him for leaving me here, all alone for, in truth, I feel more alone surrounded by hundreds of ladies of the chamber, attendants, courtiers, servants or any form of humanity coming into the palace. For any reason.

Jane Dormer knocks at the door and enters when I bid her to. She asks if she can get anything for me or if I would like company. I smile wearily.

"Yes, Jane," I say quietly. "Come and sit with me by the fire."

The fire crackles and the flames leap up suddenly sending a reflection of moving light and fire on to the opposite panelled wall. The bright light from the window is fading very slowly and is replaced by the many candles now lit. It changes Philip's expression slightly when I study the portrait closely, just as if he had listened to my remark earlier and was now replying to me.

"I feel closer to him when I come in here," I tell her. "So silly of me, isn't it?"

"No, Mary," she responds with feeling. "I can understand your mood. I think I would feel the same."

"You're a good friend," I tell her, "even if I don't believe a word of it."

"I speak truly," she insists.

We sit contemplating the brightly coloured portrait in silence for some time. Sometimes, I even imagine he is smiling at me from the portrait, and I feel a warm glow. It does not last. Jane is studying the picture almost as intently as I do.

"What say my ladies?" I ask. "Do they laugh at me?"

"No, indeed. They curse the king for spending so much time away from you and the kingdom."

"Ah, no, they must not do that," I say starkly. "He has so much foreign territory and the constant threat of war to attend to. He is forced to spend time on such responsibilities."

When I lost my baby, that was when I needed and missed him most, I think ruefully. But time has not healed the rift I felt then and, every day that passes, I feel more desolate. I do not share this thought with Jane.

"Does he not look fine standing there, posing impressively for his portrait?" I ask, thinking out loud rather than speaking to Jane.

"He does, Majesty," she responds softly, nodding agreement.

"Thank you for your company, Jane," I murmur quietly. "Now we would wish to be alone for a short time."

She leaves quietly without uttering a single word.

Francis looks smart indeed in his dark blue doublet and, although his eyes shine brightly, his expression is a compound of apprehension and determination. I turn back to the window where the snow lays thick upon the ground and beyond the limits of my vantage point, the Thames is completely frozen over.

"I know I risk your censure and possible anger," he tells me. "But I feel I simply must speak out."

"Say it, Francis," I command. "Say it, get it off your chest, do."

"It is this," he continues. "All reports reaching me indicate that excessive numbers of people are attending the recent burnings of clerics."

"As they do."

"In their thousands," he goes on. "Far more than ever

before. And the mood of all, Catholic and other church followers alike, is angry and in sympathy with the heretics."

"No doubt they are," I agree. "But also in fear and trepidation of what will befall them if they practise heresy."

"Perhaps," he concedes. "But it does indicate that Your Majesty is becoming most unpopular with a vast section of the population. I felt it my duty to speak out."

"Well, you have done so, Francis and much good may it do you," I tell him earnestly. "Understand this. Monarchs will always be unpopular for those acts they must authorise for the good of the realm. I will never shirk from my duty to this country and stamping out heresy is, and will remain, top of my list."

"Then there is no more to say."

"Not on that subject, no. We are heartily sick of hearing opinions about it."

Even as we speak, there is a planned conspiracy against me of which I am aware and there are agents of mine working to bring the traitors to justice. Sir Henry Dudley is suspected of being the ringleader and he has plans to recruit our enemies in France in what is thought to be yet another attempt to remove me and put Elizabeth on the throne. My people are watching him and his henchmen closely and he will not be arrested until we find out the full extent of his treachery. Neither will any of the others be taken into custody yet but, when the time comes, full retribution will be handed out.

At least I can be absolutely sure that this time Elizabeth is not involved. She was put in a conveniently placed manor house near Oatlands Palace when we moved there and kept under observation. She was allowed to proceed to her home at Hatfield House a short time ago but watched carefully. I also have spies in her household and her letters are intercepted before she receives them. I cannot be too careful.

Sir Francis prepares to leave but I detain him.

"A word, Francis. I suspect the brewing of another heinous plot against my person and may require your services to bring it to a satisfactory conclusion."

"Whatever I can do to assist," he offers. "I am your faithful, most loyal servant."

"Yes, you are, Francis," I agree. "At least when not meddling in affairs that do not concern you. Thank you. You may go now."

SIR FRANCIS ENGLEFIELD'S DIARY

WHITEHALL AND OXFORD, EARLY SPRING 1556

THE QUEEN'S HEALTH AND STATE OF MIND DO NOT IMPROVE although she has now taken to odd behaviour to add to her mysteries. She will jump up suddenly in the middle of a group of her ladies in waiting and disappear, sometimes for more than two hours. Nobody knows where she goes or what she does. She is known to spend much time sitting and gazing at a portrait of the king she likes very much and also to wander through the kitchens, looking for all the world as though she is inspecting everything and everybody. She is also known to be in and even seen in her privy chamber and then suddenly, she has departed, and nobody can tell where she is headed.

Today she has the usual grim, weary expression and signs a sheaf of papers I hand to her without so much as a glance at their contents. She could easily be signing a death warrant and not knowing whose.

"I have an assignment for you, Francis," she announces flatly.

"Yes, Majesty," I reply cheerfully.

"I want you to travel to Oxford."

I could ask why but it hits me at once that in three days'

time the lately removed Archbishop of Canterbury, Thomas Cranmer, is due to be executed. This is an event to which I have given much thought and it brings back memories of Gardiner, on his death bed, reciting the last hours of Bishop Hooper in all its horror.

"You want me to watch Cranmer die?" I ask, grim faced.

"Don't get ahead of yourself Francis," she says. "First, he is due to make a public recantation in the market square."

"He's already recanted four times," I tell her.

"Five."

"Well, what could possibly be the point of another one?"

Although the queen's expression has been dull and grim and her manner listless over the past few months, she does become quite agitated and her eyes glint brightly whenever she talks of Cranmer. The very name seems to inflame her and precipitate an outburst.

"I don't trust him," she complains. "He is as slippery and slimy as a barrel of eels, that one. I want to be sure he does recant again, In public. In the market square where thousands will hear him."

"Surely," I suggest quietly, "if he has recanted and accepted the Bishop of Rome as head of the church, he should now be pardoned?"

The queen shakes her head vigorously. Do I think, she asks, that she should forgive the years she lived as illegitimate? Falsely accused of being a bastard when her mother and father's marriage was as legally sound as any could be. Forced to see her mother humiliated and sent to a country retreat while Henry went through a form of marriage to Boleyn. And do I think it forgivable that she was forced to act as servant to Boleyn's child, Elizabeth. Cranmer, she states, was guilty of initiating all this and a lot more besides.

"That man will receive no pardon, Francis," she states angrily. "If he recants in public, that will be some small atonement for his multitude of sins."

I raise an eyebrow but accept that I must prepare to witness yet another execution.

It occurs to me as I arrive in the City of Oxford that Cranmer, most staunch supporter of the Church of England, must have recanted to save his life. And even several recantations have not been enough in his case. The rain has been persistent today and, although I have a heavy coat and a thick cap, I still feel damp and uncomfortable. A notice on an oak tree informs me that because of the inclement weather, the recantation by Cranmer will take place at St Mary's Church. I hurry to the spot.

A remarkable number of people are clamouring to get into the church but only those known to the stewards are allowed in. I move in slowly behind a group of four people and I am close enough behind them for the odour of damp clothes to rise up. I walk down the aisle and nod to Sir John Browne, whom I have met and know slightly. He indicates a space with a gesture and I sit next to him. I find myself distracted, as usual in these circumstances, away from the high structure by the altar. Instead, I choose to look with interest at the bright colours in the stained-glass windows.

A shuffling sound behind us heralds the arrival of the mayor, aldermen and Lord Williams, leading the unfortunate man lately styled archbishop. He shuffles past our pews wearing the most unseemly, tattered clothing, no doubt picked out for him to heighten his degradation. As soon as he gains access to the altar, Cranmer kneels and starts to pray. Then he rises to his feet, eyes stained with tears, and receives the leave to speak from Doctor Cole.

"Good people," he begins in a gravelly voice, filled with emotion. "I had indeed intended for you to pray for me, and I thank you for it. Every man desireth, at the time of their death, to give some good exhortation. That others may remember after their death and be the better thereof."

There is a hush in the church with everybody present

waiting to hear the late archbishop recant in this public place. Then a murmur of whispered voices is heard rumbling along as the pause becomes longer.

"And now I come to the great thing which troubles my conscience more than anything I did or said in my life. That is, the setting abroad of writings contrary to the truth."

A gasp is heard throughout the church at these words. Browne turns to me.

"Great God in heaven, the man is not going to recant," he says. "He's changed his mind."

"I here renounce as things written with my hand, contrary to the truth, which I thought in my life and written with fear of death and all such bills as I have written in my life since my degradation: wherein I have written many things untrue. And whereas my hand offended in writing contrary to my heart, my hand shall be first punished. For if I may come to the fire, it shall be first burned. And as for the Pope, I refuse him, as Christ's enemy and Antichrist with all his false doctrine."

Doctor Cole admonishes him furiously for dissembling, his voice cracked with fury: "You are a disgrace, Sir."

"Alas, Sir, I am a man that all his life loved plainness and never dissembled till now against the truth. I am most sorry for it. As to the sacrament I believe I have taught it as in my book against the Bishop of Winchester."

Much noise breaks out, with shouts of heretic and traitor from the assembled crowd as the onetime archbishop is bundled swiftly out of the church by Doctor Cole and the guards then marched down to the stake. It is wet underfoot and under a deep grey sky as he walks along with two friars desperately, no doubt, trying to persuade him yet to recant and save his soul. I follow, weaving this way and that to avoid the surly, unruly crowd who bump into me frequently with no help from my servants who have been separated in the move out of the church.

At the stake he is asked by a fellow of Brasenose college, in a loud voice, to revert to his former recantation but he refuses vehemently. The Spanish friars shake their heads in disbelief.

"We should go from here," the taller of them states. "For he is with evil."

"As to my former recantation," Cranmer says, "I regret it sorely for I know it was against the truth. I stand by my latest words for I know them to be God's truth."

"Make it short, be done," Lord Williams bellows, anxious to proceed with the execution.

Cranmer takes off his ragged, dirty clothes and stands ready in his shirt. He drops to his knees, says another prayer and then stands up and begins to shake the hands of friends and people sympathetic to him. The man from Brasenose is most persistent and again tries to persuade Cranmer to see the light, as he puts it and recant now, before it is too late. Cranmer refuses and makes clear that he will not be persuaded. The Oxford man is disgusted and shouts out to those people that shook hands that they have offended God. He is placed in the centre of the wood pile and a chain is fastened around his waist.

The fire is lit and roars up brightly on this dull, grey day. True to his word, Cranmer extends his right hand and thrusts it into the fire before the flames reach past his midriff. He shouts out, "This hand has offended," in a loud, croaking voice and actually holds it in the fire until it withers and burns down to a cinder. I stand shocked and amazed that he can withstand the pain and not cry out, but he remains still until his right arm drops off and the flames engulf his body. I try to look away but once here, again, in this truly horrible situation, I am mesmerised and find I cannot take my eyes from the spectacle.

The scorched shirt burns away, and the blackened body and face remain static, burning fiercely now as the tongue blackens too and the gums seal up and, mercifully, the man dies at last. I stand still, oblivious to my servant's entreaties to come away and return to my horse. The people are either standing around in awed, shocked silence or drifting away about their business. A few spots of rain drizzle slowly down on this dismal scene as several dignitaries come forward and shake my hand before departing. Some speak to me, others do not. I say nothing.

As I stand there with the stench of burning flesh mixed with rainwater, and the black sludge at my feet just three or four inches away, I make a solemn vow that I will never, ever, witness this barbaric act again, even if it means surrendering all my offices of state and position on the privy council. Enough is enough.

The queen wears a face of thunder which does not sit well with her dishevelled hair. It seems her hair has resisted all the blandishments of the brush and, together with her pallid, wrinkled face, she presents a sorry sight. My report on the events in Oxford have both pleased and annoyed her sorely.

"I just knew that slimy toad would avoid recanting in public," she complains. "It was always a likely tactic."

"He made quite a business of explaining his reasons, too," I contribute.

"As he would," she responds.

I finish my report leaving no detail unmentioned. Even the foul weather is given due consideration along with those present legally and those, like the friars, who chose to add their contribution.

"Did you stay to the end, though," she asks, eyes bright as she searches my face. "Did you see the snake die?"

"In considerable detail," I tell her, shuddering as a picture reforms in my mind.

The queen settles in a high-backed chair and her mood

gradually changes. In the silence that ensues, I am very conscious of the rain beating against the window and a sudden howl of wind. Then a smile forms on her face.

"At least I have the pleasure of knowing," she begins, "that the principal architects of my poor mother's shameful treatment are now dead. And the added satisfaction of knowing they died badly and painfully."

"Except Wolsey?"

"Oh, the cardinal was a victim himself," she replies. "As much sinned against as sinner."

"And he was hounded out of office."

"The deaths of Thomas Cromwell and now Cranmer give me most satisfaction."

"Stephen Gardiner?" I enquire, tongue in cheek.

"I forgave him," she muses thoughtfully. "He had little real involvement. He swung this way and that but never renounced his Catholic faith. Not in any true sense.'

And I think to myself, he died peacefully in his bed at the last. A sinner who repented. Then, as I see that the queen is in a forgiving mood, I ask her to excuse me from attending future burnings of heretics.

"Of which there will be many now and in the coming months," she admits. "We are, though, inclined to excuse you, Francis, if you have not the stomach for it. I think I can find another loyal councillor to report accurately to me."

QUEEN MARY'S DIARY

LONDON, SPRING 1556

THE SIGHT OF CARDINAL REGINALD POLE IS PLEASANT TO MY eyes. He has done much to present a truly English form of Catholicism in our land, not ideally viewed by the Bishop of Rome but then, as I point out, we are not in Rome. He has held masses in St Paul's, instructed the clergy to educate and explain the ways and paths of God and helped me so much in my bills still going through parliament to restore our country fully to true Catholicism. As the cardinal who came closest to being appointed as the next pope, he was the only true candidate to become our Archbishop of Canterbury, although he did not accept the offer lightly and had to be persuaded.

"I hope that I will fulfil that high office with due reverence and humility," he says.

"We are sure that you will," I assure him.

All is reasonably well in our land although there is one matter that I do feel I must discuss with the cardinal. When three heretics in Bishop Bonner's diocese were found guilty and sentenced to death, they appealed to Cardinal Pole for mercy.

"You absolved them completely, Cardinal, all three," I complain.

"They recanted," he tells me. "And, as repenting sinners, I felt, in this case, that this was the right way forward. I gave them penance and absolved them."

I remind him quietly of my policy on heresy and how determined I am to stamp it out, once and for all. He nods, acknowledging my words carefully.

"You will recall, Your Majesty," he continues, "when we first met on my arrival in England, that I expressed the view that caution and moderation should be used?"

"I recall," I tell him frostily. "Although you should perhaps, my Lord Bishop, remember that I, as supreme monarch, have the final say on all matters of government including spiritual disputes."

The cardinal acknowledges quietly that I am indeed sole final arbiter, and he is, in all concerns, my loyal and faithful subject. He must, however, do his duty as he sees it, to God and the church and for the benefit of the people. "As the Bible teaches us," he continues, "there will be more joy in heaven over one sinner that repenteth than over ninety and nine just persons…"

"Yes, we take your point," I assure him. "I hope, however, that you and I are not going to disagree on this."

"Much better by far, though, I humbly suggest," he adds, "to lead people on the path of righteousness rather than punish them severely for inadvertently stepping off it."

I leave it there. I do not want to fall out with him as he is too important to me and to this realm in the full restoration of the Church of Rome. He has done much already to reinstate the monasteries, particularly Benedictine and in general and specific education of the priests. I ask if he be ready for his consecration as Archbishop of Canterbury.

"A post I regard with awe," he tells me. "But I am ready."

I need the cardinal to be in London and have so instructed him, so he is sending his proxy to Canterbury. Robert Collins,

Canon of Christchurch Canterbury, his commissary, will install for him.

It is a Sunday, March 22nd, known as Passion Sunday, that Cardinal Pole is consecrated Archbishop of Canterbury, in the conventual church of the Friars Minor of the observance of the order of St Francis at Greenwich. Nicholas, Archbishop of York, Primate of England and my Lord Chancellor, conducts the ceremony.

I sit in the old church, which is heavily draped in cloth of gold with diverse hangings on the walls and many cushions for comfort. Daylight shines brightly through the church windows as an additional sign of God's Grace on this solemn but joyous occasion. It is a great pleasure and delight to me to see a new and glorious Catholic archbishop consecrated here today and I could only wish that my husband and king, Philip was here to share that joy. Bishop Bonner of London and six other bishops look on as the ceremony proceeds. The Pope's letter is read by David Pole, Archdeacon of Derby.

We move into the parlour and the archbishop takes the oath as I watch the proceedings carefully. It is all done with great solemnity, as indeed it should be, the voices of the participants pitched high in a spiritual manner. I think my Lord Archbishop of Canterbury, as he must from this time forward be called, looks magnificent in his bright ceremonial robes. Standing close I see him more clearly than ever before and become aware of his light blue, friendly eyes and gentle, serene expression.

In the church, the Archbishop of York says Mass at the high altar. So many lords, earls, bishops and other titled people are here today, more than ever collected in one place since my wedding to Philip. I know Reginald will be a good archbishop and a stabilising force for the good people of this country. As the ceremony finally ends, I think of how much good has been done here today and how I must work tirelessly to build upon it.

I do not have Philip by my side and regret that with every day that passes but I do have the cardinal, now my archbishop. He has kept his promise to my husband to take care of me, visiting regularly, praying for me constantly and sending little parchments containing wise words. There was once talk of him and me marrying but it came to naught. Somehow, I could always only think of him as a churchman and a good one but never, ever, as a lover. What I must arrange in the coming week is the gift of lands to him now that he must live in the style and fashion of an archbishop. I intend to hand him farms and land in Chevening, Wrotham and Bexley and the manor of Charing, all in the county of Kent.

"A goodly ceremony, supremely well-conducted," he says. "Do you know, with all the years spent in Rome and Europe generally, I had quite forgotten how well we do things here."

"Only the English could manage so lavish a ceremony," I tell him.

"Yes. And Nicolas, he does well as Bishop of York and here today but how does he fare as chancellor?"

"I must say he is doing well," I respond. "He is becoming as good a politician as he is an archbishop."

"One other small matter," he continues, lowering his voice a little. "Elizabeth. Is she safely returned home?"

"She has now returned to her home in Hatfield," I reply. "I placed no further hindrance to her going."

"That is good,"' he says. "I do not think you need have any further concerns regarding her loyalty."

"I hope you are right, My Lord," I reply quietly.

"I met and spoke with her some time ago," he goes on. "I have to say I was impressed by her strength of character, resilience and honesty. Of course, her religion is to be regretted but as she keeps it and, overall, her opinions, to herself, I am convinced that nobody need fear her."

I nod but make no response. I do not feel I can ever trust

her, and, for many reasons, I can never like her. But the archbishop's word is good enough for me. In the event that she continues to live quietly at Hatfield and in peace, I shall contentedly leave her in that state.

QUEEN MARY'S DIARY

❦

GREENWICH, SPRING 1556

Heresy and rebellion everywhere I look. Is there no end to the treachery of those subjects who favour the new English church? I have to look over my shoulder everywhere I move, even in the parliament house or talking to members of the privy council. It is a cold day for this time of year, although sunshine occasionally breaks through. What am I to do with so few people I may truly trust? I may spend time with my ladies but not long. Their conversation is, for the most part, bright and chirpy and I am unable to join in. If I am listless, as I usually am, I may go to my presence chamber and sit there alone, secure in the knowledge that none will come in to disturb me. The latest treachery seems now to have been rumbling on for more than a year. I expect it has; I hardly know. Jane will seek me out, though, if I remain alone for more than two hours, but she is one of the few I do trust. Her and Francis Englefield.

I must collect my thoughts into some semblance of order, even if I am weighed down by pain and grief. Sir Henry Dudley is the latest traitor to plot and scheme against my person and replace me with Elizabeth. He has recruited some of the most prominent and important people in this land in his nefarious endeavours but every one of them will be rounded up if they are not secured already. In the Tower, they are interrogated assiduously, and I have ordered torture for those whose lips remain sealed. An hour on the rack will loosen their tongues, I'm thinking. Or removal of their body parts if it comes to it.

I gaze out of the window at a clear blue sky. Birds hover, suspended in air before flying down to land on a bush or bench. It is the loneliness that is most soul-destroying and yet, feeling as I do day after day, I do not seek company. When I have it, I have little to say. I have, of course, my absent husband Philip to thank for a significant part of the failure of this latest gross treachery. He signed a pact with France to secure the peace of England, Spain and that troublesome country.

I am conscious that Sir Henry is a relation of that other rebellious tyrant, the Duke of Northumberland, and his daughter in law, Jane Grey. Henry Dudley is now lying low in France but, if he ever should return to these shores, I will have his head on a spike on London Bridge before the day is spent. Dudley approached the king of France for money and men to invade us but with the fragile truce recently signed, he received no help from that quarter. As to Elizabeth, all the people involved in that latest outrage were and are close to her. What to do with her? I write to Philip for advice.

Philip is of opinion that Elizabeth is not involved and counsels me to leave her alone. He even suggests setting free her faithful servant Kat Ashley, whom we were interrogating. She will never implicate her mistress, so it is best to let her go. I am convinced that Philip's words are dictated by his desire to protect his fragile peace plan, but he is right, of course. For the good of the realm, I go along with it.

"Travel down to see Mistress Ashley, Francis," I request. "Tell her she will not be troubled further, nor her mistress, so long as she obeys the ruling not to return to Elizabeth."

"Yes, Your Majesty," he replies contentedly. "Although I had planned to return to Reading to check on reports of much civil unrest in the area."

"Go to Reading by all means," I tell him. "But tend to Mistress Ashley first."

"Yes, of course," he agrees and continues tentatively: "Are you convinced, though, of Elizabeth's and Ashley's innocence?"

"Of course not," I respond, "but with Philip's advice and that of the archbishop, I see no other path to follow."

"I seriously doubt she was involved," he says. "And, in any case, she would never admit it if she were."

"Well, leave Elizabeth to me. I will write to her personally."

Francis Englefield will not let me down. I may trust his best efforts in all I demand of him and would wish that I had others like him around me. I thank him for the work he did to track down the perpetrators of Dudley's evil scheme and uncover their outrageous behaviour. So many treacherous men, members of parliament, lords and knights, all in league against me. Of course, I must acknowledge the good fortune that stemmed from the King of France refusing to have anything to do with the rebels. And the warning by the English ambassador in France that there was a plot afoot to "deprive Mary of her state". There were so many of them that nobody seemed in overall charge and that is one reason it failed.

They planned an invasion force that would land on the Isle of Wight and march to London. Another, Sir Anthony Kingston, was to raise forces in the west and they even schemed to cause diversions, with fires, in London as they planned to take the crown treasure from the tower. I can hardly believe there was so much treachery and so many people, many of them nobles from Buckinghamshire.

"Henry Peckham, the member for Chipping Wycombe,

shocked me," Francis tells me. "I always thought he was the most loyal to the crown."

"They are all loyal to the crown until they turn, Francis," I say. "I trust nobody, and I see treachery all around."

"Not from me, Your Majesty."

"No, not from you, Francis, but there are few like you. Do you know what the archbishop, Reginald Pole, told me? A man named White, an official at the Exchequer, became frightened for his life and confessed the whole plan to the archbishop. They bribed the wife of the teller and then made an impression of the teller's key. So much outrageous planning and stealing."

"They even bribed the keeper of the star chamber at Gravesend and the customs official to let their boat pass harbour with all the stolen silver on it."

Fortunately, that last plot was uncovered by Francis and his two assistants and stopped before it could start. More than 20 people were rounded up at the point when the rebellion broke down and, with some torture, which I authorised, the whole sordid scheme was unravelled. Many will die, some will remain in the Tower. Francis enquires about the man who confessed all to the archbishop. He was buying his freedom.

"Let him stay where he is in the Tower for now," I instruct. "He can cool down and repent his sins at leisure."

SIR FRANCIS ENGLEFIELD'S DIARY

ENGLEFIELD HOUSE, BERKSHIRE, SUMMER 1556

It is difficult for the man to be heard above the whoops, shouts and ugly calls of the ever-increasing crowd. He stands on a large box in front of an assortment of rough-looking fellows, mainly farm labourers and market workers. Fires have been lit in the road, right here in the centre of Reading town and there is noise everywhere. The man is dressed in fine-quality doublet and hose, far different from the people ranged in front of him. He speaks treasonous words about Queen Mary and refers openly to her great cruelty.

"Do my ears deceive?" I ask, dumbfounded.

"They do not, Francis," Sir Thomas informs me, smiling.

The crowd is increasing by the dozen every few minutes, it seems to me as a casual observer, positioned to one side of the road with Thomas. The noise rises and falls, mainly rises, and the speaker has to shout loudly to be heard.

"That fellow would be thrown into the Tower in London," I suggest. "Without ceremony."

"He would here, normally," Thomas informs me. "But the magistrates are working day and night and he knows how to pick his time."

"How so?"

"So many cases of felony to try. They have increased a hundredfold since last year's poor harvest."

"Do you know him, Thomas?"

"I believe he's a very wealthy merchant," Thomas tells me, looking carefully at the orator. "Lives in the manor house at Tilehurst, I think."

He should be apprehended and thrown into prison immediately, but I am not on state business just now and rounding up guards to deal with him does not appeal at this moment. Neither it seems does it appeal to Sir Thomas who appears to find the whole incident quite amusing. Does Thomas not feel the urge to do something?

"It's happening all over the country at present, Francis," he responds. "You don't know the half of it."

"Evidently not."

"You stop one incident and another 10 break out from here to Cumberland."

Thomas suggests a visit to a clean, well-positioned alehouse that he sometimes frequents, and I join him for a tankard. The noise outside the inn is still almost deafening as the speaker is being cheered and whistled at. Thomas gives me some details about the growing unpopularity of the queen and government that has been fermenting here and in diverse regions across the country. I tell him that much time, effort and resources have recently been spent in bringing to justice a considerable number of rebels, most of them from the aristocracy.

"Or the government," he suggests.

"Or both, in some cases."

The noise does not abate as we part with an arrangement to meet on the morrow with a plan to ride out if the weather be conducive. I ride home swiftly, the summer breeze on my cheeks and the goodly feel of the fine young grey horse beneath my thighs. He is a present from Catherine, bought from the extensive stables of a close friend. Such a ride, on such a clear warm evening, is exhilarating.

"You stay away for months and then spend your first day home in an alehouse," Catherine complains with a frown creasing her pretty face.

"Hardly that," I protest. "Mostly visiting estate management folks and farm incumbents. Thomas and I enjoyed a swift tankard of ale at the end."

At supper, I eat heartily after a long day. Salmon sallet to start with, salmon fillet strips and thin-sliced onion, lemon juice and olive oil. And violets. Catherine, too, has a healthy appetite today and we always enjoy our fish days. We continue our repast with trout, a large, delicate fish, which our cook has prepared with great skill and then sample crab, whiting, young pike, tench, and oysters. Strikes of pimpernelle, a delicious small eel dish come along next. I inform Catherine about the scene in Reading early this evening.

"Yes, I'm well aware," she retorts calmly. "Your wonderful queen is much hated now, it seems."

"She's not my queen," I tell her irritably. "She is our sovereign queen and should be treated loyally and with respect by everybody."

"Then perhaps she should refrain from burning people," she replies haughtily, cutting trout with her knife before transferring it to her spoon.

"Heresy must be stamped out," I respond. "If it spreads too far, we are all doomed."

"She goes too far, Francis. You must realise that."

We are offered lobster tart but, with the amount of fish and vegetables we have consumed so far, we both decline. Neither of us, though, is able to resist some sweetmeats. Catherine samples sugared almonds and I take a portion of delicious egg fritter, made to perfection with cream, cloves, mace, nutmeg and saffron. The scent of these dishes is enough to inflame the senses before we take a mouthful. But we eat slowly, sensuously, as the lute and flute players in the gallery fashion a slow, sonorous ballad.

The music occasions us to linger with sugared almonds and scented marzipan balls in front of us, if we can find room for such sweet delicacies. The lute player provides a sweet refrain and I settle back intent on the melody. In London, I find little time for music, much to my dismay.

"I worry about you at court," Catherine murmurs wistfully. "One day you may say the wrong thing and end up on the scaffold. Or chained to a stake amid the flames."

"No need for alarm," I tell her cheerfully. "I instigate punishment for traitors when necessary, but I am always on the side of law and order."

"Surely you have done enough," she pursues. "You could relinquish all your titles and retire to a gentle, peaceful existence in the country."

I smile indulgently. "I will, no doubt," I assure her. "When I reach the age of 50."

"And if you fall foul of the queen before that?"

I shake my head. I try to convince her that my position is secure and ever will be. I trust the queen and, more importantly, I am one of the few people that she trusts implicitly. Catherine in turn shakes her head. She lists those that have died that were once held in high esteem. Northumberland, Wyatt, Throckmorton, Jane Grey.

"They were traitors, Catherine," I protest. "I am not and never will be."

But she remembers further back. Those that died when she was a small child and even before she was born. Henry killed without compassion and sometimes on a whim or as revenge for the sins of another family member. She sites Margaret Pole, the archbishop's mother. And, she says, Mary is her father's daughter.

"She is not the monster you suppose," I insist.

"I'm not convinced," she argues. "And young Jane Grey, she was no traitor but the victim of unscrupulous men. They manipulated her into a position she had no desire to fill."

"I grant you that," I say softly. "Jane should not have died."

Gradually, slowly, we are moving towards a truce. We retire to the bedchamber and put on our nightclothes silently. We take it for granted that we will occupy the same bed on this night. As I lay with her, caressing her hair and face gently I tell her that the queen is not entirely without remorse.

"She suffers from dreadful dreams," I explain. "She sees awful ghosts in her nightmares. Cranmer in flames, Lady Jane Grey, headless and bleeding. Hooper in flames with no arms, just a pile of cinders at his feet."

"She tells you about that?" Catherine asks, incredulous.

"Only very infrequently. When she is in deep depression, although that state is becoming more regular these days."

"God's breath, how ghastly."

I say we have talked enough and now I tell her I want to make love and fuck her. We stretch out luxuriously in the bed, curtains drawn around us and we kiss slowly then, as I enter her body she sighs softly.

A fine summer morning with a clear blue sky. My new young grey trots along briskly as I spot the approach of Sir Thomas from the direction of Reading. He rides a fine stallion with a black coat that shines like silk. We wave and meet up easily at the road post we had designated last evening as our starting point. At first, we trot along easily on the road to Newbury, vapour rising from our horses' bodies in the early-morning air. We give our horses the chance to canter forward then and cover three miles or thereabouts swiftly. As we slow right down again to an easy trot, we do not speak and cover some distance in silence. We pass the old chapel building in Thatcham Village and continue to St Mary's Church. The sight of that building reminds me of my conversation with Thomas yesterday.

"How about this area?" I ask Thomas but as he looks puzzled, I add: "Our discussion last night?"

"The unrest, the agitation?" he asks. "Oh, just the same. It's all over, Francis."

With the sun shining down now on the fairly new tower of the church, everything looks so peaceful in this village and a million miles away from the executions. I speak my thoughts to Thomas. He nods slowly.

"I want to show you something," he tells me.

We ride out again and take the road to Newbury. As we pass St Nicholas's church, Thomas tells me that three young men were tried there for heresy just over a week ago by the Sheriff of Reading. We ride on through fields until we reach the area of Enbourn and halt our horses at Sandpits. We dismount.

"Over there, you can see the ashes," Thomas states, pointing. "By the pond."

"A burning?" I enquire.

"Jocelyn Palmer, a young Catholic, and latterly master of the grammar school as he had been originally," Thomas continues.

"When was this?" I ask.

"No more than a week ago," Thomas answers. "He and two other young men were accused of denying the Pope's supremacy and saying that the priest had shown an idol in church."

Thomas explains that Sir Richard Brydges, the sheriff, had offered Palmer a farm and to find him a wife and 10 pounds a year if only he would show repentance but the man told him that they were good things but there was one thing better, the truth of almighty God.

"After that, it was straight to the stake," Thomas continues.

I stare at the remnants of charred wood, ashes and blackened slime that remain on the spot. Thomas suggests that a tankard of ale would be a good idea, so we ride to the nearest good inn. We sit at a broad, rough table and I take a swig of ale.

"It's right here, on our own doorstep, so to speak," Thomas says. "But all over the country and everywhere, it is accompanied by protesting, angry citizens. Revolt could break out anywhere."

"Yes, I can see that," I tell him.

Thomas, who seems to have studied it in great depth, is talking about the decline of the cloth trade right here in Newbury. Lost markets have never been replaced, although the hope had always been that the king would open some up to England when he married Mary.

"It never happened," Thomas says regretfully.

"Mary has worked hard pursuing new trade markets," I say, defensively. "We sent a delegation to Africa only recently. And to Russia."

It is a delicate balance indeed. We align ourselves with Spain through our king and queen but, if we go to war with our enemy, France, we lose a lot of trade with that troublesome country. And as Philip remains abroad serving the interests of his many dominions, the queen sinks more heavily into depression.

"To new trade outlets," Thomas calls optimistically and we clink our tankards and drink deeply.

Outside, a shepherd is herding sheep along the main highway. The sun shines down on the green pastures and this rural scene is one of peace and tranquillity. I look out of the casement and wonder at the stillness all around.

"What we need to remember," Thomas is saying, "is that those young men that burned believed just as passionately in the truth of their religion as we do in ours. It seems our sons, grandsons and great-grandsons will have to learn to come to terms with the English church followers and both religions will need to live in harmony. Side by side."

QUEEN MARY'S DIARY

GREENWICH, SUMMER 1556

IN THE PARLIAMENT HOUSE, IT IS ROWDY. NO ONE MEMBER CAN agree with anything another says. If one says hot the man next to him immediately shouts cold. I despair of all of them but as usual I have little desire to be here, only duty and a will to get things done that should be done.

"I want further plantations in Ireland," I remind them. "In all the previously designated locations."

They will not refuse me, but will they get on with it and pass all the necessary legislation? I have other things on my mind, though, as I take my leave and call for my litter to take me back to Greenwich. The streets are quiet on the way back and most of the people we pass are silent. Most doff their caps or bonnets but there is no cheering.

At Greenwich, I go straight to my presence chamber where I will have solitude. I send for some state papers I intend to look through but make no alterations or issue instructions. Time for that when I feel less lethargic and without head and minor belly pains. I can and do sit for two hours doing nothing except looking out of the window at a bright blue sky and watching the infrequent bursts of sunshine.

The papers, when I do finally look through them, are only fit to depress me further. All are old and most are those that I have put off with intention to deal with another day. If that day should ever dawn.

My ladies will be wondering why I am not in their company, being amused or entertained by them but they know I must not be disturbed in this chamber. Under any circumstances, save declaration of war.

I call for sweet wine and biscuits and then ask Jane Dormer to join me. Her sweet smile and well-presented appearance generally are welcome but even she cannot shake me out of my melancholy. I ask her to sit with me, though.

"How fares Your Majesty?" she asks.

"Weary," I respond. "And not in goodly humour."

A servant approaches to pour wine, but I wave her away. I invite Jane to fill our crystal goblets.

"You should rest more, Mary," she tells me. "Do less state work. Others can be assigned to take the strain."

"The chance would be a fine thing," I respond.

A distant bell chimes and it strikes suddenly at my cold heart, reminding me, for no good reason, of wedding bells, weddings and great, happy ceremonies. I sigh deeply.

"I write frequently to the king," I tell Jane sombrely. "I tell him what is current here in London and remind him often of how much I miss him and how much I am longing for his return to these shores. And what do I get in return? News of his lands in the Low Countries and the problems in Naples, Rome and his new responsibilities in Spain."

Jane smiles sadly. "Men are not romantic as we are, Majesty," she says. "Work, good food and a full belly keep them happy."

"Well, I hope no more than that, Jane, I really do. If I thought he had a mistress, it would break my heart in two."

"No," she tells me, smiling, "not the king. He cares only for you."

THE TITIAN PORTRAIT

"I do understand," I say soberly. "He has so much more responsibility since the emperor was taken gravely ill and handed over all the lands to Philip. The poor man is dying, Philip says, and will not see the year out. Although with all I know and all I understand, I still crave the odd word of affection."

"As do we all," Jane replies. "But who of us can fathom the minds of men?"

I clink my crystal with hers gently and somehow force a smile. She is right, of course, and I am not alone among women. If I had given birth to a son and heir, it would have been so different. I think back to the way he stayed by my side, for the most part, when I thought I was with child. His gentle ministrations. His concern. But then came the worst time of my life when my belly receded, and I was alone and forlorn.

He will return to England soon, Jane feels sure, and lavish sparkling jewels, furs and satins on me and all the love and affection he has been unable to bestow on me while he is away. I smile. When Philip wrote to me most recently it was to request finance for the war against France that he thinks is now inevitable. A visit to England may be necessary, he suggests, if he be required to assist me in persuading parliament to provide money and army for a war. No word about missing me or looking forward to being here with me. But fool that I am, I look forward to his coming home with all my heart, whatever the initial spur to hasten his arrival.

We travel down the Thames to Windsor Castle where I will stay for a while. My ladies are all happy and full of gaiety as the country air and pleasant surroundings of Windsor suit them very well. I must confess that my main reason for going is that I feel safer leaving London in summertime. Although we have seen no outbreak of the plague for some time now, that is not to assume we are immune. And instances of influenza of a particularly virulent type have broken out. Also, the hideous sweating sickness that kills so swiftly and arrives so suddenly and without warning. We will all be much safer in Windsor Castle in summertime, one sensible idea that I must have inherited early from my father, Henry. At the first sign of any outbreak of plague or pestilence, he was moving down river as fast as his oarsmen could convey him.

We arrive in the afternoon of a hot day with sunshine bathing the fields and a clear blue sky above. The familiar grey stone walls of the castle and the building overall is a delight to me, as it has been to many who came before me. High up, in my privy chamber, looking out at the sparkling river below, I begin to feel at home, in much the same way I do at Hampton Court. The Court, though, has too many sad memories at present and, much as I love the place, I cannot bear to go there. It may take a good two or three years before I can return in comfort.

I try on a new velvet and satin gown that I have not yet worn. There is a tightness.

"Just here, under the armpit?" Margaret Douglas asks.

I nod and she pulls and prods the fabric this way and that. Margaret is one of my most skilled needlewomen and the first I always turn to with new clothing. Servants would do a good job, but Margaret has a special knack.

"I'll fix it in two shakes of a lamb's tail," she tells me cheerfully.

"Thank you, Margaret."

When she has taken her measurements and left me, I am ready to sign the "urgent" state papers that Francis Englefield insists must be dealt with promptly. He is kind enough to compliment me on my appearance and I am aware that the extra efforts I have made in the past few days have made me feel I carry more of a sunny disposition. My ladies say that it is the expectation that the king will be returning soon that puts me in good humour and they may be right. My problem is that if and when he does return, it is more for the requirement of English support overseas than to be with me again.

"So Philip is now fully crowned King of Spain?" he asks.

"And has been for some time, Francis," I respond.

In truth, the emperor has now handed over complete responsibility for all his territories to Philip as he continues to live but is too gravely ill to continue as a sovereign ruler. The threatened war with France, though, is troublesome, although I am inclined to support it. Francis shakes his head.

"Parliament will vote against it, Majesty."

"Of course they will," I agree. "I expect nothing less."

I remind him that the French were much involved in the recent abortive rebellion initiated by the villainous Henry Dudley, still cowering in that land. And a much bigger shock than that was the French ambassador. Ambassador de Noailles departed from these shores for France in great haste when the plot was uncovered.

"I would be inclined to support such a war," I tell Francis.

"For King Philip?"

"For the safety and security of our people, Francis," I inform him irritably. "The French are our biggest threat."

"Parliament will fight you tooth and nail."

I become impatient. I remind Francis that I have suffered constantly with those who would overthrow me here. I am not prepared to stand idly by when a foreign country, and a hostile one generally, supports our home-grown traitors. Is there no peace to be found anywhere?

"Tell me where you stand on this matter," I command.

He hesitates and looks uncomfortable. He takes some time before replying and, when he does, I am already sure of his answer.

"My instinct tells me to support you," he tells me. "But my heart feels strongly that it is wrong, and I must not."

"Thank you for being honest, Francis," I say coldly. "Now you may leave."

He goes out without another word. Francis has his little moods and speaks his mind always and I admire him for that. But he has never let me down in the past and I doubt he will do so on this occasion when it comes down to it. There is more at stake here than just a fight with the French. Battles with those troublesome people have been going on for hundreds of years. There is also the question of my husband Philip and what he needs. Part of the agreement with the privy council, when we married, was that Philip should advise us in matters of war with other nations. We depend on the security of the alliance with Spain and must not go against them.

Philip has written to me twice on this matter and he obviously feels it to be of major importance. I am his wife and would wish to support him in any way I reasonably can. If he tells me war is inevitable, I am not able to refuse him troops and money from this island. Nor would I want to; he is my husband and I love him dearly. Philip will receive the support he needs, and I will get the necessary backing from the privy council. On that I am determined.

QUEEN MARY'S PRIVATE JOURNAL

WHITEHALL PALACE, SPRING 1557

THE COBBLES ARE NOT YET DRY, EVEN THOUGH IT HAS NOT rained for two days. Cold and grey all around me with the streets practically deserted and the ice on the surface of the Thames not fully melted yet. It is dull, bleak and full of bad odours in the street outside the palace. If it were not absolutely necessary to be here now, I wish I could be at Hampton Court or even Windsor. No bad odours there or clanking carts rumbling past together with the constant clip, clop of hooves on the cobbles. Out there, in the country, the first green shoots of spring are just appearing on bush, tree and hedgerow. The air is fresh and, if the rain holds off for more than five hours, the sky is blue.

Today is not the day for gloom or melancholy, however. At least the weather is clement, and it is brightly lit on this fine morning in my privy chamber. Surrounded by all my ladies, not one absentee among them, all chattering joyfully and everybody indulging in embroidery or sewing furiously. Voices are bright and sibilant with the occasional rippling peal of laughter but I make no fuss, whatever is said. Today I feel more like them than I have in the past year, expectant and cautiously optimistic in a manner that has eluded me for far too long.

"I'll wager you can't wait for Thursday, Majesty," Jane Dormer says.

"On the contrary," I reply, laughing, "I have no choice but to wait. As I have for the past dreary year and a half."

"Absence makes the heart grow fonder," Susan suggests.

Margaret is saying she has a cousin who knows a sea captain and he told her that if the winds are any more than light, it can hold up a ships progress by more than a day. Wouldn't it be terrible, she says, if the king's arrival were more than a day late?

"Thank you, Margaret," I say. "Ever the optimist."

"Well, I say it will be good for us all to see Philip at court again," Jane contributes. "It's not as though we had a supply of good-looking men about the place."

"As long as you just look and don't touch," I say to Jane, smiling.

"I wouldn't dare touch," she responds. "Anyway, he can be quite stiff and formal."

"Oh, I wouldn't say that," Magdalen contributes but then seems to realise what she has said and blushes deep red from forehead to neck. She stops her embroidery and twists her hands together nervously.

"Do you know something we don't, Magdalen?" I ask, teasing her a little.

"Oh no, Majesty," she replies nervously, shaking her yellow-haired head furiously.

"The king wouldn't even notice a little mouse like you," Susan adds with a grin.

"No, no, of course not," Magdalen responds indignantly, tossing her head, and everybody laughs.

I sit back in my high-backed chair and feel a contentment that I have not experienced since the day Philip sailed away from me at Greenwich all that time ago. The ladies all seem genuinely pleased for me and no doubt they have missed seeing his handsome face in the gallery from time to time. It will certainly brighten up the court, no matter where we are currently domiciled.

"Of, course he isn't the only man with looks," Mabel suggests. "Begging your pardon, Mary, but Francis Englefield is not unpleasant to gaze upon."

"Be careful, Mabel," I tell her. "He, too, is happily married."

"Yes," she answers ruefully. "The best ones always are."

"And the count wouldn't be pleased to hear you say so," I add.

There is more laughter, and our frivolous but contented mood stays until it is time for dinner. That repast, too, will be pleasurable, I do not doubt and there is also the joyous thought that very soon now I will not be eating meals on my own.

I walk purposefully into the chamber where my portrait is, smiling to myself because I realise I do not need to look when I have the real thing here. It is still good to gaze upon the portrait, though, even if I do come in here at least three times a week when we are at Whitehall. And it is all that is available just now. Philip tells me the first thing he must do is catch up with his Spanish councillors before he can even breathe. If I needed to catch up with my English people before I could breathe, I would be long dead by now.

It is a good hour and twenty minutes before he honours me with his presence, but he knows just where to find me.

"You never sent it back, then?"

He gazes intently at his own portrait as if he does not recognise the subject. In his blue tunic and soft satin hose, he is just as fine a spectacle as the picture today. Not so many jewels in the picture, though.

"It is mine," I tell him. "It will never leave this chamber while I live."

"Is it so special?" he wonders, looking at it critically. "It was sent here from the Low Countries somewhere, I believe?"

"It is special," I tell him. "More so when I am alone."

"All I recall is the merry song and dance Titian led me," he says thoughtfully. "The man was a menace."

I smile, trying to envisage Philip sitting dutifully for his portrait for hours when he thought he could be using his time more profitably. Somehow, I cannot picture him posing for long hours in silence.

"There was nothing but fuss and bother with that man," Philip continues. "Move a fraction of an inch and he would shout and screech like a hyena. You would think he was the king and I the hired craftsman. One time he spent hours trying to find a shade of pale blue paint. The colour was not quite right for him and the replacement even worse. He would not continue until someone found it for him and even then, he complained and fussed. I very nearly kicked him down the staircase towards the end."

"Poor Philip," I commiserate. "What you went through to provide my picture."

"You needed to see what you were getting," he says, grinning.

"Well, I love what I got."

"We must get on, Mary," he tells me, straight faced. "I have much to catch up on tonight."

Surely not. My face looks crestfallen, and I tell him that we should spend time together on his first evening back home. Unfortunately, he tells me, it will not be possible. He has a mountain of state papers to plough through. Then he looks terribly serious and says we must go through his request for militia from England. They will be sorely needed. And finance; the coffers at home in Spain are almost empty now.

THE TITIAN PORTRAIT

"Let us go through to the presence chamber," I suggest. "Nobody will disturb us there."

We walk through the corridor and come across Francis Englefield in the long gallery, looking out of the window at the Westminster street. Three well-dressed men on horses are the only people abroad, I notice, as we stop and look down.

"Sir Francis," Philip greets him. "I am in your debt, Sir. I understand you have helped to look after Her Majesty when the archbishop was not available."

"My privilege and pleasure, Majesty," he responds.

"Well, your help and advice are much appreciated," he continues, looking at me. "Is it not so?"

"Francis is my right-hand man," I agree. "Always there when I need him."

We depart and make our way to the presence chamber. Philip suggests that we should honour Sir Francis in some way or reward him with lands. I point out that Francis has much valuable land in Berkshire and other counties and his wife, Catherine, is an heiress of the very wealthy Fettiplace family. He grimaces and acknowledges that royal gifts of land are hardly appropriate in this case.

"We are on the brink of a war with France," he tells me as we settle in the chamber. "It could blow up at any moment."

"Yes, I share your concern," I tell him.

"I need to know those men will be available," he explains, frowning.

"I will make sure they are," I tell him.

"For certain?"

"Yes."

"I will need upwards of 10,000 men, Mary," he tells me, looking apprehensive."

I assure him that, if that is what he needs for the security and safety of his country and mine, that is what he will get. Money to finance it may be more of a problem, but I will find it for him somehow.

233

"What about your councillors, though?" he asks, his face registering doubt and concern.

"They will be against it," I admit, "but it will still go through. I know how to deal with my councillors."

He shakes his head and looks as though he cannot believe it. Should he perhaps address them himself and make a plea on behalf of the country, his country and our combined future?

"No, no, my dear Philip, no. I regret that anti-Spanish feeling has never gone away since we married and that, I'm afraid, stretches to several members of the privy council. Leave it to me, my love, and all will be well."

Maybe Hans Eworth is far from the distinguished and revered painter that Titian is, but he appears to be just as fussy and finicky over getting the right blend of colours in his paints. I can see Philip looking impatient already and we have barely started. The artist makes a curious growling noise as he mixes and tries out a colour, oblivious, for the moment, to the presence of his royal sitters. Philip complained bitterly to me that he is losing precious time on affairs of state and it took me a considerable amount of time persuading him to sit with me. The man simply works too hard.

"Where do you want us?" Phillip asks in a gravelly tone.

Eworth shakes his head irritably and bids us wait a minute longer. Five minutes pass. He is still arranging his paint palette with painfully slow movements. Finally, he surveys the chamber, eyes up and down, peeking into dark corners.

"The queen on the right on the high-backed chair," he suggests, "and you, Majesty, on her left."

We move into the suggested positions dutifully with the window, one panel open, behind us. The light is good today and the walls behind us provide an attractive backdrop. He

THE TITIAN PORTRAIT

has his head on one side and then suggests a higher chair for Philip so that he appears fractionally taller than me. It is arranged. Then the artist shakes his head, says no, no, no and wants Philip standing but leaning back slightly. With me sitting and Philip standing, he is taller than me. Eworth seems content.

"Are you doing any painting today?" Philip enquires irritably.

"Sketches, drawings," Eworth responds curtly. "It will help me and save Your Grace standing later. Once I have the outlines perfected."

I am being very patient, all things considered, but then I do want a portrait. I want one of us both together. Philip may tire of the whole thing suddenly and walk out. I dread this occurring.

"All right, get on with it, then," Philip mutters.

But now he wants to arrange the way our hands are positioned and requests permission to touch them. I grant it and find his hands are heavy and feel clammy. Perhaps he is nervous, but he does not show it. Quite the opposite. The way he has placed my hands is not exactly comfortable. He gives Philip a small scroll to hold. Just when we think he is about to start the preliminary sketches, he stops.

"A small dog," he exclaims. "It would be good."

"What?"

"At your feet, Majesty. It is homely and pleases the citizens to see such a domestic scene."

"Does it?" Philip snaps. "Perhaps you would like to go out and buy an animal?"

Eworth thrusts out his lower lip. "There must be one or two at court."

"The Marchioness of Exeter has two very tiny animals," I say swiftly.

"Ah, excellent, Majesty."

A courtier is dispatched speedily and soon returns with

two of the smallest dogs I have ever seen in my life. The artist places them exactly in position in front of my feet and the message from the marchioness is that they are as docile as ever you could wish and will not move an inch.

"Are you sure they are not rats?" Philip asks disdainfully.

Eworth begins to draw on his parchment, his face a model of concentration. I dare not sneak a peep at Philip as I can sense his growing impatience. The dogs may be docile, but they do occasionally yap, for no apparent reason.

On the day Hans begins painting, he is slow, meticulous and very annoying. He asks if the window may be closed as he is sensitive to draughts. It is a hot day, but we agree, and he closes it but leaves it open on the painting. The ways of artists are beyond my comprehension. I shall be glad when it is finished, and I know Philip will. He has been irritable and snappy with me all the way through it. Even so, I still want a picture of us together and I will endure what I must endure for that purpose.

QUEEN MARY'S PRIVATE JOURNAL

HAMPTON COURT AND WHITEHALL, SPRING 1557

DAYS OF REFLECTION AND PLEASURE AT HAMPTON COURT ARE not working out quite as I expected. Do I ask too much of my husband that he spend some time with me during the day? I think not. He has been locked in conference for three hours today and joined me only when I sent for him with a message that it was a matter of some importance.

"I remain uninformed of the nature of this important matter," Philip says stiffly.

"I just want you with me," I tell him. "Is it too much to ask?"

I sit on the stone seat watching and listening to the waterfall as it cascades down. Thin sunshine brightens the day but there is an early spring chill in the air. I try to smile reassuringly but Philip has a face like thunder. I tell him I have missed him these past 18 months or so and crave his company.

"I was engaged in delicate diplomatic business," he snaps.

"Which will wait, surely?" I respond.

He shakes his head and sighs. I continue to gaze at the scene all around me, contented but somewhat disturbed by his harsh words.

"So, there was no important matter," he complains.

"It was important to me," I murmur softly.

Philip sticks his hands in his tunic and faces me. I resist the urge to smile but he does look rather ridiculous when he behaves in a pompous manner. It does not suit his character.

"I have the responsibility for several kingdoms, Mary," he begins pompously. "Not just one, like you. I think it is high time you understood that and realised that my time is precious."

"So you have no time to spend with your wife?" I ask, exasperated.

"I didn't say that," he answers. "We will be together at dinner and supper."

"Is that all? Is that my only allotted time?"

I do not want to fall out with him. I have missed his company so much these past melancholy months and want to make up for it now. I tell him this, but he is quiet, not answering my questions but sulking really, like a small child. I try my best to make peace with him and he responds slowly to my overtures. He informs me that he currently is in difficult negotiations with an ambassador and three other diplomats and all must be resolved before nightfall. I must let him go now and return to the fray.

"I will make it up to you tonight," he promises, and I nod my head and smile.

"Be sure that you do," I say.

In the bedchamber, the fragrances of sandalwood, musk and jasmine hang in the air. The king keeps his earlier promise, caressing me in bed then pleasuring me slowly. This and his warm caresses are what I have waited for all these last, lonely months and I surrender myself to his erotic embraces completely. Then we lie together, not ready for sleep but talking softly of all the places he has been to and seen, the exotic places and the people therein. It is yet early in the evening and I am content that we retired shortly after supper.

THE TITIAN PORTRAIT

Philip draws back the bed curtains and smooths down his night attire.

"You are not leaving?" I ask, disturbed.

"I have a shoulder pain developing," he tells me gently. "I would not disturb your sleep for anything so I will spend the rest of the night in my privy bedchamber."

"Oh," is all I can manage to say.

"It is a recurring problem," he asserts, "and one the physicians seem curiously unable to treat successfully. You will be more comfortable alone."

I tell him I would gladly put up with a little disturbance to spend the entire night together, but he responds by saying it would be unfair to me and he would never forgive himself if I had a really bad night. Tomorrow he is trying a new potion that the physician is bringing so we should be fine for the next evening. He sounds so sincere that I am almost convinced that his thoughts are for my comfort alone. Almost. He kisses me and bids me sleep soundly. Then, suddenly, he is gone, and I am left alone with my thoughts.

He does consent to spend the next afternoon with me and even refuses to see one of his Spanish diplomats when a request is made. We are both most comfortable by this time with French wine and marshmallows to help us become mellow. I ask him to continue his intriguing tales of his journeys through all the territories for which he is responsible and his tales are most entertaining. And illuminating. The number of high- born ladies who have made themselves available to him is exceeded only by the number of times he has had to rebuff their advances. This he emphasizes over and over again. When I wonder idly how he comes to get himself into such situations, time and again, he assures me, fervently, that it is impossible not to, in his current position as King of Spain, England and various other colonies.

"You could ask your courtiers to keep them away before

they gain access to your various chambers," I suggest, as a pang of jealousy and pain invades my being.

"Easier said than done," he responds. "Sometimes they have access to state chambers before I arrive in them myself."

"Well, I just hope and pray you are being completely honest with me," I reply. "If I found that you lied to me and tupped foreign whores, I'd have your prick cut off."

He laughs raucously. "If you could get past my courtiers and guards, you probably would."

"You are being absolutely honest with me?" I ask, shaking nervously at the very thought of his being unfaithful. "You would never give way to temptation?"

"Not in a million years. You are my queen and my wife and I am a man of honour."

He sits there looking at me with an amused expression on his face. I desperately want to believe him, and I love him so much. I could not bear it if he should be false to me. I persuade myself that he was honest in telling me about these incidents. He could have kept it to himself And I would be none the wiser.

"Will you come to my bed tonight?" I ask. "And stay until morning?"

"That is my intention."

We spend the entire afternoon together. Long after the candles are lit and lavender is wafted through the chamber, even until the light outside has failed altogether. I notice before we go to supper that he has a frown upon his face and I ask, solicitously, what ails him. He says it is nothing, but I am persistent and insist on his speaking up.

"You meet with the privy council soon?" he enquires.

"Two days from now. At Whitehall."

He wonders if it will be possible for one or more members to block his requirement for troops and finance. I tell him there is no chance and he need have no worries. What about rebels?

"I know how to handle them, Philip, each and every one," I tell him confidently. "I haven't been Queen Regnant for more than three years without learning a trick or two."

I have already given him assurance on this matter in past weeks but now he has sought it once again. It is obviously a major concern to him. He need not have any worries.

QUEEN MARY'S DIARY

WHITEHALL, SPRING 1557

WHILE THE COUNCILLORS ARGUE AND ARGUE AND FAIL TO reach any agreement on anything, I remain in my privy chamber and bide my time. They have little reason to question my actions over the past two years to make our realm safe. I have bolstered the strength and effectiveness of our armies and, in particular, brought our navy up to date. I scrapped all the ships that were defective, and there were many, repaired all of those that were worthy of it and built 16 new galleons. Our naval treasurer has adequate funds for the upkeep of all vessels, and we now have 21 good ships in the fleet. This ensures our safety, should any country be ill advised enough to invade us. And it should keep us secure for many years into the future.

I have also stabilised our coinage, which was in a sorry mess before I came to the throne.

And still, they argue and cannot reach agreement on whether or not to support my bill to enter the war against France. In support of our good friends in Spain, with whom we are aligned. There should be no question. Francis Englefield returns. I have asked him to keep me informed.

"They are at each other's throats," he informs me. "No agreement."

"Consensus?"

"No chance."

I tell him that I want the meeting suspended, as of this moment. I wish each member of the council to come to my privy chamber individually, one by one. Francis warns me it could take hours, talking to every member.

"No matter," I inform him. "Send in William Paulet."

I know exactly what I am doing, although I can see from Francis's face that he does not think I do. If it takes the entire day, I intend to see this matter through. And achieve the outcome I desire.

My Lord Treasurer is now 74 years old. He should be the least of my problems. He has served in councils that go back to my father's father. Competent enough in his office, he is showing signs of age and feebleness. Not surprising of course, in one of his years. He enters the chamber and I make him welcome. I smile broadly. "How long have you been of service to me William?" I ask.

"A good number of years now, Majesty."

"And before that my father, my half-brother and grandfather."

He nods and smiles at me.

"I want this resolved swiftly," I tell him. "If the king thinks our ultimate safety depends on war with France, we should embrace the prospect. With the might of Spain and our own military prowess, we cannot fail."

He is looking thoughtful but makes no response. "I know you won't let me down, William," I say softly. "I can depend on your loyalty."

He begins nodding his head slowly.

"I was sure I would have your support," I say warmly. "I would not ask if it wasn't of prime importance regarding the safety of the realm. Thank you, William."

I ask to see William Paget next. He is a different kettle of fish, compared to Paulet, but I will secure his support. When he comes in, he is looking quite belligerent and unmoving. I begin by going through some of the disasters we have suffered over the years to the French. I tell him I understand his reluctance to go to war, but I am thinking of the ultimate safety of the realm. I know some councillors will be obstinate and pig-headed but I know, too, that he is a man of honour and I really need his support at this crucial time. He is one of the few men in my council who do, truly, understand. I desperately need his assistance in this matter, and I do hope he will not let me down. I depend on him so much in these important affairs. He gives me the sort of look that says I know what you are doing but I can also see he is flattered. And likes it too. He promises me full support even though he has his reservations. I thank him profusely.

And so it goes on. They troop in, one by one, and listen to me respectfully. I try to probe each one for the strengths and weaknesses I know they have. I appeal desperately to their loyalty. I tell each one how much I depend on him specifically. I finally have the support of all my councillors except one. I have left Francis Englefield until last.

"I suppose you think you are very clever," Francis suggests, smiling widely.

"Not at all," I reply indignantly. "If the queen of England cannot depend on the loyalty and support of all her councillors, what can she depend on?"

He grins again. "Well, you've won," he concedes. "They will pass it through now automatically."

"So," I ask demurely, "may I depend on your support too, Sir Francis?"

"I can hardly refuse now, can I?"

"Well, thank you, Francis. I knew I could depend on your loyalty. As always."

He shakes his head negatively and actually takes a seat beside me without being invited. He says he hopes I am fully aware of what I have done. The costs involved with a force of men in a war against France will be prohibitive and the coffers will barely support it. Lives will be lost. But the king will be delighted and much indebted to his English queen. Philip may not have much influence over English government affairs, but he knows which strings to pull to make his queen dance to a tune.

"Have a care, Francis," I warn. "Do not go too far."

"It is time I returned," he says, not heeding my words. "to my carefully prepared colleagues."

"Give them my love," I reply brightly.

It takes only 40 minutes for Philip to appear suddenly in my privy chamber. I dispatch Anne and Jane together with Margaret and Magdalen who have been in with me since Francis departed. Philip has a broad smile on his face, and he immediately plants a kiss on my lips before either of us can say a word.

"Well done, Mary," he tells me. "You have excelled yourself, is it not so?"

"Well, Sir," I respond, "I must indeed have done something noteworthy if it can prise you away from your Spanish diplomats and attendants."

"We will celebrate" he announces, ignoring my comments.

I suggest some of the finest sweet French wine, but he is more inclined to drink strong ale. I call for both and we are soon clinking drinking vessels.

"To England and Spain," Philip proposes, raising his tankard. "And death to the French."

On Easter Sunday, April 18th, one Thomas Stafford sails to the Yorkshire coast from Dieppe. He sails with two ships, both loaded with uncouth mercenaries made up of Frenchmen and traitorous Scots and Englishmen and invades this country. Dressed as peasants in rough attire, the men stroll purposefully through Scarborough, on market day, easily overpower the 12-man garrison at Scarborough Castle and take possession of the building. This Stafford, being an ignorant and uncivilised individual, issues a proclamation claiming that Philip is surrendering the chief strongholds of England to the Spaniards, prior to his coronation. Stafford is inciting yet another revolt, promising to return the crown of England to the true, English blood of our own natural country. He also, for good measure, declares himself the Duke of Buckingham and protector of the realm.

This creature wrote to me a year or more ago asking to be reinstated as Duke of Buckingham. He has no claim on the title and was duly informed of the fact. Now he appears again, ready to vex me further with his insane plans. He proclaims that I have lined up 12 of the best castles in England and plan to hand them to my husband who, in turn, will fill them with thousands of Spaniards. Worst of all, the man is a nephew of Reginald Pole.

"He has followed me around Europe on more than one occasion," the archbishop says.

"Does he suffer from madness?" I enquire.

"I'm inclined to think so," Pole answers, laughing. "Yes."

We are indebted to Doctor Nicholas Wotton, our ambassador in France, who informs us of Stafford's plan before it is completed. How he obtained his information, we know not but suffice to say it addressed the safety of our citizens. It does not say much for the French king and his people that they should orchestrate this treachery and, it would seem, supply ships and men. In the meantime Stafford is enclosed in Scarborough Castle, chivvying his band of brigands, screaming that I am an unfit queen and waiting for hundreds of thousands of Englishmen to join him and start the rebellion to overthrow us. It will not happen.

"Understand, Majesty, I always sent him on his way," Pole adds. "Told him to return to England and behave himself."

"What manner of man is he?"

"An exceedingly sick one," Pole tells me. "Of course, in my capacity as God's servant on earth, I should speak kindly of all men, but young Stafford makes it difficult indeed."

Stafford issues a proclamation, declaring himself Lord Protector and governor of this realm. He invites the populace to withdraw their allegiance to the king and queen. It takes but a short time for Henry Neville, the Earl of Westmorland, to recruit local militia and storm Scarborough Castle. He easily overpowers the rebels and takes Stafford and the rest of them prisoners.

"He is the grandson of the old Duke of Buckingham," I muse. "Which only makes it even worse, of course."

"A disgrace to his family's good name," Pole says.

Stafford is tried and convicted of treason and goes to the scaffold on Tower Green. He is beheaded. And I am left wondering why I went to so much time and trouble to persuade my councillors to back my request for war with France when Stafford made it easy. His treachery, aided and most likely financed by the king of France, makes war now inevitable.

"Did he really think he could just call for another rebellion and hundreds of thousands of men would just roll up at Scarborough?" Francis Englefield asks me.

"We are at a loss to answer that question, Francis," I tell him, smiling broadly.

"The danger, it seems," Francis continues, "is not just from bright, well-educated commanders but lunatics as well."

War with France is now inevitable.

. . .

Summer 1557

If I thought Philip was giving me less time than he should before, it was nothing compared with the past few weeks. Since war was agreed and my councillors were suddenly in favour, he has all but disappeared. I send a diplomat to France to advise them that we are declaring war. The king of France is caught off guard, it seems. According to my emissary he questioned my intent in considerable detail and repetitiveness. Finally, it appears, the message sank in and was not dismissed as a bad joke.

Philip is engaged all day and most of the night in war conferences. He receives new Spanish commanders and others almost daily. I wait for him at supper, but he rarely comes. I wait in bed at night but often fall asleep before he arrives. Mostly though, he sleeps in his own privy bedchamber.

"I must have a few hours' peace," he complains, joining me at nightfall.

"You should," I advise. "I have almost forgotten what you look like."

He smiles knowingly and bids me not to exaggerate. If I knew the volume of work, he has ploughed through in the last few days I would be more understanding. The sheer volume of arrangements to be made, commanders to be appointed and troops to be recruited is enormous. I tell him I do sympathise, but I thought I had a husband and now I am not so sure.

"It will begin to slow down now," he continues, "but I urge patience from you, Mary."

"Please forgive my unreasonable demands," I say, tongue in cheek.

"Not least of my problems is your English commander in chief," he complains. "He demands guns, ammunition, carts and waggons to be ready in France and more. Where am I to find carts and transport in a country we are at war with?"

THE TITIAN PORTRAIT

"Do we retire to bed now?" I ask.

He frowns. "I will join you for a brief hour," he tells me, "but I must then retire to my bedchamber."

I have long since learned not to argue as it does me no good. He is full of reasons why he cannot calm down completely and sleep and would only keep me awake. All night long. He cannot subject his English rose to such treatment. I shrug and settle gracefully for an hour of passion.

He has decided on Saint Quentin for his decisive battle. It is a strategic location and will aid their major thrust for victory. He is confident he will be victorious. At dinner he eats beef, mutton and wild boar with relish, but I am struggling with a small platter of pheasant and various small birds. All are tender and delicious, but I am sore at heart. I know not why except my usual worry that he will leave me, and I will lose him. At least I have him with me for once and I tell him so and confess my concerns.

"I shall not be fighting myself," he assures me. "I will be co-ordinating and controlling from some distance away."

"That's a relief, then," I tell him.

Before we finish our marzipan and jellies, he asks if I can guarantee at least 8,000 troops.

"It's a tall order," I muse, "but I will instruct the exchequer in the morning."

I feel much satisfaction and relief that I have strengthened our armies and struggled, successfully, to see that we have sufficient monies available for war. He is known throughout Christendom as Philip the prudent, but I feel I deserve the title more than he does. I ask the one question I do not want to ask and have been avoiding this past month.

"When do you leave for Spain, Philip?"

"Very soon now. I must go, is it not so?"

"But you will return soon?"

"As soon as I can," he replies starkly. "You must understand, my flower, that I cannot give you any definite dates."

He tells me of the problems of war, his commitment, his duty to other territories such as Naples, the Low Countries, Rome, too. I have heard it all a thousand times before and all I care about is to have him here. By my side. There is a cold chill in my heart now that will only get colder still.

QUEEN MARY'S PRIVATE JOURNAL

~~~

GREENWICH AND WHITEHALL,
SUMMER 1557

CAN I DARE TO HOPE? THE PAIN AND MISERY OF MY FAILED pregnancy two years ago would be completely erased if I were now pregnant. I run my hands over my swollen belly and swear that it has grown considerably bigger in the past 24 hours. I've had a long time to come to this realisation but always held back because of what happened last time. This time, there must be no mistakes, no errors. When I waved Philip off on his ship at Greenwich, I was desolate and tearful, but this might bring him back to me in good time.

"You are considerably swollen there," Dr Owen states, prodding my belly gently as I lay back on my bed.

"But is it pregnancy?"

"We can't be absolutely sure," Owen states, annoyingly. "How long since you last menstruated?"

"Six months."

"Six months? Why haven't you called me in before, Majesty?"

I remind him that he examined me thoroughly in May last and, in any case, I was reluctant to say anything for fear that history was repeating itself. Yes, he says, but six whole months? Then, he wants to know if I have any pain there. I tell him I do not but, in truth, there is a little nagging pain. He does not need to know at this stage. What I need is an opinion.

"Am I pregnant, Doctor Owen?"

"I think we can say a cautious yes," he tells me. "I must emphasize that I can't be certain, though."

Philip departed to his war with 7,000 soldiers. He wanted eight but was lucky to get what he did. Parliament argued fiercely as usual, but eventually agreed to 7,000. I miss him dreadfully, of course, but he does write to me regularly. He was only with me for a breathless five months but if his frequent visits to my bedchamber have done their job then I am content. This will bring him back to me much sooner, perhaps.

I could wish his writing to me was less about the difficulties of transporting men to the battleground and the number of casualties each day and more about missing his wife. I tell him I miss him over and over but get nothing of a tender nature in response. Now is not the time to think about such things or dwell on them, though. I do not tell my ladies, not yet, only Jane Dormer.

"Second time lucky, I'm hoping," I tell her.

Jane looks stricken.

"What is it, Jane, what's wrong?"

"I worry, Mary," she tells me, eyes wide with apprehension.

"Don't worry, I'm fine," I assure her. "This time it is the real thing. I feel it in my bones."

Jane is the one, of all my ladies, that I trust and depend on for good advice. She is my female Francis Englefield. If I could have only one lady in waiting, it would have to be her. She may not be a duchess or a marchioness. Well not yet, anyway, but she is my friend and my companion. I value her good intentions.

THE TITIAN PORTRAIT

"Do you have morning sickness?" she asks solicitously, her eyes once again wide with concerned enquiry.

"Not this time," I say quietly. "Although my appetite for fresh pears knows no bounds."

"I urge caution," she informs me. "Do not take it for granted. I do not wish to speak out of turn, but I am worried that you may be misled."

I pat her hand. I tell her that I appreciate her concern and do not blame her for speaking out and risking offending me. I have a good feeling about my swollen belly this time and feel sure that it heralds the birth of a prince. Philip visited my bedchamber on many occasions this last time, although I do not share that information with Jane. There is little doubt in my mind now. Although, I reflect, great care will be needed as my age is against me in childbirth. I am in my forties, after all.

Coming in from a brisk walk in the grounds, past the tennis courts and the tilt yard, I just miss a sudden downpour of rain. I settle down to write out my will, leaving nothing to chance. In the event of my death in childbirth, I stipulate that I wish my husband Philip to act as regent for our child until he is old enough to rule alone. That is a precaution that needs to be addressed. I sign it in the presence of my lawyer and a witness. Jane is once again most pale of face and subdued, but she witnesses my signature in silence.

"You will be fine, Mary," she assures me after the lawyer departs. "You are strong and robust."

"I don't feel strong or robust," I complain, "but every sinew in my body will be stretched to ensure a safe birth."

Philip writes to me from the battlefield. It is a horrible letter. Our English and Spanish forces have beaten the French and the bloody battle is won. We lost 1,000 men, but our enemy has lost 3,000 and three times that number taken prisoner. Including the commander-in-chief of the French armies. Philip informs me that he visited the scene of the battle a day after it ended and was appalled at the carnage he witnessed. A great field lay before him splattered with twisted, blood-stained bodies, some with limbs ripped off. Blood, slime and flesh lay everywhere. Philip tells me that he stood there, unable to move, tears forming in his eyes. He surveyed the terrible scene and vowed there and then that he would never take up arms again or fight with his men in any war. Poor Philip. I wish he would leave now and come home to me.

"My poor boy," I say. "He is extremely sensitive, but few realise his strengths and weaknesses."

"And a strong, resolute leader of people," Francis replies. "Our combined forces have done very well."

"Indeed, they have," I agree. "'It is a fine tonic for me in my present condition."

"Yes," he says. "And perhaps you should rest more now that you need to save your own strength."

If only I could. I must ensure that my new legislation to increase taxes is passed through parliament. I will also chivvy my people who are pursuing new trade routes to Russia and other parts that would improve our revenue. This bloody war must be paid for, but it will take some time, I am thinking.

In my privy chamber the ladies are solicitous for my comfort and welfare. Gertrude tells me I must take a certain amount of rest every day. Eleanor and Magdalen bring me extra cushions and soft, colourful fabrics to enhance my gown. Margaret knits soft woollen baby clothes. And I sit here with a smile on my face and eat the ripe pears that Jane has sent for.

I do not sleep well. Since Philip left from Dover, I am restless at night, tossing and churning, unable to get off to sleep. When I do finally drift off it is only to see the ghosts in my dreams. My father is always there, Henry, as he was and as I remember him as a small girl. So fine a man, upright and well-proportioned, handsome too. In the dreams, though, he is always just out of reach and, when I try to step forward, to approach him and speak with him, my feet become clay and I can't move. I cannot move either when I see archbishop Cranmer, as he was but now surrounded by fire, petals of flame bursting out of him and lighting up the air.

Sometimes my dreams are milder and easier to accommodate. Henry leads a fine white horse and I remember the animal from my youth. He was my horse exclusively and none but I could ride him. In my dream, though, it is Elizabeth that sits on the horse and my father looks proudly at her. I try to move forward and reach my horse, but I cannot do so. My legs are set in stone.

Worst of all is a recurring dream of my cousin Jane Grey. She walks towards me in bloodstained smock, and she is holding her head out to me, the eyes staring horribly. "Look what you have done," she says, and I always scream loudly at that point and wake up perspiring profusely and deeply troubled. On these bad nights, my Mistress of the Robes, Susan Clarencieux, comes rushing in to comfort me.

"Shush, shush, shush, be still, Majesty, be still," Susan says clasping me to her bosom. "It is just a bad dream."

"It was so real," I whisper, shaking all over. "All that blood."

Susan is worldly-wise and patient. It is why she is retained as Mistress of the Robes. She soothes me gently, as a troubled child would be comforted by his mother. She dabs my forehead with linen doused in lavender oil and makes my cushions more comfortable. The ghosts of bad people come out to haunt us in dreams, she tells me, but they are but shadows and cannot harm us. When she is finished ministering to me, I find I have forgotten the ghosts and slip back easily into peaceful slumber.

Since discovering my condition, I tend to stay in quiet, darkened chambers in solitude. My ladies-in-waiting I do not wish to see or converse with. One by one, I summon them to my privy chamber or wherever I have chosen to remain for maximum solitude. Rumour has reached my ears that, while Philip was here, a strange Spanish woman, very tall, dark-skinned and with black hair, was seen around our palaces. I question all my ladies in turn, but nobody knows or claims to have seen this creature. Not even any of the servants will admit to having seen her. It makes me extremely uncomfortable but there is little I can do. Perhaps Jane Dormer can throw some light on the subject.

"I believe the king did have a Spanish servant matching that description," Jane tells me.

"And he brought her over from Spain?" I enquire. "I would have thought there were more than enough Spanish servants here already."

"The story goes," Jane continues, grinning, "that she was extremely proficient at trimming his fingernails."

I shake my head in disbelief but there is nothing I can do about it now. This creature went when Philip went so, presumably, she follows him to battlefields and other places brandishing her special nail clippers. I sincerely hope she did not offer any other service to him. Thinking about Philip just now and his speedy departure when we declared war on France is hurting me. He is gone again and I do not have any idea when he will return. And with his letters all about the war and its aftermath, what is the future for him and me? My miserable state must be difficult for Jane. Sadly, I am too full of my own troubles to care.

"How are you feeling now?" Jane asks, large eyes widening again.

"The baby does not kick," I tell her, "but my belly continues to expand."

She thinks I can only rest most of the time and try not to let recent events upset me. I do not tell her that headaches have commenced again and a little pain in my groin and legs. All associated with the forthcoming birth, no doubt, but I do not want her fussing, well-intentioned though she surely be. What is of much more worry is that I asked Archbishop Pole to write to Philip and advise him that I was with child. This, he assures me, he did in great haste, but I have received no response whatsoever from Philip. It is too cruel. The war consumes most of his time, but I am his wife and soon to be the mother of his child.

"Why are men so heartless and thoughtless, Jane?" I ask her miserably.

"They simply do not think clearly," she answers. "We and they consider different things important."

I go to my privy bedchamber and have the heavy drapes drawn to shut out the daylight. It is raining heavily again and the slashing of raindrops on the window outside is intrusive. I hope the storm will pass quickly. I instruct the servants to wait outside my chamber in case I require anything. Susan, too, is on hand in case of need. I lie back on the bed and clutch my prayer book in my hand. I say a prayer to God to deliver my baby safely as tears well up and run unchecked down my cheeks. The slashing rain reduces to a light shower. The harvests will be bad this year, again, and many people will starve. The economy of the realm will need to be bolstered up, but I am too tired, too sick and too worried to think about it now. I lay both hands on my extended belly and gently, oh-so-gently, rub and caress the tender flesh.

SIR FRANCIS ENGLEFIELD'S DIARY

~

ST JAMES'S PALACE AND HATFIELD
PALACE, HERTFORDSHIRE, SUMMER 1557

I RISE EXTREMELY EARLY AND WRITE A LETTER TO THE KING. I appraise him of the queen's concern and ask when he is planning to return to these shores. I tell him he is much missed by all at court. I am not happy about his conduct. It is not my place to question a king's activities, so I keep my most private thoughts out of the letter. I do feel that he has treated the queen badly by not returning as soon as he heard about the pregnancy. Not that many people at court really believe it is a genuine pregnancy. Maybe Philip shares that view, although he did write to the privy council recently saying he was delighted that the queen was with child. Added to all this, there are rumours still flying around court that he had a Spanish woman here on his last visit and was seen scurrying along to her bedchamber at all hours of the day and night.

I'm still comparatively early as I approach the queen's privy chamber, where I am bid to report.

As I reach the doorway, I am waylaid by Susan Clarencieux and Jane Dormer, the queen's most trusted ladies. They look stern and troubled.

"She is not here," Susan tells me.

"She is in her privy bedchamber," Jane adds politely.

"Is she unwell?" I ask.

The women trip over each other in attempting to voice their concerns. Jane tells me the queen has been in her bedchamber for five days, barely moving out at all and having food brought to her. The heavy drapes are drawn night and day and all she does is lie there, gently massaging her belly and rarely talking.

"May I see her?" I enquire.

"Oh yes," Susan assures me. "She requires me to bring you along and, as Mistress of the Robes, remain present as you talk."

"Very well," I respond quietly.

Jane, her big eyes widening, tells me she is extremely worried. The queen seems to be losing interest in life and fading away. She implores me to persuade her that she is much missed and try to get her to leave the bedchamber. Susan implores me to do whatever she asks without question. And to talk her out of staying in her bed.

"Well, I'll do whatever I can," I tell them.

"One other thing," Jane suggests, "try to get her to join her ladies. They will talk to her and flatter her and, I hope, cheer her up."

"Do not worry too much, ladies," I tell them. "The queen is tough and resilient. She will come though her bad patch."

"I hope you are right, Sir Francis," Jane says gloomily. "I have never, ever before, seen her quite like this."

"God go with you, Sir Francis," Susan adds.

We walk down the gallery, all three of us, and Jane departs before we reach the bedchamber. As we enter, I am aware that the room is musty and very dark. One solitary tallow candle burns. I ask for more candles as we settle down on stools near the bed. Mary's face is grey and drawn. She appears wrinkled, more so than I have noticed before. She is sitting up in bed now, but I notice her hands caressing her tummy under the coverlets. Her hair is wispy but has been brushed, I note, possibly by Susan earlier.

"You find me in a sorry state, Francis," she murmurs. "I much regret that."

"Be of good cheer, Majesty," I reply. "It might never happen."

She lets out a little rippling laugh, but it causes her to cough briefly. "I fear it already has," she offers.

"Can I do anything for you?" I ask quietly.

"Yes," she replies, quite eagerly. "Visit the Lady Elizabeth for me."

"Today?"

"Yes please, it's a short ride to Hatfield. I brook no delay."

It is far enough even with a good, young, healthy horse but I say nothing of that.

Her voice is a little strained and she is somewhat breathless, but she makes it clear that she wishes me to convey her best wishes to her half-sister and tell her that all is well and she need have no concerns whatsoever.

"So why am I going?"

"Talk to her at length. Be her friend; she quite likes you; I am told. Find out what she has been doing and what is on her mind. Find out, if you can, who she is with and who are her close companions and advisers."

"That will be no problem," I assure her, to gain her confidence. "Would you, Majesty, be prepared to do something for me in return?"

"If I can, Francis," she responds, frowning. Not an encouraging look.

She needs to get out of her bed, put on fresh clothing and get out into the courtyard. Take exercise and spend at least an hour with her ladies. Probably more. There is no way of putting all this politely without causing offence. So, I suggest getting out and breathing fresh air into her lungs. She shakes her head and says that she does not feel well enough. I urge her to try to leave her bed.

"I am weighed down by grief and pain, Francis," she tells me in a stark tone.

"Fresh air and limb movement is a wonderful tonic, Majesty," I offer cautiously.

"I think not," she replies. "Although I thank you for your concern, Francis."

I leave the chamber and am set upon by Susan and Jane. I admit my initial failure but tell them that I have sown the seeds in her mind and now it just needs to be reinforced. I urge them to find Dr Owen swiftly and get him to go to her. He will tell her much the same as I, I feel convinced.

"I've never seen her in such low spirits," Jane confesses, face bleak.

"It is an extremely bad moment through which she is passing," I admit. "But she will bounce back."

"I don't know, Sir Francis," Jane responds. "I'm not so sure." Susan merely shakes her head sadly.

"And ask Owen to give her a pick-me-up potion," I suggest, "when you find him."

The ride to Hatfield is fresh and exhilarating. No sun but, more importantly, no rain and little breeze. Dry and grey all around with few large carts or carriages to hinder progress. Farm labourers in white smocks are the only bright spots on the landscape on such a dull morning. I pass a goodly number of other travellers on horses and many nod to me as they pass. So many beggars are abroad. When I reach Barnet, there appear far more farm workers in the fields, trying to salvage something from what is, overall, a disastrous harvest.

The Old Palace has stood now for many years but still looks bright with those ancient, light-brown-coloured bricks gleaming. I ride through the quadrangle and two stable lads take my horse. I request a good rub down for him and then some oats.

A servant takes me to Elizabeth's privy chamber. She greets me dressed, as is her usual manner, in a plain purple gown and black kirtle. It is most ordinary but yet so perfectly fitted to her frame and made of fabrics of such high quality that she presents a most attractive figure. She wears few jewels but those she does have are most strategically placed on her person. Her bright-red hair is the first and most striking aspect of her appearance that I am aware of. She is smiling.

"You are welcome, Sir Francis," she tells me. "It is always a pleasure to see you."

"The pleasure is all mine, Lady Elizabeth," I reply.

She smiles again. "Be comfortable, Sir," she implores me, leading me to her unseasonable fireplace where the fire burns brightly. "Be seated and rest well after your journey."

"We meet in far happier circumstances than last time," I say, stretching my legs swiftly and then pulling them back decorously.

"We do," she acknowledges imperiously. "Although you should not think that outward appearances represent my full and unencumbered freedom."

"No?"

"Not really. I know full well there are servants around me who report to attendants who in turn send messages to the queen." She smiles ironically. "I know they are there, but I do not know who they are."

"An unusual situation," I reply, frowning as I am puzzled by her remarks.

"It is rather, isn't it?" she agrees. "But my good half-sister does not trust me as far as she could throw me. Which, of course, isn't too far."

She pauses to ring a bell and instruct the scurrying servant to bring wine, sugared almonds and marzipan balls. She trusts that I could do with a refreshing taste of wine after my journey and a sweetmeat or two. I tell her it is good to see her

THE TITIAN PORTRAIT

in fine fettle and cheerful. Not like the previous occasions when we met.

"Sadly, I do not completely rule out the possibility of assassination," she states coolly. "It is always there, around me, the possibility."

"I am convinced you need have no worries on that score," I tell her, with sincerity.

Her smile returns yet again and lights up her face, which has a healthy glow. I am conscious of her bright eyes, so intense and her prominent, well-chiselled nose, a feature of her face I am more aware of seeing in such different circumstances to the past.

"I am unable to share your well-intentioned optimism," she informs me. "Why, for example are you here today, Sir Francis? Not that we are not pleased to see you."

"The queen wished me to convey her good wishes to you and assure you that all is well," I answer. "There will be no further problems."

Elizabeth laughs. "She wanted you to come here and find out everything about my everyday activities," she states flatly. "Who advises me, who are my closest friends."

I say that that is untrue. It is merely a goodwill mission on my part. I feel a little guilty but remember that my loyalty is to the queen and only her. The queen would like to know how she is faring and if she is content but that is all. Elizabeth nods and tells me I am a reliable and faithful messenger. She admires that in a man. Her expression becomes serious.

"You may tell my dear sister," she begins, "that I would be far more content if I could have my most faithful servant Kat Ashley returned to my household. Mary forbids her return to my service."

"She was found with seditious books in her possession," I tell her quietly.

"Mary and I see sedition differently," she replies. "But no

matter. What of the queen, my good half-sister? How is she faring, Sir Francis?"

"Sadly, not well," I answer truthfully. "She stays in her bedchamber for hours and appears to have lost her ability to enjoy life. She misses the king sorely and I fear he will not return to her."

"Ah, that is sad," she replies. "And, with Philip away, no chance of a new pregnancy."

As I debate in my mind whether to mention the new pregnancy, Elizabeth tells me it is time for dinner, and we may go to the banqueting hall now. She asks me if I am happy with fish as it is that day here. There is a fine dish of boiled salmon to start us off with rosemary and thyme and seasoned with saffron. A large pot of ale has been included in the cooking and it is quite delicious. Next up is a boiled porpoise with almond milk and that, too, is extremely tasty. I find I have quite an appetite and eat plenty, as bidden to do. I particularly enjoy crayfish cooked with herbs and fine spices. And some delicate but tart-tasting crab. I have plenty of strong ale to wash it all down, but I notice that Elizabeth eats quite delicately, taking portions of everything on offer but only extremely small amounts.

"What you asked earlier," I begin, tentatively, "with regard to the queen's pregnancy. A short time ago she announced that she was pregnant."

"Ah, now I must confess that such a rumour had reached our ears."

"But I wouldn't attach much credence to it," I continue. "Most people at court are of opinion that it is just another ghost pregnancy."

"Ah. Poor Mary. While I do not pretend to feel much sympathy for her current condition, I must admit she has been sorely tried of late. Does her health improve slowly or is she still sinking?"

"She is holding on," I say, giving little more away. "But

who do you depend on most for advice in these difficult times Lady Elizabeth?"

"Well, I did wonder when the probing would begin," she says and laughs out loud. "Not that I have anything to hide. William Cecil, the Lord Burghley keeps me well informed."

We end dinner with marzipan shapes of vivid colour, gingerbread and a selection of fruits and jellies. Once again, Elizabeth picks daintily at a very few sugary items and as I am at my own limit, I also pick at one or two only. Sweet spiced wine is served to conclude. She tells me of two other advisors that keep her informed, as she puts it, but insists that it is only to keep her up to date with events. At court and in the country generally.

Elizabeth assures me that there are no intrigues going on that she has heard of and that, of course, if there were, she would distance herself from them immediately. She lives a quiet life now and is happy and content to do so. She is, she insists, biding her time.

"Waiting for what?" I enquire boldly.

"To see which way the wind blows," she replies honestly. "After all, if Mary should sink further and not recover, I should be queen of England."

"Yes, of course," I respond, "you would, wouldn't you?"

A day that has been dull and grey all through, turns suddenly in the late afternoon. Rain begins and gradually increases until it is a thunderous downpour. I look over to the window and the rattling rain thrashing against it with dismay.

"It looks as though I'm going to get a soaking returning to London," I murmur.

"You can't ride back in this," Elizabeth says. "You'd catch your death of cold."

I shake my head, but she tells me I must stay here, in

Hatfield. She will provide a fine chamber for my comfort and I can set off early tomorrow morning, after a hearty breakfast.

"It's extremely kind of you," I tell her.

"Nonsense," she replies. "It will give you time to see that I have no assorted traitors assembled in dark chambers, plotting the queen's downfall."

I shake my head and observe that I never suspected anything of the sort but realise, of course that she is having fun at my expense. It is the twinkle in her eye that gives her away, something I have often observed in Catherine, at home, when she is in frivolous mood. Catherine says I lack humour but then I think there are some things that are just not funny and must remain so.

"Are you familiar with Hatfield Palace, Sir Francis?" she asks.

"Not really," I respond. "I came here once many years ago."

"Let me show you around," she offers and commences a walk round the old palace that I find most absorbing. I look at the great hall and the fine, high-ceilinged reception rooms as well as a walk down to the main banqueting hall. In such a fine old palace, many years old but very much fitted out for life today, it is no surprise Elizabeth is content. As we walk around, she gives me some history of the place.

"Let us go and have supper now," she suggests as our tour around ends.

I nod contentedly.

"The heavy rain will have subsided by tomorrow morning," she reasons. "Then you can be on your way." The twinkle returns to Elizabeth's eye. "I wonder what Mary will make of your spending the night with me, so to speak?"

QUEEN MARY'S JOURNAL

HAMPTON COURT, AUTUMN 1557

I DO BELIEVE THE MOVE TO HAMPTON COURT HAS DONE ME SOME good. Little enough, perhaps, in real terms as my head aches, the leg pains continue, and the bad dreams are increasing in severity. But now I am over the sense of shock, pain and humility I endured at the loss of my baby here some time ago. If I could look forward to the safe birth of my present baby now, it would be a real blessing. I do have some pain in my belly, though, and Dr Owen is concerned, saying that should not be so. At least I can rise every morning now and have done since Francis and the doctor advised me so strongly to do so, in the summer.

My ladies work so hard to cheer me up that I feel indebted to them for their warm loyalty. Susan brings me a new sweet French wine that has a tangy, spicy flavour in spite of its overriding sweetness that is most agreeable. Magdalen has brought me some new bright-red marzipan balls that are sweet and delicious. I know they are trying to find delicacies to feed to me because they are alarmed at my loss of appetite. I have not eaten well at dinner or supper for many months now and Owen insists that I need to eat more to feed the baby. My moods change from day to day. Some mornings I am as bright and sprightly as I was when Philip was here beside me. At others I am as low as the ground and feel unable to pull myself out of bed each morning. I make a concentrated effort to do so, though.

"Some more sweet marzipan, Majesty?" Magdalen asks, smiling sweetly. I take some and eat it, more to please her and the others looking on. Susan and Jane are particularly distressed, as I see from their expressions. Eleanor calls a servant to refill my wine crystal.

"Will I walk with you in the grounds, Majesty?" Magdalen asks. "'Tis a fine autumn morning."

"No thank you, Magdalen," I respond. "My belly is heavy today."

"It would do you much good," Magdalen continues, her youthful enthusiasm spilling over.

Eleanor, Susan and Jane turn on her with fierce expressions. Jane asks her not to harass me. I know when I am ready to take exercise without her intervention. They all seem over hard on her. She is incredibly young and means well. I ask them gently not to scold her; she is thinking only of my welfare. As are they all.

I tell them I must go to the confinement bed chamber and check that all is in readiness for my lying in. I ask Jane to accompany me, and she rises up, a concerned expression clouding her pretty face. It is dark indeed in the chamber, the heavy drapes drawn at the window to prevent even a glimpse of daylight. There is a musty smell to in the room and only three scented candles are alight to alleviate the gloom.

"I should perhaps move in here today," I suggest speculatively.

"Not yet," Jane replies. "It is too soon."

I look at her and see the familiar eyes widening. She is concerned for me. I am thinking that if I moved in here now, I would be quiet, peaceful and not have to get out of bed again until the babe was born. "Shall we see what Dr Owen thinks?" I ask.

"Yes, good idea, Mary," she agrees, perking up at my words.

"I will receive him in my privy bed chamber," I tell her. "He can examine me there."

I walk slowly to my bedchamber and prepare myself for examination. When Owen arrives, he has the midwife with him. I lie back on the bed and they examine me. First the midwife, who prods my belly with her stubby fingers and causes me some pain. I cry out and she apologises. Dr Owen is more careful, gentle, probing gently into the flesh and nodding from time to time, a frown of concentration on his face.

He goes over to the midwife and I hear them in subdued, whispered conversation for what seems a long time. Finally, she leaves, and Owen approaches my bed.

"Should I go into isolation now?" I ask. "It is early, I know, but I am weary and feel a longer rest would do me much good."

"Your Grace," he begins portentously. "I much regret that I must inform you that you are not pregnant."

"Don't be ridiculous," I say, in panic. "Of course, I'm pregnant."

He shakes his head sadly. He reminds me that he brought in two other doctors last week for second opinions and they were both in agreement. So is the midwife. He has now reluctantly reached a final decision and can state, categorically, that there is no baby in my belly.

"Surely not?" I almost whimper. "You must be mistaken."

"Regrettably not. Your stomach is getting smaller rather than larger, as I have just ascertained. I am extremely sorry."

My hands move immediately to my distended belly and I run my hands over the surface, I prod gently in the middle and experience a slight, dull pain.

"It is now my belief," he continues, "that you have a slight infection in your stomach and a temporary blockage that causes it to swell up and then deflate. I will mix up a strong potion to help restore your stomach size to normal."

It is God's punishment that I must face. I have failed to restore my realm completely back to the Catholic church and there are still heretics out there, even though more than 200 have burned.

I lie back in my darkened bedchamber for some time after Owen departs and cannot bear seeing anybody. I will not face councillors or my ladies or anybody else in my present humiliated state. I need two weeks at least of self-imposed isolation in my privy chamber. Only one exception will I make; Jane Dormer will be summoned as my one and only companion.

I sit in my darkened privy chamber with all the curtains drawn. I have not retreated like this for more than a week now, but a sudden flurry of depression came over me unexpectedly. Silly, really, as I was just getting back to something like normal routine after a few weeks of self-imposed isolation. I even thought to go and spend time with my ladies. But I do go up and down frequently, bright and perky one minute, deep in a state of utter desolation the next. Not surprising, I imagine, given what I have gone through in the last year.

Now I am seeking to recover a sense of balance and equilibrium as I see the familiar and mostly welcome face of Jane Dormer peering round the door.

"May I come in?"

I beckon her in and agree to her lighting some candles. The scent wafts up suddenly to provide pleasant odours in the recently stuffy chamber. Jane tells me she came to see if she could get me anything or maybe I would like to return to the ladies with her or even go for a short walk in the grounds outside.

"No to all suggestions," I respond. "But I thank you for your concern."

"You should come out of the darkness, Mary," she says tentatively. "It would aid your recovery."

"The darkness encloses me," I tell her. "It is part of my existence now."

"You are strong," she declares in a vibrant voice. "You will come through."

I know she means well so I cannot be angry with her. "Come with me, Jane," I invite. I take her along the long terrace and into my private chamber where I keep my most cherished possessions. Inside I call a servant to light candles and I sit in my high-backed chair and ask Jane to sit with me. The portrait always looks subdued in colour and content at night, but it is still a vibrant work. The colours are so natural-looking, bright. I look up at the portrait and take in the oh-so-familiar picture.

"He will never return to me now," I say, sadly.

"Oh, in time, surely?" she blurts out, not knowing really how to respond but, I suspect, doing so impulsively.

"No," I insist positively. "If there had been a baby, an heir, but…"

We sit in complete silence. My eyes wander away from the portrait and towards the blue wisps of smoke curling up slowly from the candles. Shadows dance unnervingly on the walls. I breathe deeply.

"You know, Jane," I begin slowly, quietly, "I fell in love with his portrait, this painting. I never really had the man's love. It has taken me a long, long time to realise it. He wanted an alliance between our countries. I wanted his love."

She makes no reply but, in the charged silence, she puts her hand over mine and squeezes it gently. There are no more words to say, and I think Jane has understood that. I feel the warmth of her hand and find it comforting. Far more so than if she had made another protest suggesting Philip would eventually return. And, in any event, I am too busy controlling my deep emotion and making sure I do not start to cry. I have shed enough tears in the past 24 hours to last a lifetime. I am all dried out. We sit there for a long time and not another word is spoken.

After reaching down into what felt like the depths of despair, I feel cleansed. I stayed alone for three more days keeping everybody from me, even dear Jane. Today I feel bright and lively, with a sense that all is not evil in this world we inhabit. Because I have spent so much time alone, in the dark, it is time now to pay due heed to my appearance. The ladies rally, to a woman and all go out of their way to help.

"It is not as though I go on a state visit, even," I protest but then laugh.

"You wear clothes well," Eleanor tells me. "Why not take advantage?"

Central to all this fuss and performance is my new purple satin gown. It is laced with velvet and has cloth of gold inlays. Susan is smoothing down the shoulders as Magdalen, on her knees, attends to the hem. When they have smoothed out all the wrinkles between them, I must say that I feel good. Then I take a seat and allow Susan to finish off the effect by brushing out my hair. It has been a long time since I last took any trouble over the way I look, although I have to admit that I enjoy it.

Finally, I am persuaded to apply a little lead-based cream to my face or, rather, have it applied by young Magdalen. Jane supervises the operation carefully.

"Not too much of that stuff, Magdalen," I tell her.

"It suits your complexion, Majesty."

"It clogs up the pores, too," I complain. "And makes it difficult to move my face muscles."

We all laugh but I do like what I see when I see the reflection. I feel a good five years younger and, best of all, I look it.

The letter I receive today confirms everything I said to Jane a short time ago as we gazed at the portrait. Philip writes to warn us of an impending attack on Calais by the French. It is our last outpost in France and must be defended vigorously. That said, I am saddened but not really surprised to find that there is nothing in the letter of an affectionate nature towards me. It is purely an informative document. I must call together the privy council and take urgent action. First, though, I will seek Francis's advice.

"This is serious," I say. "We should send reinforcements immediately."

"Yes, agreed," he responds, "but extremely difficult."

"How so?"

The problem, Francis advises, is that it will be difficult, if not impossible, to recruit enough men. The ravages of the influenza epidemic sweeping the country now has caused thousands of deaths. Many, many more are incapacitated by the disease.

"The Duke of Rutland would be our best choice as commander," he advises.

"I'm inclined to agree."

"We must act quickly, though," he continues. "If we are to hold Calais."

"All right, Francis," I agree. "I will call an immediate emergency meeting of the privy council. Time is of the essence."

SIR FRANCIS ENGLEFIELD'S DIARY

ST JAMES'S PALACE, JANUARY 1558

IT IS THE WORST POSSIBLE NEWS. THE EARL OF RUTLAND WAS equipped with as many troops as he could muster and set sail for Calais at the beginning of this month. Unfortunately, the French commander, the Duke of Guise, had moved with lightning speed to move thousands of men across frozen marshland and seize the harbour from the seaward side. They took the harbour entrance and the fort and occupied it. The French bombarded the town with such force and fury that our forces were unable to enter. After a fierce and bloody battle our troops were ordered to surrender, and we lost our last European colony.

"I hear they had 30,000 men," William Paulet says.

"Yes, we had no chance against such numbers," Nicholas Heath adds. "And no chance of raising more than 3,000 with this influenza epidemic."

I look around at the grim faces before me and share their misery. Calais has been an English colony since King Edward captured it way back in 1346. Now it is ours no more. I cannot agree with the Archbishop of York's estimate of our having sent only 3,000 troops. My information is that they recruited men who could barely stand, so weak were they recovering from influenza. So far more than 3,000 went. And those poor wretches keen to take the work with so little available after a third poor harvest in a row. We could never have put out 10,000, though, never mind 30,000.

"Some of our men were not fully fit," William Paget adds.

"There is little point in trotting out excuses," Heath retorts angrily. "It is lost and done with and we must face that unpalatable truth."

"Edward will be turning in his grave," Paget adds.

There is a silence in the chamber until Paulet pipes up with a question and looks directly at me: "Who will tell the queen?" he wonders.

They all look towards me and somebody murmurs: "Fucking French."

"Yes, all right," I concede. "I will do the job nobody wants."

"Good man," Heath offers and a chorus of "hear hears" is heard.

I go to my office first. It is not my desire to put off the duty. Rather is it that I do not quite know how to put it. The queen has been showing slow but steady signs of improvement lately. The glint is back in her eye when a subject dear to her heart comes up. Even so, she seeks news and progress reports from privy councillors independently. She has not been near meetings for some weeks now. At least she has resumed dressing well and is always well attired in fine, elegant gowns with plenty of jewels attached. Her face is less pinched, and she keeps her hair well brushed. This sort of news, however, is not going to help.

I meet Jane Dormer in the long gallery and find that she has already heard the news. "It might well set her right back, Sir Francis," she suggests. "Oh dear."

I ask Jane to walk down with me and she goes in to see if I will be welcome. I am. The queen is sitting by the window in a favourite spot and is gazing out at the clear blue sky and the ice-encrusted landscape outside.

"Have a seat, Francis," she offers, looking relatively cheerful. "Talk to me."

"Always a pleasure," I tell her, "but unfortunately I am the bearer of bad news."

"Is there any other kind?" she enquires.

As I have decided to take the plunge right away, I continue in that manner and give her a swift summary of events in France. I offer my opinion that our troops were considerably outnumbered on this occasion, even allowing for the large contingent of Spanish soldiers.

"That cuts deep into my heart," she replies, looking stunned. "You could not have brought worse news."

"I am aware," I admit.

"Our territory since, what, 1340?"

"Forty-six."

"And our last outpost in France."

I tell her some of the remarks by councillors and she shakes her head sadly and says never mind King Edward, her father would turn in his grave and churn up the ground under Windsor Castle if he knew. It is truly the saddest, saddest day. Then she appears to crumple before my eyes. Her shoulders sag and when I look into her face, the eyes seem suddenly dulled. This is, all things considered, the worst time for her to receive news like this. I should be on my way about my business but it occurs to me that I cannot leave the queen in this state. Especially as she is alone and has none of her ladies in attendance.

"I appear to be cursed, Francis," she complains bitterly.

I shake my head vigorously. "No, no, do not say that, Your Grace."

"What else can I think? We are not yet fully restored to the Catholic church. Heretics are still abroad denying the Pope.

Our coinage is in need of reform and I haven't even completed that yet."

"You've worked hard on it and it will go through," I assure her. "As to the full restoration, that will go through in time. And you have plenty of time, Majesty. You are only just under five years into your reign."

"Yes," she replies, looking thoughtful, "and I need to achieve a considerable amount more in the next five years."

"You've certainly brought great improvements to our militia and navy," I assure her. "Both were in a sorry state indeed under Edward."

"Keep talking, Francis," she bids me. "I need all your reassurance and I need it badly. We are at a low point indeed in our reign and I crave your indulgence, reminding me of the few things I have achieved so far."

Lady Magdalen Dacre stands at the altar looking extremely attractive in her black velvet gown, laced with crimson facings and wearing many precious stones. She has a gold mantle, and her smile is radiant. The bridegroom gives her a look which seems to say: You are looking lovely and this will be over soon, and we can take it easier. For now, enjoy every minute as you are the centre of attention. Sir Anthony Browne himself looks quite happy on his wedding day. He is 10 years older than Magdalen, but they make a handsome couple as the marriage ceremony continues.

"She will have her work cut out," the queen observes, "looking after the twins of his first marriage, Mary and Anthony."

"His first wife died in childbirth, did she not?" I ask, remembering hearing something about it.

"She did, sadly. But Anthony has a fine young bride in Magdalen."

I am pleased that the marriage ceremony is being

conducted here at St James's Palace and even more so that the queen is attending. Had it been further afield, I doubt she would have gone. This has obviously taken her out of her deep melancholy mood, at least for a time. The queen has always been close to young Magdalen, who was a Maid of Honour at her own wedding to Philip in '54. Both are very pious and spend long hours in prayer. This is indeed the tonic Mary needs in such times of trouble. She also thinks highly of Anthony, who held her train at her wedding, I seem to recall.

At the banquet in the great hall, everybody eats heartily and good French wine flows freely. The long tables accommodate Magdalen's brothers and sisters, Anthony's relatives, diverse noblemen and women, bishops and attendants. Music from lute, flute and viol fill the air with lively jigs.

Magdalen curtsies to the queen at the banquet and Mary smiles broadly, takes hold of her shoulders and kisses her forehead. Anthony bows low to the queen.

I sit at the long table allocated to councillors. So much wine is being consumed that I fear there will be many sore heads on the morrow.

"They make a fine couple," Sir William Paulet is saying, raising his goblet in salute.

"Indeed," Paget agrees, also indulging himself with fine wine.

"There was a story going round court at one time…" Paulet begins and then stops.

"Yes, go on then," Paget requests.

"No, no, it can't be true."

"Come on, William, spit it out."

Looking at them I fear that both have consumed more wine than either can reasonably handle. The baron is very red in the face indeed but, like everybody present on this happy day, all are in contented, frivolous mood. All within earshot are now looking keenly at Paulet.

"Well, I did hear that the king once took young Magdalen to his bed," Paulet says and then shrugs his shoulders.

"You shouldn't listen to malicious rumours," I suggest, frowning.

"It came from an impeccable source."

"Well, I for one don't believe a word of it," Paget says and drinks more wine.

"Think about it," Paulet continues regardless. "Young girl of what, 17 at the time? A handsome Spanish king makes a fuss of her. Is seduction so unlikely?"

"Do not let the queen hear you," I suggest. "Unless you wish to be separated from your head."

"No, I don't," Paulet replies, grinning. "I've grown quite attached to it sitting there above my shoulders."

"There are times," says Baron Paget, "when I am pleased that Philip has returned to Spain and is unlikely ever to return to these shores."

I turn my attention to the musicians. The lute, flute and viol erupt in sonorous harmony above the many assembled, restrained voices.

SIR FRANCIS ENGLEFIELD'S DIARY

ST JAMES'S PALACE, SPRING 1558

The bedchamber is rather stuffy as I open the door and walk in. A mixture of ambergris and musk is heavy in the air, blended unfortunately with the odour of the sickroom. As I move closer to the bed, the smell of rosewater is added to the mix, so strong now. The queen is sitting up in bed with many feather cushions behind her head. Her face is pale, white almost and her eyes a little sunken. Oddly enough, she does not look too unwell, and her features are composed naturally, as though she were sitting in the privy council chamber.

Susan sits a short way from the bed calmly knitting. She looks up and directly at the bed every few minutes, as though she expects the queen suddenly to leap out of bed. And do what? The queen is almost motionless; only the flicker of an eyebrow is occasionally noticeable.

"Take a seat, Francis," the queen instructs. "What news for me?"

"Very quiet, really, Majesty," I reply. "No news from France."

I ask her how she is feeling this morning and she responds by saying she feels absolutely fine. Her words are clear, giving the impression that she is just suffering from a mild

THE TITIAN PORTRAIT

malady. Susan looks up at me with a sort of sad, pleading look in her eyes. What does she expect me to do?

"I need your immediate attention to an affair of state," the queen blurts out suddenly, fixing me with one of the glares I used to find quite intimidating.

"Yes, I'm at your service," I tell her.

"Philip writes asking when his coronation will be," she continues. "He is really getting most impatient."

I look at her. I am taken by surprise, but her expression is bland. She could have just as well have asked for a sweet biscuit. I look over at Susan in sudden panic, but she just shakes her head negatively, swiftly, and drops her eyes to her wool.

"I understood you had decided not to proceed with that," I say quietly.

"Philip is agitating," she informs me. "Says he should have been crowned king last year."

I do not know how to respond to that, so I remain silent. The queen closes her eyes and appears to drift off to sleep. Susan watches her, trying to ascertain whether she really is asleep. Finally, she is satisfied.

"She is suffering with fevers," Susan whispers to me.

"At the moment?" I ask.

"Oh yes, she will wake suddenly. The fever comes and goes," she whispers, looking haunted.

"She looked almost fit and well as I came in," I suggest.

"Yes, it is difficult to gauge. Often her speech is as lucid as yours or mine."

"But not its content?"

"Yes, often it is," Susan goes on. "That is why it is so confusing."

I nod. The queen appears to be sleeping soundly, peacefully. Her breathing is smooth and ordered. I ask Susan how long she has been like this. She tells me that after two weeks of almost total silence and staying in bed complaining of pains in her head, belly and legs, she became calmer. Began talking regularly, calling for Susan herself or Jane Dormer. At first, her speech was perfectly natural, just as always. Then she began to wander and say strange things. Dr Owen told her it was a fever that would come and go.

Susan gets up and goes to the bed to wipe the queen's perspiring brow, very gently, with a rosewater-soaked handkerchief. The queen stirs and opens her eyes then closes them again. Susan blinks and returns to her stool.

"You could go," Susan suggests. "I am sure you have things to do. Jane and I take it in turns to watch over her."

"She sent word that she wanted my opinion," I reply.

Susan smiles. "It was probably the fever talking."

"I can wait," I tell her. "I have nothing pressing at this time."

All is silent in the chamber for several minutes. In the heavily perfumed air of the room everything appears to be at a standstill. Then the queen stirs, and this time wakes up, blinks, looks wide-eyed and struggles into a sitting position in the bed. Susan goes over quickly and assists her, adjusting the cushions behind her head for maximum comfort. Susan gives me a bleak glance and asks the queen if she can get her anything.

"Water."

Water is brought and Susan helps her drink.

"Wine now."

Wine is brought and the operation is repeated as before.

"We must send more troops to France," the queen says, looking directly at me.

"Yes, I'll attend to it," I tell her.

"Make sure you do," she insists. "I do not want Philip left stranded in a field in France, unable to fight."

She leans back on the cushions but appears restless, agitated. Then she starts to get out of her bed. Susan, alarmed, goes over to her swiftly and attempts to restrain her. The queen shakes her off angrily and tells her that if she wants to get up, she will get up. It was not so long ago that everybody was begging her to rise and take more exercise. I suggest gently to Susan that she allows her to get up and helps her. Susan looks at me and then turns, helps the queen out of bed and wraps her nightgown tightly around her.

The queen walks over to the window very slowly, Susan at her elbow all the way. She looks down at the road and calls me to come over.

"It is a bright summer morning," she says. "I wish I felt well enough to walk in the grounds."

"Time enough when you feel a little better," I reply.

"The thing is," she retorts, "I do feel a lot better now. No more pain in my head, or belly, or leg."

"That's good," I respond cheerfully.

"It is ridiculous, Francis," she informs me lucidly. "One minute I feel low as low, talking nonsense and the next I am perfectly fine."

"It is the fever, Majesty," I suggest. "It comes and goes. When you shake that off, you will be fine again."

She looks bright and composed now. I am relieved to see and hear her sounding like her old self. She looks down and remarks on how suddenly the leaves on a tree below have sprouted and multiplied. Two days ago, the tree was bare. The cobbles in the street below are messy with horse dung and various litter of an unpleasant nature. Straw is spread out in a heap, probably the leakage from a broken bale fallen from a cart.

Jane Dormer enters the chamber. She is dressed in a bright green robe with velvet facings. Her face is radiant, her expression reassuring. She nods to me and tells Susan that she will take over now. Susan gives her brief instructions and then leaves the room.

"How is she?" Jane whispers to me.

"Talk to me, Jane, not about me," the queen reproves her lady-in-waiting.

"There's your answer," I respond, smiling broadly.

Jane's smile is infectious. She is obviously pleased to see her friend appear so well. The queen remains gazing out of the window as we watch her carefully. Suddenly she slips and almost falls but I am able to catch her swiftly as Jane holds her hand.

"I suddenly felt a little dizzy," she announces.

"Best get back to bed, Mary," Jane suggests, frowning.

Jane and I steer her back to bed and Jane assists her into it as I call for Dr Owen. He arrives with a nurse and attends to the queen as Jane, and I wait just outside the door of the chamber. We are both grim-faced.

"She is so up and down," Jane says. "I don't know what to do for the best."

"Just be there," I tell her.

"I'll never leave her," she replies, looking set and determined.

As the doctor and nurse come out and Jane goes back in, I ask Dr Owen if I can have a quick word. He dismisses the nurse and looks at me with pursed lips, his eyes small and piercing.

"What is wrong with the queen, doctor?" I ask.

"I believe she suffers from a growth of some kind in her belly," he responds thoughtfully. "It is something that causes her stomach to swell up and then go down. Hence the phantom pregnancies."

"Is it a threat to her life?" I ask.

"Not alone, I don't think so," he answers. "But the various pains in her head and legs are another matter."

"Will she recover?" I ask bluntly.

He glares at me intently for a few seconds. "I can't honestly give you any firm reassurance, Sir Francis," he says. "The varied pains and general malaise are bad enough. But I worry about the state of her mind, too. The up-and-down swings of mood are most worrying."

He can see I am upset. He touches my arm and tells me to pray for her. "I will bleed her in the morning and that will help to dispel any increase of bloated flesh."

I thank the doctor and walk back towards the queen's chamber. He calls to me before I can enter the room.

"One last thing, Sir Francis," he calls, as he approaches me. "We can deal with the physical ailments and hope to cure them. What we cannot deal with is her will to live. If she loses that, all is lost."

SIR FRANCIS ENGLEFIELD'S DIARY

ENGLEFIELD HOUSE, BERKSHIRE, AUTUMN 1558

A LATE SUMMER DAY, VERY STILL, QUITE WARM, VERY DRY. Up here, at the top of the hill in Whiteknights, it is quiet, hardly any breeze at all. Looking down at the town below, it seems there is little activity there either but I am sure it is just an illusion. Reading is a busy, active place with farm folks selling corn and other wares.

My black horse snorts and shakes his head as I pull gently on the reins to hold him steady. I wait by the milestone as that is our designated meeting place and reflect how very mild, how peaceful it is in a spot like this on a rare, warm autumn morning. Late afternoons and evenings are chill now. Autumn breezes carry a warning of winter to come and are already active in late August. I reflect that, although our climate is terrible overall with excessive rain, such as we have seen these past three years, I like living here in England. I would find it hard indeed to leave these shores.

I gaze out to left and right and wonder if Sir Thomas has misunderstood my suggested meeting place. A farm worker in white smock passes by and touches his cap to me. He goes on past the oak tree and out across the field. All is still quiet, not a man, woman or child to be seen. Not even the clip clop of a passing rider. In the distance now, I pick up the faint, muffled sound of church bells. To break the silence all around me. Then a cart comes into view and a gentleman passes in his coach and the peaceful silence is shattered. My horse is getting restless. As I look up to the blue sky, a horse and rider trot up and come to rest by the side of my mount.

"Been here long?" Thomas asks, by way of initial greeting.

"Ten minutes maybe," I respond. "Just thinking how unusual it is. Warm weather for once and still and quiet as the grave."

Often is around these parts," he tells me. "Seems a world away from the bustle of the town down there."

It is still quite early, but Thomas tells me his lips are parched and wonders if I can suggest a remedy. I suggest a ride down the hill and a stop outside the nearest welcoming-looking inn or tavern. He nods, mentions that there is one not more than half a mile distant and he finds it difficult to coax his horse past the place. It stops and refuses to budge. It is not too long before we dismount, walk into the straw-floored establishment and arm ourselves with two large tankards of ale. We find a wooden bench by a heavy oak table and settle there, under the window.

"How is the queen now, Francis?" he enquires between taking large mouthfuls of ale.

"Sinking fast," I reply sombrely. "I wouldn't leave her normally, but I do need to talk to Catherine urgently."

"I'm sorry to hear that," he says. "Is there no hope?"

"Her physician is of opinion that she may see out the next few weeks but little, if any, after that."

He tells me that there have been many rowdy meetings in the town lately and calls for her to stop the burnings. There have been agitated calls for her to be overthrown and Elizabeth installed as queen.

"That may happen sooner than they think," I reply. "And with no need of violence."

"What ails her?" he asks.

"A most painful growth in her belly, mainly," I inform him. "But her mind is in turmoil and she has outbursts of calling out at night and talking gibberish. She is also prone to a form of sleepwalking and wailing at night."

"Sounds dreadful."

"It is. Most strange of all is that she has periods of quiet, peaceful conversation and talks lucidly with her companions."

We drink up and decide to replenish our tankards with ale. I feel sad to be the bearer of bad news about our queen and not too sure I should be sharing the news I have. Thomas is discreet, though, and it will be public news soon enough anyway. I remain silent for a minute or two and gaze out of the window. Few people are abroad this day. In the distance I can hear a hurdy-gurdy being played. Thomas asks if the queen is being made comfortable.

"Yes, on that score we need have no worries," I tell him. "Jane Dormer and Susan Clarencieux are with her night and day."

"All through the nights?"

"Yes, they take turns. She frequently becomes quite agitated during the nights."

Susan is loyal and dedicated, I explain, Jane even more so. Jane is her unselfish, faithful friend and her favourite among all the ladies. Jane would not leave her alone at night even if her own health were suffering. I offer to keep him up to date by letter of all new developments although, as he points out, news of the court travels fast these days. He is likely to know an hour or so after me.

We ride together out of the town and head towards Englefield House. At the corner near the ash tree, we part company. I tell him I hope we meet again before too long. Thomas grins. "I spend most of my time in Oxford these days at colleges," he informs me, "and don't get much time in Reading. So, it could be a long interval."

"Unless we meet up at a funeral," I say in grim tones. Then I gallop away at pace.

A troupe of players in colourful harlequin costumes entertain us for an hour. The leading performer, a man wearing a distinctive black-and-white costume and with a cap sporting an enormously long feather approaches and bows low. Catherine applauds him contentedly, grinning, and I follow. They troop out of the banqueting hall swiftly and the musicians enter the gallery. On this occasion, Catherine has arranged for two flutes, two viols, sackbut and viola da gamba. They strike up with a merry air straight away.

"You say she is dying?" Catherine asks. "Is there no hope of recovery?"

"Unfortunately, not. Dr Owen gives her two weeks."

Catherine raises an eyebrow slowly and returns to cutting her roasted swan portion. I take a drink from my ale tankard and then concentrate on the wide variety of beef, mutton, pork and various game in front of me. The music has an infectious, lilting rhythm to it, but I do not really feel in a mood to appreciate it.

"And what will you do when she dies, Francis?" Catherine asks in a cold voice. "What will you do?"

"I can't stay here," I tell her calmly.

"Can't stay in your own home?"

"I don't mean this house," I tell her irritably. "I mean I can't stay in this country."

All will be different when Mary dies and her half-sister is proclaimed queen. As a trusted friend and adviser of Mary, I will be seen as the instigator of the heretic laws and the subsequent burnings of hundreds of people. It would not be long before I was arrested on some charge, genuine or otherwise, and thrown into the Tower. Then, sooner or later, execution would follow. I will not stay in this country long enough for those things to occur.

"So where do you plan to go, Francis?" Catherine demands.

"To Spain," I say lightly. "We can start a new life."

"Oh no, Francis, not me," she almost snarls. "I'm an Englishwoman and this is my home. This is where I am and where I stay."

"You are my wife, Catherine," I remind her. "Where I go, you should go."

"Not to Spain," she asserts. "Not anywhere abroad. Are you sure you have given this enough thought?"

Have I? Quite some time ago it was that I began writing regularly to Philip, our king. He had first contacted me with a request to watch over the queen as her health appeared to him to be failing. As to recent events, Philip is most aware of what is happening now. His last few letters have made it clear that he would be happy to offer me sanctuary in Spain, should I want or need it. And a pension.

"We could be comfortable in Spain," I tell her. "Start a new life together, forget the past."

"I shall never leave this house," she tells me firmly. "And I could never live in Spain."

There does not seem to be a lot more to say. I call for a portion of pheasant and lark in a special sauce and eat. Slowly and with gradually diminishing appetite. Catherine, too, appears to be struggling with her supper, but she calls for strong wine and drinks liberally. The musicians suddenly strike up a most lively melody that seems totally unsuitable for our present mood. Thinking about it, though, melancholy music would be even worse. They do slow down the tempo now, though, as we pick at a large selection of sweetmeats.

"How long have you been planning this. Francis?" Catherine asks, her eyes piercing into mine.

"I haven't planned anything," I tell her truthfully. "Just letters to Philip and his to me." I look closely at her and see she does not believe me. "And suggestions."

"Suggestions?"

"Yes, he said there would always be work for me and a place to live. If I ever needed it."

"Strange man," she muses. "He abandons his wife and then offers a home to her adviser. Why?"

"He thinks I'm a good Catholic," I tell her. "And he can use me."

"Yes. I hadn't considered that."

We finish supper and return to the library. The musicians are still playing but we leave them to their airs and jigs. Catherine sits by the empty fireplace and frowns. She expresses deep regret if this will herald the parting of the ways between us, but she will never consider Spain as home. Have I given any consideration to what will happen to her if I leave this country?

"I have," I assure her. "My lawyer has been instructed and will make provision for you."

"I wish to stay in this house and live here until I die."

"Then you shall do so."

Catherine flashes an ironic smile. It has not escaped her attention, she informs me, that I must have foreseen that she would not accompany me to Spain. Sadly, I admit, it had occurred to me. But I was hoping she would be open to persuasion. She shakes her head sadly and takes a long drink of strong French wine. I sit down next to her and say that I hope we can discuss this further, in the coming weeks and months. I do not plan to go anywhere until all my affairs are in good order.

"What went wrong between us, Francis?" she asks sadly.

"I really don't know," I answer, truthfully. "Maybe we can talk it over and put things right."

"I don't think so," she responds. "Do you?"

"Perhaps, perhaps not."

The night is dark outside and the air pure, warm and clean.

I lie in bed in the darkness and listen to the creatures of the night outside. It is lonely in London, especially at night-time but so it is now, here, at home in Berkshire. Normally I can sleep soundly back home, usually as soon as my head touches feather cushion. Not so tonight, I lie awake and wait for the sleep that does not come. My personal problems merge into those that await me in London when I return and that stifles sleep further. I feel sure I am making the correct provisions for the future, but Catherine and I have been together for a long time now. It will feel strange without her.

Virtually sleepless, I stagger through the day, ill at ease. Relentless rain falling does not improve my mood. In the grounds, it is soft and muddy underfoot. I think about the queen and wonder how she is today. I really should be travelling back. I eat little, picking at food delicately, like a maid. In bed again, I wonder if sleep will come on this night. I think it will. Catherine stirs and sighs softly. I reach out to her, half-expecting her body next to me to be an illusion that will fade as soon as I attempt to touch her. The flesh is real.

"Before you go," she whispers.

"Before I go."

I caress her gently but with desire and soon we are wrapped in a passionate embrace. Bodies joined, face to face, her tears wet on my cheek. We are together as one. Perhaps for the last time.

JANE DORMER'S DIARY

ST JAMES'S PALACE, AUTUMN 1558

Her breathing is uneven with short bursts followed by almost frantic panting. I feel so helpless when she is asleep like this and in discomfort. I can do nothing to help alleviate her pain and suffering. It is extremely early in the morning just after the dawn. Pale, greyish light seeps in through the window where the drapes are not quite level. Yesterday was almost peaceful. The queen slept most of the day and when she awoke, in fits and starts, she was mostly lucid. The day before was horrible, even the usually calm Susan lost patience with her. I remain calm and collected. At all times. If I feel agitation coming on, I just remind myself, forcefully, that her suffering is 10 times worse than mine. It is a good discipline. But she is so thin, it breaks my heart to look at her. Only her poor extended belly looks bigger than it should and that is out of proportion with the rest of her. If only she would eat more it would help her health enormously. She picks at food like a bird. When her breathing becomes loud and panting, I know she is waking up.

"I can see a row of angels in front of me," she blurts out suddenly before she is completely awake.

"Can you, Mary?" I ask, tears beginning to burn my eyes.

"Oh, I know it was just a dream," she tells me. "But sent by God to help me. Such beautiful cherubic faces. The row of angels looking straight at me. So glorious."

I help her to sit up in bed and push up the cushions behind her back and head. Her hair is wild and grey and in such a mess. I ask if she would like me to brush it for her. It will not be easy with her in bed, but she would like me to do it. I call for a brush and a servant brings one to me. I begin brushing.

I have been with her most of the night. Susan was feeling rather the worse for a headache, so I suggested she take a few extra hours' sleep. I struggle to find a position to brush out the queen's hair and manage, with some contortion, to get it looking tidier. She appears more cheerful and tells me she has had a good night's sleep. I am so relieved. The bad dreams have been troubling her quite a lot in the past few days. I mop her brow gently to remove the perspiration.

"I hope God will forgive me for my failures," she is saying, almost whispering. "Although I will find it more difficult to forgive myself."

"Oh. Don't torture yourself," I cry out. "God will bless you."

"No, no," she replies. "I have made too many mistakes as queen of this realm."

"Nonsense," I respond. "You have served your subjects well."

"I must pray for God's forgiveness," she continues, "before I die."

"Don't say that Mary, please," I implore. "You are not dying." Tears start to flow down my cheeks. She shakes her head.

"Don't cry, Jane," she says. "You have served me well. But I know the end is near."

I am unable to stem the flow of tears, hard as I try. I snuffle and blow my nose and struggle desperately to control my emotion. Mary reaches out a hand and pats mine as though I were the invalid and not she. When Susan enters the chamber, she finds me in a sorry state. I struggle again to compose myself and explain to Susan that the queen has had a reasonably good night's sleep. She tells me to get along now as it looks as if I am in a bad way myself.

I join the other ladies and they are full of questions that I find it difficult to answer. Eleanor offers to sit with the queen for a few hours so that I can get some extra sleep. I tell her I will be fine after three hours or so in bed. I do not want to leave Mary's bedside for long. Magdalen, wide-eyed, asks if she may visit the queen. She has come to court especially.

"A little later, Magdalen," I tell her. "I'll send for you at the right time."

I should go straight to bed now, but I go to find Francis Englefield. He is busy with state papers, although he greets me cordially enough. I advise him that the queen had a good night.

"That is a blessing, anyway," he agrees. "I should have returned sooner, knowing her condition."

"She has been asking for you," I inform him. "Several times."

"Yes, I'll go to her soon. I had unavoidable business back home in Berkshire."

I ask him if he thinks there is any chance of the queen rallying. He shakes his head and tells me that he thinks it extremely unlikely. She is too weak now, unable to live more than a few days. I turn away to avoid Sir Francis seeing my fresh tears, but he touches my arm lightly and tells me not to be upset. I am the one person who has cared for her and never turned my back on her, all through the years of her reign.

"Which is a mere five," I say sadly.

"Almighty God decides the length of a reign," he informs me. "And who should question God in his wisdom?"

I nod, understanding what he means. I am now so tired I could lie on the cold stone floor at my feet and go off to sleep in an instant. I hurry to my bedchamber. At first, I worry about all the things churning in my mind, but sleep comes swiftly and refreshes my exhausted body. On return to the long gallery, I find Magdalen looking forlorn. I ask her if she is making her way to the queen's privy bedchamber.

"Yes, I must talk to her," she tells me.

"What about?"

"I want her to forgive me," Magdalen states sadly. "For not serving her as well as I should and for being a sinner."

"Best go to the chapel for that," I suggest. "Confess all."

"Oh, I've done that," she replies eagerly. "And received absolution."

I gaze at her quizzically. She is not, I sincerely hope, planning to mention to the queen the night the king embraced her, and she allowed him to kiss her. Her eyes widen in sudden fear.

"No, of course not, I wouldn't dare, would you?"

Magdalen looks stricken. I ask her to sit with the queen and try to cheer her. Make goodly talk about how well she is looking today, even if she is not. Cheerful talk to brighten her, not sad words about sin and sinning.

"But I want her to know that I care for her and wish her well," Magdalen says, still looking sorrowful and her big eyes moist as she tugs nervously at a strand of her blonde hair.

"She knows that, Magdalen," I tell her, smiling. "You've always been a favourite ever since you were a bridesmaid at her wedding."

She begins to cry, and I bid her wipe her eyes thoroughly and plant a smile on her lips. And stop immediately before she sets me off again. We walk down the corridor together and enter the bedchamber. Sir Francis is by the bedside and Susan jumps up, eager to be on her way. She brings me up to date telling me the queen slept for an hour then awoke and

THE TITIAN PORTRAIT

started talking gibberish. She was calling for a certain bishop to be burned immediately but Susan managed to quiet her down. She has been lucid and calm for the past 20 minutes. Susan departs and Magdalen and I wait, ready to be called forward but prepared to stand here indefinitely.

It is not long before I realise that the queen is delirious. I bid Magdalen wait by the door and move forward to assist Sir Francis. "I want to go to Hampton Court, and I want to go now," the queen shouts. Sir Francis is somewhat at a loss, but I move to swiftly mop her fevered brow.

"I'm only ever truly happy and content there," she tells us.

"It shall be arranged," Sir Francis tells her, playing along faithfully but if I know her the queen will not be thinking about Hampton Court or anywhere else for long. I try to calm her by soothing her with gentle mopping of her brow again and smoothing down her rumpled nightgown.

"I will not do it," she snaps suddenly, angrily. "I will not be insulted in this way." I try to calm her down, but she is so agitated now that it takes the combined efforts of Sir Francis and me to settle her again. Even so, her eyes are bright as she stares straight ahead and begins breathing heavily.

"I will not be a servant to that brat for one minute more," she continues in a strange, fluting voice that is unfamiliar to me. "Elizabeth can call and call, but I will not respond," I realise what is happening as her fever transports her back into the past and reassure her that I am with her and all is well.

The fever passes as swiftly as it arrived. She is asleep again now, breathing calmly and peacefully for once. Sir Francis says he must be going so I assure him I will attend to all the queen's needs.

"And could you take Lady Magdalen with you, Sir Francis?" I ask. "The queen is not up to any more visitors today."

He nods an assurance and they both leave the chamber. The queen sleeps for an hour and is relatively calm all through. As she awakens, I am aware that she is looking very content, peaceful in fact.

She looks up at me, begins to realise slowly where she is and who I am, and she smiles.

"I was having a wonderful dream, Jane," she whispers. "The choir of little angels was back, singing softly to me and I was back playing in the grass at Hampton Court, the sun was shining brightly, and my father was striding across the lawns towards me with a big smile on his face. My mother was there somewhere but she was out of sight and I could not see her. I called to her, but she did not answer."

She pauses and frowns as though trying to work out why she could not see her mother. Then, quietly and smoothly as before, she continues. "It was a clear, hot day, and we were all content. It was just the three of us and the servants and Elizabeth was nowhere to be seen."

"It was before she was born," I suggest softly.

"Yes, that's right," she goes ahead, still frowning in concentration. "But now I do have to talk about Elizabeth."

"You do?" I ask apprehensively.

"I don't have long to live now," she begins. "No, don't look at me like that, Jane, the truth must be faced. I have wrestled with myself long and hard over this but a short time ago I named Elizabeth as my successor and the next Queen of England. And tomorrow, I would like you to take all my jewels to Elizabeth and hand them to her as a gesture of goodwill."

"Oh," I murmur, "I see."

She is silent again, frowning, but suddenly perks up. "Well, it is only right and proper. She is my half-sister and my father's daughter and, whatever I think of her personally, she is next in line to the throne."

. . .

I set out early in the morning in the royal coach, conscious of the gravity of my assignment. I have with me the royal jewels, attendants and guards and the roads to Hatfield are almost afloat with rainwater. It rains relentlessly. We plough through mud and artificial lakes of water, a cold, wet, miserable journey. I am conscious of the honour that Queen Mary has done me. I carry this precious cargo to the woman who will be our next queen. Sadness sweeps over me as we plough on through the rain sodden countryside.

At Hatfield house, all is quiet. I am received and my cargo safely taken by trusted attendants. I am taken to Lady Elizabeth's privy chamber where she stands in plain but high-quality robes by a roaring fire.

"Come forward, Jane," she says. "You are welcome to my home."

I thank her and advance timidly into the room. She bids me sit by the fire to get warm after my journey and she sends for hot spiced wine for me.

"What late news of my sister?"

"She is near the end," I tell her. "Hanging by a thread."

"A thread of iron, if I know her," she suggests.

"No, no, Doctor Owen gives her less than a day," I splutter and, as I think about the queen's fate, the tears start again in my eyes and roll down my cheeks. Elizabeth bids me not to get upset, she knows how fond I am of the queen and my love and loyalty do me great credit. I should warm myself by the fire after so wet and windy a journey and drink heartily of my cup of spiced wine. I sip the wine, which warms me physically and try to compose myself.

"The queen has named you as her successor, Lady Elizabeth," I tell her. "By Saturday, I wager, you will be Queen of England."

"Yes, Jane, I suppose I shall," she agrees. "I shall do what I can to continue the good works she has started. I give you my word of honour on that."

I thank her. She tells me that, for all the misunderstandings that have existed between her and her half-sister, she has studied Mary's reign with much interest and learned much. It cannot have been easy, coming to the throne as the first woman regnant, a monarch in her own right and not merely the wife of a king. Some of her speeches have been inspirational. Her work with the military and the Navy have bolstered the safety of the realm. Her control of parliament has been impressive, too.

"She would be pleased to hear you say those things," I tell her.

"Sadly for her, she never will," she replies. "Where we part company, and I make no bones about, it is on the future of the church in England. I will restore the true religion of this country back to the people."

"You and I will never agree on that, Lady Elizabeth," I tell her sadly.

"No, we never will," she agrees, smiling. "Live and let live, though. That is my motto."

"I am with you there," I tell her boldly.

Now, though, if I am rested somewhat, she intends to see that I have a good dinner and some strong wine to prepare me for the journey back to London. I must be of stout heart, she insists, and of good cheer for the future can be bright indeed if we all work together to make it so. I force a smile and agree with her, but I cannot share her optimistic outlook. For her the future is assured and full of wonder but for me it is uncertain and unknown.

SIR NICHOLAS THROCKMORTON'S REPORT

⚜

DATED NOVEMBER 17TH 1558, WHITEHALL, LONDON

There is a sombre air over Whitehall on this day. Only hushed voices are heard at the palace and in the Lords and Commons. My mission is to break news of great import to the Lady Elizabeth and I can ill afford any delay. I ride furiously to Hatfield, spurring my good horse on constantly to greater speed. The animal responds splendidly, almost as though he realises the importance of our mission. The ground is still soft from the incessant rain but at least, today, it is fresh, cold and dry. The sky is clear and bright. We encounter slightly harder ground in Hertfordshire where few have ridden lately. I am able to spur my horse on even faster, but the animal will need a good rest and feed when we arrive.

At Hatfield I am received with solemnity. Perhaps my hasty arrival, grim expression and unexpected appearance give some clue to my mission. I am told that the Lady Elizabeth is walking in the grounds, taking the fresh, biting air in her stride on this cold November day.

"I will find her," I announce.

I walk out through the ground, warmer now that I have ceased to ride at speed and no longer receive the swirling winds from fast motion. I see her walking slowly towards the big oak tree where, I am told, she loves to sit and read her books in the summer. She is well wrapped up against the cold air and her face is slightly flushed. I reach her side and bow to her.

"Sir Nicholas."

"By your leave, Madam," I begin hurriedly, "I am come to you from London to give you important news."

"Please proceed."

"Madam, early this morning, your half-sister, our gracious Queen Mary died, and you are about to be proclaimed Queen of England, Ireland and France."

I hand her Mary's ring as a symbol of her death. She takes it solemnly.

"To quote the Bible," she replies, smiling, "this is the Lord's doing and it is wonderful in our eyes."

She puts her hands together, raises her eyes towards the sky and is most likely saying a short, silent prayer. I wait until she is finished, and she bids me accompany her into the house. In her privy chamber, I am invited to sit by the fire with her and she orders strong, spiced wine for us both. Her questions come thick and fast. "When did my sister die exactly?"

"Early, I am told. I do not know the hour. She received mass and the viaticum, the Holy Communion for the dying and was able to make the appropriate responses before slipping into unconsciousness."

"Was her death peaceful?"

"I am told it was. She was so peaceful at the end that her ladies thought she was feeling better and merely sleeping."

"That is good. Did she utter any last words?"

"Not at the last as I understand it. The day before, she voiced the opinion that, if she were opened after her death, Calais would be found engraved on her heart."

"Yes, that was most unfortunate. A terrible loss to the realm. Perhaps inevitable though, in the long run."

THE TITIAN PORTRAIT

When she asks when the proclamation will come, I tell her that it is most likely being made at Whitehall at this very moment. If not, within the next hour. She smiles contentedly and drinks. I tell her the members of the council will be arriving soon. She raises an eyebrow.

"Many will be disappointed," she informs me. "I intend to have a much reduced council. I am of the opinion that a large, unwieldy council causes confusion and not much gets done."

After a pause, she speaks of the sorrow she feels for her sister and of the burden that is now placed on her shoulders. But she adds that she is God's creature, ordained to obey his appointment. She will seek God's grace to aid her in her bid to minister his heavenly will. She says she will require the service of her councillors to make a good account to almighty God and leave some worthy achievements to posterity on earth.

JANE DORMER'S DIARY

WHITEHALL AND WESTMINSTER ABBEY, DECEMBER 1558

WE GO IN SLOW, MOURNFUL PROCESSION FROM ST JAMES'S Palace to Westminster Abbey. Queen Mary's body has lain in state here since her death on November 17th. Her body lay there under the cloth of state and I frequently went there to be alone, to be peaceful and to be near her. Now we head slowly towards the Abbey, the coffin draped in cloth of gold and with a full-sized wooden effigy of the queen, which is crowned and carries a sceptre and orb on top. Margaret Douglas, Countess of Lennox, Queen Mary's cousin, is the chief mourner.

We follow the funeral chariot, her loyal men and women all in black. Head to toe. At each corner of the chariot a herald on horseback is positioned bearing a banner of the four English royal saints. Mary's ladies, headed by Margaret Douglas, follow on behind. Margaret was Mary's loving cousin, and I am pleased that she is chief mourner.

We halt at the great door of the abbey and are met by four bishops and an abbot, who censes the coffin and the effigy before it is taken inside.

Queen Mary's body will rest overnight, guarded by 100 poor men, all in black robes and carrying torches. The queen's coffin is draped in purple velvet. Here she rests again before the funeral service tomorrow. I was so pleased that Mary slipped away out of life so quietly and peacefully. After all the pain and strife leading up to her last day, the end was gentler than I could have hoped for. She went through the last rites as though talking amiably to a friendly priest. Then she lay back on her cushions, smiled, reached out and took my hand in hers for a few seconds before closing her eyes and going to sleep for the last time. As we walk slowly back to St James's Palace, my grief wells up again and I feel a restriction in my throat. I must control my emotion for tomorrow when I say my final goodbye.

The funeral mass is heard in solemn, hushed silence. All the nobles and members of the privy council are gathered to pay their final respects. Paulet and Paget look bleak and cold in their black robes. Arundel inspects his fingernails. Heath appears fidgety and perhaps feels that he should be conducting the funeral mass. Sir Francis Englefield appears calm and somewhat detached, sitting some distance from the rest of the councillors. All the ladies, and I include myself, sit very still and wear sad, grim expressions as befitting the occasion. But all feeling the grief deeply and genuinely. Dorothy and Eleanor hold hands tightly, their expressions bleak. Magdalen is weeping silently and surreptitiously wiping her eyes from time to time.

The Bishop of Winchester, John White, begins the funeral sermon. He has written a poem to extol the virtues of Queen Mary.

How many noble men restored
And other states also
Well showed her princely liberal heart
which gave both friend and foe.
As princely was her birth, so princely was her life:
Constant, courtise, modest and mild;
a chaste and chosen wife.

Well showed her princely liberal heart.
Oh, mirror of all womanhood.
Oh, Queen of virtues pure.
Oh, constant Mary, filled with grace.
No age can thee obscure.

The bishop pauses and gazes upwards in the silence that follows. Susan nudges me and then whispers: "He planned to end his poem there," she continues frivolously, "but our new queen wasn't having that."

"How do you know?" I ask softly.

"I have my sources," she continues and grins. "The next bit is by Elizabeth."

Mary now dead, Elizabeth lives,
our just and lawful queen.
In whom her sister's virtues rare,
abundantly are seen.
Obey our queen as we are bound,
pray God her to preserve.
And send her grace, life, long and fruit,
and subjects true to serve.

"He was never going to get away with not mentioning her," Susan whispers and giggles.

The bishop continues: "She was a king's daughter, she was a king's sister, she was a king's wife. She was a queen and by the same title a king also. She had the love, commendation and admiration of all the world. She was never unmindful of her promise to the realm. She used singular mercy to offenders. She used much pity and compassion towards the poor and oppressed. I verily believe, the poorest creature in all this city feared not God more than she did."

He goes on to wish Elizabeth a prosperous reign and then adds: "If it be God's will."

"I wouldn't care to be that bishop tomorrow morning," Susan whispers mischievously.

Her regalia is offered to God by the bishop. Her draped coffin is taken to the north aisle of the chapel of Henry VII and placed in a vault. We all follow and break our wands of office and throw them into the grave. "The queen is dead, long live the queen," the heralds proclaim.

SIR FRANCIS ENGLEFIELD'S DIARY

WESTMINSTER ABBEY, DECEMBER 1558

So significant and so final. As we break our wands of office and throw them into the grave, we are aware of a new age dawning. The queen is dead, long live the queen. As I look into the vault and think back to the years of Mary's reign, short though they were, a bitter sadness enters my soul. I stand in the Henry VII chapel and I am unaware of people around me for a minute or two. Familiar faces incline to give an inclination of a nod or even a sombre smile as they pass by and file silently out of the chapel. I gaze up at the spectacular, intricately carved fan roof, the golden colour gleaming brightly.

I walk slowly out and back along the aisle to the main part of the abbey. This magnificent building, I am thinking, was where Mary was crowned queen and now is her final resting place. It is an ancient structure, housing the remains of many sovereigns, so Mary is in good company. Once a church, once a cathedral, it has been called many things. Now the Benedictine monks are back, it is similar to its original function.

I stand by a pillar and look down towards the altar. Hushed voices occasionally break the heavy silence. Bishop White stands talking to another cleric and both look as though they have just received painful, heavy blows. They are deep in agitated conversation; something has gone amiss but who can say what?

"Built in 1269, I am reliably informed," says Elizabeth, appearing by my side silently. "A magnificent building."

"It is indeed, Your Majesty," I agree, recovering swiftly.

Elizabeth looks straight at me and I notice that familiar twinkle in her eyes. It is still there.

"We meet again, Sir Francis," she is saying. "And once again under different circumstances. I suppose going from mere noblewoman to Queen of England in one swift leap is somewhat unique."

I laugh and agree it is something special. She never expected it to happen when it did, she tells me, but adds that things seldom work out the way we expect them to. Do they?

"I don't know if you noticed," she asks, "but that unsavoury bishop, White, in his sermon, quoted a piece based on verses from Ecclesiastes which come out as: 'I praised the dead more than the living, for a living dog is better than a dead lion.' The slimy creature was referring to me as a dog."

"Surely not," I protest.

"Oh, he meant it," she assures me. "I wonder if he thought he might get away with it?"

"He won't, will he?" I ask, grinning.

"I shall deal with him in the morning," she informs me.

He will be punished, of course he will, but he is an insignificant speck of dust compared with affairs of state she will now have to concern herself with. Day and night, endlessly. She intends to build on many projects that her half-sister started and had not time to finish. Along with many new items of her own that have long occupied her thoughts. Now is the opportunity. First though, the appointment of a new and much smaller privy council.

"Not with you in it, Francis," she tells me. "I like you, but our religious differences are likely to be unsurmountable."

"I understand."

"I wonder if you do. I bear you no malice, on the contrary, gratitude."

"I only ever did my duty. As I saw it."

She tells me she has no doubts on that score whatsoever. In any case, it will be a much smaller privy council, which, she thinks, will be far more efficient. And very few, if any, who favour the Roman church.

"So what next for you now, Sir Francis?" she enquires genially.

"Oh, I think I'll attend to business locally," I tell her cautiously. "In and around Berkshire."

"Won't you miss the excitement and intrigues of the big city?"

"Not for one half-second."

She laughs. "Well, the very best of good luck to you," she bids me. "By the way, were you aware that the king wrote to me proposing marriage?"

"Philip? No, I most certainly wasn't," I tell her, genuinely shocked.

"Not too many people were," she responds, smiling. "Of course, I told him exactly what he could do with his proposal. I am no Roman and never will be. Nor will the good citizens of this realm be if I have my way."

The bells are tolling mournfully for the late queen. Soon they will be ringing joyfully for the new one. Her words have cut into me deeply and I know what people must expect now. A new reign. A new broom sweeping clean. Sweeping away the good that Mary managed to do? Or building on it and fashioning a new order on the back of it? Time will tell. Elizabeth prepares to leave. Her courtiers are hovering nearby purposefully. The guards stand ready.

"Time I was on my way," she states. "Goodbye, Francis."

"Goodbye, Majesty."

She sweeps out imperiously, followed by her retinue. I

walk down the aisle to where a little knot of the late queen's ladies-in-waiting have not yet dispersed. Margaret and Eleanor stand-alone looking forlorn. Magdalen stands with her husband looking curiously appealing in her all-black attire, her yellow hair glistening where it peeks out. Susan and Jane are together in intense conversation. I did not know they were friends outside of the court. Chalk and cheese, though. I approach them.

"A sad day," I begin. "A good service, though."

"So sad," Jane agrees. "But all credit to our new queen, she managed a thorough and well-planned funeral. No detail left to chance."

So much is true. Whatever differences the two sisters had in life, in death, Mary was given a magnificent funeral. Elizabeth was the architect and the builder, ordering and approving every aspect from the order of movement to Westminster from Charing Cross to the carved effigy of Mary that was placed on top of her coffin. Even the bishop's poem had to feature an added stanza, written by Elizabeth. It was planned down to the last detail. Although now it occurs to me that the entire spectacle was designed to pay homage to Mary and draw attention to Elizabeth.

"So, what next for you then, Susan?" I ask.

"We are going to live in Spain," Susan tells me, indicating Jane.

"We?"

"Yes," Jane confirms, grinning. "Together, The two of us."

"I had no idea you two were close friends," I tell them thoughtfully.

"Why not?" Jane asks. "We were both very close to Mary and spent much time in her company and with each other. And you know, Sir Francis, we shared vigils at her bedside until the end."

"Yes, it makes sense," I agree, smiling. "Well, I too will be heading for Spain before too long, so we may all meet up again."

They both express their surprise. "You, Sir Francis?" Susan queries, as Jane looks on with puzzled expression.

"Yes," I say. "There is much to do there that perhaps I can no longer do here."

They both nod their heads as though understanding the underlying suggestion in my comment. I tell them I must make a move. "Oh, by the way, ladies," I say before departing, "that information is not for general distribution. I would be obliged if you kept it to yourselves for now." Again, the two heads nod in agreement and I pass on down the aisle.

Outside the air is chill, biting. I walk slowly down to the river and stand on the bank gazing out at the swiftly moving crafts. It is a time for change and renewal. And new plans.

SIR FRANCIS ENGLEFIELD'S DIARY

ENGLEFIELD HOUSE, BERKSHIRE, JANUARY 1559

The inn in Reading is busy with farmers, merchants and others, all swilling ale or small beer. The rushes on the floor, newly laid earlier, are already soiled and browned with mud trodden in by many feet that have walked through constant rain this morning. I wait by the fire on this cold day, tankard in hand. My nephew shares not just my name but my fair hair and light-blue eyes. He is tall, too, as I am. He arrives within 10 minutes of my own arrival, acquires his tankard of ale and approaches me with a winning smile on his chubby face.

"You haven't changed, Uncle," he assures me.

"Nor you," I tell him cheerfully, although it is some years since we last met.

We click out tankards together and take a long drink of ale. The crowds are noisy and I suggest finding a quieter spot in the inn, but it is difficult. The landlord, on request, supplies us with a small back room he keeps for meetings. We sit at a large oak table near a smaller but fiercely burning fire.

"Is it true you are bound for Spain?" he asks, and I nod an agreement. "Not for some time yet," I tell him. "But plans are in hand."

"And Catherine?"

"No, she will not leave England."

He is sorry to hear that, he confesses. He had always thought we were a well-suited couple and bound together for life. I smile ruefully and tell him that it was never a passionate love match, but we have strung along together for a goodly number of years. I am thinking that I have never had a passionate love match and am unlikely to have one now. My most intense and satisfying union has been my relationship with the late queen Mary and that was completely chaste. I do not tell him that, though. My true passion in life, if I have had one, has been the restoration of the Roman faith in England and working towards that has sustained me this past five years. Together with the queen, it was proceeding very satisfactorily but now is ended. I have deplored the burnings at the stake and said so, frequently, but have never deviated in my desire to see heresy stamped out and the Church of Rome fully restored in England. Mary and I were always at one with that desire. For me, the restoration of the true church has been paramount. A matter of life and death in extreme circumstances. Indeed, in many cases it has meant death rather than capitulate to an antichrist religion. Sir Thomas More and many others come to mind.

"What will happen to Catherine?" he asks.

"She will be well provided for," I assure him. "Whether she chooses to live in her own extensive manors or at Englefield House, the choice is entirely hers."

"How can I be of service, Uncle?" he enquires, studying my face closely.

"In the event that my activities abroad should cause trouble," I tell him, candidly, "I wish to attempt to secure my lands and properties. At some stage in the future, I intend to put them all in your name. With the one proviso that I can revoke the grant at any time by presenting you with a gold ring."

THE TITIAN PORTRAIT

"I see," he replies, frowning in deep consideration of my words. "Quite a responsibility."

"It is," I agree. "Are you prepared to take it on?"

"Of course, Uncle. I will do whatever you require me to do," he states, his expression intense.

"Good man."

"It will all be drawn up legally and without loopholes by my lawyers."

"These activities you plan to pursue in Spain..." he begins and stops abruptly.

"Are best left undiscussed for now," I tell him sombrely. What he does not know cannot hurt him and will not be drawn from him if he has no knowledge to impart. I scarcely know myself at this stage, although I know I plan to link up with other English Catholics who have departed from these shores.

I buy him more ale and express my gratitude for his willingness to help. We have always had a good relationship, young Francis and I. Not that we have met up often or visited each other but we have always been cordial when we did. We drink up and then fight our way out of the crowded bar, rowdy farmers, shepherds and merchants now becoming wild and even pugnacious on this market day.

We ride side by side through the town and come to the milestone where we part ways.

"Come to dinner tomorrow," I shout, as Francis moves off at a steady canter.

"Yes, love to, thanks," he calls and then urges his horse forward again.

The fields around Englefield are wet and windy. It is a bleak outlook as I ride up the pathway to the house. Under a grey sky, all is still except for the slow crossing of a deer, not far from the house. I dismount and hand the horse to the stable boy. It is icy underfoot from yesterday's shower of snow.

Catherine is extremely quiet at dinner. We get through some rich boar, chicken and sundry venison, hardly speaking. Only later in the afternoon, when we are seated by a well-stoked fire, wood crackling merrily in the grate and armed with goblets of strong French wine, does she broach the subject.

"When do you plan to leave, Francis?" she asks, brow creased in a frown.

"Not for some time yet," I tell her. "I have work to clear up here first."

Catherine is glaring at me with an expression I can only describe as barely concealed hostility.

"What will you do in Spain?" she asks quietly.

"Make friends, get to know people," I say frivolously.

"No, Francis," she responds, "what are you really planning to do? Or is it a secret?"

I shake my head and tell her that I have no secrets from her but, on the other hand, there is no mystery and nothing to be secretive about. After the last five years, a quiet life with little responsibility would suit me rather well. I will meet up with other Catholics, most likely, and indicate my support. I will spend much time in prayer, asking for forgiveness and guidance.

"Could you not stay here in England and support the church in your own way?"

"What way is that?" I ask rhetorically. "Drum up recruits to rebel against the new queen? I crushed enough to know that rebellion does not work."

She suggests there are other ways, but I shake my head again. I tell her that when the late Queen Mary died, followed within about four hours by the archbishop, Reginald Pole, Catholicism in this country died with them. I have no desire to do anything specific but equally, no desire to ruffle royal feathers here and finish up in the Tower. Or worse.

"It might not come to that."

"It might not," I agree, smiling. "And pigs might fly."

"And I say again, what will you do?"

Still smiling, I rise, kiss her forehead and walk over to the window and look out. A bleak vista indeed. "I am invited to the Spanish court by Philip, the king." Icicles are forming on the leafless trees. Branches black and spindly. "He promises me a pension." The sky is overcast, but the fields and pastures are green and vibrant. "There will be work for me but what form it will take, for the moment I know not." Catherine will be well taken care of by both my estates and her own extensive manors and lands. I watch a peacock strutting across the grass. "Work will be plentiful, I expect." I will miss England and Catherine and wonder if she will miss me. In Spain, the sun will shine and the climate will be agreeable.

Dear reader,

We hope you enjoyed reading *The Titan Portrait* Please take a moment to leave a review, even if it's a short one. Your opinion is important to us.

Discover more books by Derek Ansell at https://www.nextchapter.pub/authors/derek-ansell

Want to know when one of our books is free or discounted? Join the newsletter at http://eepurl.com/bqqB3H

Best regards,

Derek Ansell and the Next Chapter Team

You might also like:
The Bradgate Heiress by Derek Ansell

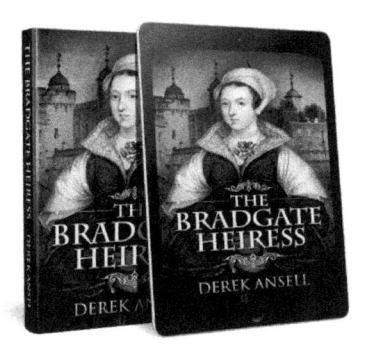

To read the first chapter for free, please head to:
https://www.nextchapter.pub/books/the-bradgate-heiress

AUTHOR'S NOTE

JANE DORMER AND SUSAN CLARIENCIEUX TRAVELLED TO SPAIN together where Jane later married the Spanish Duke of Feria, an old flame whom she met at Queen Mary's wedding. Susan joined their household. Jane died in 1612 although Susan's death is unrecorded.

Sir Francis Englefield travelled to Spain in 1559 and was soon active as spokesman for English Catholic exiles at the court of King Philip of Spain. He travelled between the Netherland and Rome and was in contact with the Pope. Catherine Englefield died in 1586 at Compton Beauchamp in Berkshire, one of her inherited Fettiplace family estates. Sir Francis continued to try to further the cause of Catholicism, speaking up on behalf of Mary Queen of Scots. His lands and estates in England were confiscated when he refused an order from the queen to return to England and he was attainted. It took a fiercely contested court case before the lands were eventually given to the crown and later, his nephew, Sir Francis Junior managed to get some of them back. He had a substantial pension from Philip II which he lived on for the last 20 years of his life as his eyesight failed. On a visit to the

Spanish city of Valladolid, he wrote to Philip suggesting a second armada. He died there in 1596 leaving his young nephew to continue the Englefield line. England reverted to a protestant Church of England once again under Elizabeth I and remains so to this day.

ABOUT THE AUTHOR

Derek Ansell was born in North London and now lives in Berkshire. He has written two biographies of musicians and five novels. In addition to published works he is a regular contributor to *Jazz Journal*, a music magazine and *The Newbury Weekly News*, a local newspaper. *The Titian Portrait* is his fourth historical novel, the others being set in Tudor times (2) and the nineteen forties (1).

Lightning Source UK Ltd.
Milton Keynes UK
UKHW021835270421
382745UK00003B/337

9 781034 826910